MAXINE MORREY has wanted to [   ] can remember and wrote her first [   ] elf for school when she was ten.

Years passed and she continued [   ] in the way. She has written articles on a variety of subjects, as well as a local history book and in 2015 she won a contract for her Christmas romcom, *Winter's Fairytale*. Since then, she has written many more 'romcoms with depth' and wants to encourage everyone to 'Read Yourself Happy'.

She is the bestselling author of *Things Are Looking Up*, *#NoFilter*, and the Kindle UK top ten read, *The Christmas Project*, among others.

In 2024, her book *You've Got This* won The Romantic Comedy Award at the Romantic Novelists' Association award ceremony in London.

When not wrangling with words, she loves to read, sew and listen to podcasts. She can also often be found out on a gentle walk in nature, camera in hand.

You can find Maxine on Instagram @scribbler_maxi.

Also by Maxine Morrey

Winter's Fairytale

MAXINE MORREY

ONE PLACE. MANY STORIES

HQ
An imprint of HarperCollins*Publishers* Ltd
1 London Bridge Street
London SE1 9GF

www.harpercollins.co.uk

HarperCollins*Publishers*
Macken House, 39/40 Mayor Street Upper,
Dublin 1 D01 C9W8
This edition 2025

1

First published in Great Britain by
Carina, an imprint of HarperCollins*Publishers* Ltd 2015

ISBN: 9780008808624

Printed and bound in the UK using 100% Renewable
Electricity by CPI Group (UK) Ltd

MIX
Paper | Supporting
responsible forestry
FSC™ C007454

This book contains FSC™ certified paper and other controlled sources
to ensure responsible forest management.

For more information visit: www.harpercollins.co.uk/green

For James

Chapter 1

There were whole chapters dedicated to the throwing of the bouquet in the very many books I had pored over in the run-up to this day, all instructing me on How To Have The Perfect Wedding. Oddly enough, there wasn't one sentence referring to the appropriate etiquette involved in throwing your first ever punch instead. In fact, there was also a conspicuously absent chapter on what to do if your spineless fiancé decides that the actual wedding day is the best time to tell you he doesn't want to get married.

Not that it mattered. It turned out I didn't need tuition on how to punch – I was a natural, apparently. Unfortunately – or fortunately, depending on whose perspective you were looking at it from – my ex-groom-to-be hadn't even had the guts to turn up to the church at all. Which is why Rob, the best man, a perfectly nice bloke, was sat on his backside on the vestry floor, holding a hastily acquired wodge of tissues to his now bleeding nose.

'I'm so sorry!' I held out my hand to help him up and he, understandably, looked at it warily before opting to push himself up. I let my hand fall back down to my side.

'I don't know what came over me. That obviously wasn't really meant for you. But honestly? It was either you or the vicar.'

1

We both glanced over at the vicar who had paled and was now the same colour as his crisp white robe.

Rob nodded. 'You made the right choice.' He pulled the tissues away and looked at them briefly before shoving them back on his nose. 'I think.'

An awkward silence settled on the three of us.

'I really had no idea,' Rob said, his voice muffled and thick through the barrier of tissues.

I looked up at him from where I'd been staring at the crystals on my dress. Each one painstakingly sewn on by hand. My own hand. Rob looked wretched. Almost as miserable as I did. Almost. If he was lying then he deserved an Oscar. I didn't think he was that good of an actor.

'No. Me neither.' I smiled, sadly.

Again there was silence. Eventually the vicar gave a polite cough. We both looked at him. He was looking at me.

'How would you like to proceed, my dear?'

He was a sweet man. Steven, my fiancé, and I had met with him several times, going over everything, confirming to him that we were serious about our intentions. We'd sworn (not literally) that this was what we wanted, and that both of us knew that it was not something to be undertaken lightly. And yet, here we were. Groom-less.

How did I want to proceed? I'm pretty sure that the vicar didn't really want an honest answer to that question as, right now, it involved a pair of nutcrackers, Steven and a soundproof room.

'I don't know. How do you, I mean, what happens normally if ...' I couldn't bring myself to finish the question.

'Well, I can go out and make an announcement that there has been a change of plan, and request that everyone be kind enough to understand. Or if you wish, you can do it. But only if you want to.'

Oh God. What I wanted to do was throw up.

Rob answered before I could. 'I'll do it. It's supposed to be the

2

best man's job to get the groom to the church. I seem to have failed spectacularly in that task, so it should be me that goes out there to explain.'

The vicar nodded sympathetically.

'What will you say?' I asked, quietly.

'I don't know yet.' Rob shrugged his shoulders. 'It's not exactly the speech I had prepared.'

I nodded, feeling numb. It all felt weirdly unreal.

'I'll think of something. Don't worry.' He gave me a half smile, trying to lighten the moment. An almost impossible ask right now, but I appreciated the effort. The vicar moved towards the door and Rob followed. I touched Rob's arm.

'Thank you.'

His hand reached out to mine and took it, squeezing gently. 'I'm so sorry.' That was a phrase I was going to have to get used to hearing a lot …

Chapter 2

'I'm so sorry. How awful for you!'

The friend of an acquaintance of an acquaintance was passing on her condolences on my failed wedding. Even though I had absolutely no idea who she was.

'And in front of all those people too!'

Yes. In front of pretty much everyone I know. Thanks for bringing that up. Again.

'Mmm.' I made a non-committal noise and tried to change the subject. 'So, are you looking for a dress for yourself or someone else?'

'A dress?'

'Yes, I assume you're looking for a dress. Is it for a wedding, a prom or another special occasion?' I tried again.

'Oh, I'm not looking for a dress, dear. I just popped in to tell you how sorry I was when I heard he'd left you standing at the altar.'

Why is it when someone makes a comment you'd rather no one else heard, absolutely everyone in the vicinity hears it? The three other customers turned and peered at me.

'Oh, right. Well, that was very kind of you. Now, I'd better see to my clients. Thank you for dropping in.'

I turned my back on her and did my best to find a confident stride and a happy smile with which to greet the other people in my studio, hoping that they had actually come to discuss occasion wear rather than my nuptials, or lack thereof.

I glanced up at the old-fashioned station clock hanging on the wall. Nine p.m. My assistant had gone home hours ago but I'd declined the offer to walk to the station together tonight in favour of catching up on some paperwork and social media updates. I'd actually finished everything over half an hour ago but still I stayed. I loved my studio but even I knew it wasn't healthy to be here quite as much as I was. Working had been my salvation after the whole wedding hoo-ha. It was the one thing I could rely on. Even with a ropey economy, there were still plenty of people in London with money, and weddings were still big business. Luckily.

My studio had been doing pretty well for a couple of years and I knew I wanted to do more, but with the planning of the wedding and having a relationship, I just hadn't really had the time to sit and think about exactly what and how. Now, thanks to Steven, I didn't have to commit time to either of those things – which is why, the day after everything had happened, or more precisely, not happened, I had lain on my studio floor surrounded by spreadsheets, brainstorm pictograms and a plethora of other paperwork. By the end of the day, I had created a five-year plan for my business. Among other things, I wanted to expand so that I could take on a couple more seamstresses – this would allow me not only to take on more commissions, but also to get those that I did take on, done quicker and I was now determined to follow my neatly planned-out path.

'Hello?' a voice called out as the bells above my door tinkled. Damn. I thought I'd locked that after Tash had left. I got up and walked across the studio space, my one indulgent pair of Louboutins clicking hurriedly on the wooden floor.

'Hi!' I greeted Natayla as she turned back from closing the door against the wind that was once more howling down the street outside my cosy studio.

'I'm sorry to bother you. I wasn't sure you'd still be here at this time but we were passing.'

'I'm often here late.' I smiled. 'No bother at all. It's lovely to see you! How was the honeymoon?'

'Amazing!' Natayla gushed. 'Sunsets, sandy beaches, cocktails and relaxing by the pool. We didn't really do much else,' she said, then blushed and smiled shyly.

I smiled back at her and touched her arm gently. 'I'm glad it all went so well, Natayla.'

'Thank you again for making me look so beautiful.'

'It was my pleasure,' I answered, honestly.

'I brought you something,' she said, and handed me a large envelope.

Opening it, I pulled out a black-and-white eight-by-ten photograph of Natayla and her new husband. The photo not only screamed at me how much in love they were, but also showed her dress off perfectly.

'Oh Natayla! That's beautiful. Thank you so much. I shall put it up first thing tomorrow.' My client smiled her shy little smile again and I wavered.

'Only if you're happy with that, of course.'

'Yes! Yes, I am happy. Very happy.'

'Wonderful. Thank you.'

We exchanged a hug and I walked her over to the door, pausing whilst she pulled on her gloves and hat before I opened it. She stepped out and waved again, before hurrying off to a waiting car and disappearing inside. I shut the door, this time throwing the bolt before turning back.

I looked at the clock and once more thought that I really should be making a move to go home. That was the problem with living somewhere you didn't like. You never really wanted to go there. Instead, I picked up my tea and wandered over to the wall covered in beautifully framed pictures. Sipping at my drink, I let my gaze drift over the happy smiles and gorgeous dresses. I laid the latest acquisition on Tash's desk. There was no need for a note. Tash would know what to do with it. She'd been a great find and she was excellent at all the admin side of the business, and with clients, but I still wanted to increase the number of staff. Part of my business plan was to accept an intern. I'd learned so much when I'd done the same thing after getting my degree – about all different aspects of the job, things you just can't learn in college – and I wanted to give someone else the chance to have that same experience. The thought of going to watch Final Collection shows with the view to employing someone, and then helping to nurture and develop that talent, gave me something to look forward to. My gaze went back to the photograph lying on the desk of the happy couple. The look of joy and love on their faces radiated out of the picture. I touched it briefly, almost as if by doing that I could experience that same joy, just for a moment.

Taking a deep breath, I took my mug and rinsed it out in the little kitchenette at the back of the studio. I slipped on my coat and belted it before grabbing the oversized leather tote bag I carried everywhere, and headed to the door.

'When's it going to stop?' I asked my best friend, Mags, as I relayed the surprise visit I'd had during the week. 'Honestly, I feel like the prime exhibit at a zoo! I have absolutely no idea who this woman was. I didn't even know any of the people she reeled off as having told her the "devastating news" of my being jilted at the altar.'

'Just ignore the old bag,' Mags said sagely as she refilled my empty wine glass.

'She even pointed out the irony of someone who makes wedding dresses for a living being left at the altar on her own

7

wedding day. I mean, seriously! I felt like suggesting that she should join Mensa because, of course, that thought hasn't crossed my mind once!'

'Have you heard anything more from him?'

'What, since he left me that thoughtful note saying he was going to go on the honeymoon alone as it "seemed a shame to waste it" and it would be good to "have some space between us"?' I'd definitely had too much wine as I was doing finger quotes in the air. I never did finger quotes.

'Yes.'

'No.'

That was the good thing about living in London. It was big. You were much less likely to bump into people you knew than if you lived in a village. Of course, Steven knew all our old haunts, and seemed to be having the good sense to stay out of them. I imagine he'd heard about my reaction in the church. I knew Rob wouldn't have said anything out of choice but announcing that the wedding was off whilst trying to stem a steady flow of blood from his nose, together with the obvious lack of a groom, had probably meant that there wasn't a whole lot of explanation required. Steven was many things, but he wasn't stupid. He'd likely worked out pretty quickly that going to the places we used to frequent together may lead to the possibility of the term 'regular haunt' becoming more literal than figurative for him.

'How are your parents doing?' Mags asked.

Mags and I had been friends forever. We were both Army brats with our fathers serving in the same battalion, and I couldn't remember a time when Mags wasn't my best friend. When it had become clear that Steven wasn't going to make an appearance at the church, she'd automatically known that the last thing I wanted, or needed, was a crowd of people fussing around me. She'd gone over to my parents, tactfully explained the situation, then sat with them whilst my dad stared at the flower display – silently, likely imagining several different ways to kill Steven with a gerbera – and my mum repeatedly asked how Steven could do such a thing, intermittently dabbing at her eyes with an embroidered linen handkerchief. Of course, had Mags known I was about to deck the best man, she might have altered her strategy.

'They're OK. Devastated. Concerned. But OK.' I took a swig of the crisp, cool wine. 'I think so long as they know I'm all right, they'll be fine.'

'And are you?' Mags asked, looking at me directly, knowing I could never give her anything but an honest answer.

I drained my glass and thought about it. Was I OK?

'Yes. I think so. Now the shock's worn off. I still have days when I don't really want to get out of bed, but then my stubborn side kicks in and I think that I'm not going to give him the satisfaction of seeing what a bloody mess he's caused.'

Mags nodded. I knew there was another question coming.

'All right. But what about how you *really* are? That's the "showing the world I'm OK" bit taken care of, but how are you inside. Really?'

I loved Mags to bits, but sometimes I wished she wasn't quite so insightful. I fiddled with the wine bottle cork as I let out a sigh.

'I'm not sure, to be honest. He hurt me. Totally humiliated me. But I am getting through it. And that sort of worries me in a way. I mean, shouldn't I be sobbing and wailing and declaring that my broken heart will never mend? It's made me question whether he was really The One after all. I mean, I thought he was, obviously. But now – I don't know! As much as I hate to admit it, I'm secretly wondering if he actually did me a bit of a favour. Would the marriage even have lasted, seeing as I'm not pining away for him?' I took another swig. 'Of course, I'd rather he'd told me prior to the bloody wedding day!' I said, my voice getting louder as I finished the sentence.

It was the truth though. I was seriously wondering if I had very nearly made a big mistake. But the anger at Steven for humiliating me, and my parents, as well as his own, still boiled away. I

9

didn't know how long that would take to go away. I hadn't seen Rob since the wedding day either, so it was likely he wasn't too sure about that aspect either, and, bearing in mind I'd punched him on the nose last time, he clearly wasn't taking any chances. I could hardly blame him.

As if reading my mind, Mags looked over from where she was studying the label on the wine bottle. 'Have you seen Rob at all since then?'

I shook my head.

'You do know you actually broke his nose, don't you?'

I whipped my head around to face her. Thanks to the copious amount of alcohol now thinning my blood, it took the world a moment or two to catch up. I blinked, and waited a few seconds for it all to settle down. Mags pushed her own cute little nose to the side, as if to illustrate the point.

'I couldn't have! He's an ex-Army, six-foot-three rugby player and I'm …' I paused to look down at my own far less statuesque frame, '… not. I didn't even hit him that hard!'

If I'm honest, I wasn't entirely sure about the last bit. In the days following the incident, my hand, with its perfectly manicured nails, had turned a variety of shades, none of which were particularly attractive, as the whole thing became one massive bruise. And he had ended up on his bum.

'Hard enough, it seems,' Mags confirmed, a small smirk catching her lips. I saw it.

'Stop it! It's not funny.'

Her smirk turned into a grin.

'It's not!' I reiterated. 'Anyway, how do you know?'

'I saw him a few days ago. I was at Borough Market at lunchtime and he came into the pub with some colleagues.'

'Oh.'

'He was asking after you. He wanted to know if you were OK.'

'Oh,' I said again. 'What did you tell him?' I asked, after a couple more minutes.

'I just said that you were all right, under the circumstances, and that you would be fine because you're not about to let a lowlife piece of pond scum like Steven ruin your life.'

'Right. Good. OK. So long as you were subtle about it.'

'Of course.'

And the funny thing was, that actually was subtle for Mags. It was lucky that it had been Rob and not Steven she'd run into. We'd been there for every good, and every awful, moment in each other's lives and her fury at seeing her best friend hurt was probably more than my own could ever be. If Steven appeared in her line of vision any time within the next few months, there was every chance a trip to the casualty department would be in his very immediate future. I was just entertaining that idea in my head when Mags broke into my thoughts.

'I think he'd like to see you.'

'Who?'

'Rob.'

'Me? Why?' My hand suddenly flew to my mouth, 'Oh my God! He's going to sue me for breaking his nose!'

Mags spurted out her wine over my kitchen table in laughter. 'He does not want to sue you for breaking his nose!'

'How do you know? Did he specifically say that? He is a lawyer! Why else would he want to see me?'

'Izz, he specialises in company law, not ambulance chasing! Like I said, he's just concerned as to how you are,' she said, mopping up with a paper towel. 'I think he feels some odd sense of responsibility.'

'Well, he shouldn't.'

'No, I told him that too.'

'Good. Well, that's that then.'

'Excellent. Glad that's settled. Is there any more wine?'

11

Chapter 3

The screen on my phone lit up for the third time in an hour. I glanced over, read the name and pressed 'Ignore'. Again. The bride-to-be whose dress I was working on noticed.

'Do you want to get that? It's OK. I have plenty of time.' She almost bounced as she said it, her excitement palpable.

I loved this part of my job. I loved almost every bit of my job actually. It was one of the reasons I'd specialised in bridal wear after leaving Central St Martins, degree in hand. For the happiness, the joy and the excitement that came along with it all. Of course, there was the inevitable odd 'Bridezilla', but for the most part, the women that came into my studio were wonderful and fun, and sometimes a little nervous, although the champagne I provided usually took care of that bit. I loved it. Even now.

It had been over six months since my own non-wedding debacle and the pain, and even the anger, were fading more and more each day. I had come to the conclusion that I'd actually been prevented from making one of the biggest mistakes of my life. A full-on, humiliating and very public prevention, but a prevention all the same. It had, dare I say it, been a good thing. I'd even managed to sell my dress. Time really was a healer in this instance. I was moving on. It wasn't like I was about to start dating again or anything drastic like that just yet, but I was getting through it and moving on.

I looked up at the bride, smiled, and shook my head, the mouthful of pins I was momentarily sporting a handy excuse for not giving a more informed answer.

'I saw Rob again yesterday lunchtime. He said he's tried calling you but you never answer your phone or reply to any of his texts.'

'Well then, maybe he should take the hint. What does he even want anyway?'

'I don't know. Maybe you should answer the phone and find out.' Mags smiled. I rolled my eyes.

'Didn't he say what he wanted when you saw him?'

Mags shook her head and speared an olive from the antipasti platter in between us. 'Nope. Just that he'd been trying to ring you.'

'Did you tell him I don't want to speak to him?'

'I didn't know if you'd been ignoring his calls on purpose or just genuinely missed them, so I didn't like to say either way.'

'Well, now you know for sure so feel free to pass on my wishes next time you bump into him.'

I aimed my cocktail stick at the last remaining olive. It glanced off, causing the olive to fly from the table, ricochet off the lovey-dovey couple's table next to us, and bounce three times on the floor before finally rolling to a stop at the feet of the restaurant owner. He looked down at the offending fruit, then at us, then back at the olive.

'Oh my God, he's coming over!' Mags was now the colour of a beetroot from trying to stifle her laughter in the hushed restaurant. We normally plumped for the noise and bustle of a local Italian, but Mags had seen an offer for this one online and the price was too good to miss trying it out. Right now though, I was wishing we'd resisted.

'*Signorina*.'

13

I kicked Mags under the table and looked up at the man. 'I'm so sorry, it just sort of flew off the plate!'

He nodded. 'Indeed. You would be surprised how much it happens.' He smiled, gave a sweet little bow and left, gesturing to a waiter to clear away the escaped food. Moments later he was back, placing another full dish of olives down on the table, and removing the previous, now empty, bowl.

'On the house.' He did the little bow again, smiled at both of us, then turned and left.

'Excellent! Well done, Izz.' Mags dived in and stabbed another unsuspecting olive. She glanced over at the owner and returned his smile before turning back to assess which olive was next. 'I think you've pulled there!' she stated, spearing her chosen subject.

'But we could eat for free!'

Mags was again putting forward her case for why I should call the Italian restaurant bloke, after he'd made a point of handing me a business card with his mobile number written on the back. She was right. There were definite benefits. And the guy seemed nice, and was certainly attractive. So what was the problem? Why didn't I just go for it? Embrace the joys of being a single woman in the heady metropolis of London? Honestly, I couldn't give her a reason. Instead, I tucked my arm around hers and pulled her closer under the umbrella. The snow that had been gently fluttering down earlier had become heavier whilst we'd been devouring our delicious Italian nibbles.

'He was gorgeous!' she tried again.

'I know, I know. I just don't feel I'm ready to get back on that particular horse yet.' Mags raised her eyebrows, pondering the connotations of what I just said.

I pulled a face. 'You know what I mean.'

She sighed. 'I do.' She squeezed my arm with hers. 'I just don't want you to miss out on anything. But you're right. You need to do it when you're ready.'

I hugged her back. 'Thanks. And I'm sorry about the free food.'

She laughed. 'I'll get over it. Probably better for my waistline this way anyway. Oh! There's my bus. Are you sure you're OK from here?'

'Positive. I'm just going to nip in and pick something up from the studio, then go home. Here, take this,' I said, handing her the umbrella. 'I've got a spare one at work.'

'Thanks! Love you! Text me later.' She gave me a quick hug and rushed off in the direction of the stop.

I sheltered under a shop's overhang and watched to make sure she caught the bus, before turning down the road where my studio resided, the snow inflicting sharp little pinpricks on my cheeks. The silver bells I'd hung tinkled as I unlocked the front door and pushed it open. The notes I wanted were sat on my desk. I grabbed them and put the file in my bag. One of my current brides had some really interesting ideas and I wanted to try sketching out a few designs over the weekend. They were predicting heavy snow, even in the city, so staying in and keeping warm seemed like a good plan. Going back to the door, I lifted the spare umbrella from the coat rack, and stepped outside, the cold wind immediately whipping at my face. I turned the top lock, threw the deadlock, and dropped the keys into my bag before adjusting my scarf a little higher around my neck. The wind was picking up. The spare brolly I'd grabbed wasn't going to last five minutes. It was just going to be a case of moving as fast as possible to the Tube station. Belting my coat securely, ready for the headwind I was about to face, I turned back to the street, and came face to face with Rob.

'Shit!' I exclaimed, stumbling back a step and bumping into the door. The snow was settling faster now and beginning to muffle the noise of the city. Including footsteps, apparently.

Rob quickly reached forward, steadying me. 'Sorry, I didn't mean to make you jump.'

'I tend to do that when people creep up behind me!' I snapped, heart still pounding.

'I wasn't creeping up on you, Izzy. I just got here and was about to say hello when you turned around.'

I cast my glance up the street to where strings of themed Christmas lights shimmered through the snowflakes. In fact, I was looking everywhere but at Rob. I hadn't seen him since he'd gone out to make the speech at the church. I'd taken the opportunity of the distraction to exit via the side door and grab the first taxi I saw.

When I didn't say anything, Rob spoke again. 'I had a meeting with a client …' He indicated further down the road, explaining his presence in the area.

I nodded without looking at him.

'How are you?' he asked.

'I'm fine. Thank you. You?'

'Yep. Fine. Thanks.'

I waited, feeling cold and uncomfortable. 'What do you want, Rob?'

'To talk to you.'

'About what?'

Rob let out a sigh and tipped his head forward. Little flurries of snow had settled on his hair, the intense blackness of it highlighting their sparkle. He shook his head gently and they disappeared. A resigned smile was on his lips as he looked back up at me.

'I thought we were friends.'

'You were Steven's best man, not mine,' I pointed out.

'Only because you never asked me to be a bridesmaid.'

'The shoes didn't come in a size twelve.'

'Well, at least you checked before discounting me.'

I finally smiled at him. Once again, he was attuned to the horrible awkwardness I was feeling and doing his best to dissipate it. Although, to be fair, the only reason I was feeling awkward was because he was standing there. So, technically, it was his

16

fault anyway. But I knew I couldn't avoid him forever. He was right. We were friends. Yes, Steven had introduced us, but we'd also become friends in our own right. Not close as such, but friends all the same. Until the wedding day. For some reason, I'd suddenly felt like there were sides. And Rob, with his best man title, automatically fell on Steven's. I knew in my heart that wasn't fair – on him, or me, or our friendship. But it just sort of happened and the longer I went without speaking to him, the harder it got to get over the awkwardness that I knew would arise. And here I was, six months later, feeling awkward as hell.

'Izzy, please. Can we just go for a drink, and talk?'

I shook my head, noticing that the dampness of the air was beginning to put the curl back into my carefully straightened hair.

'Is there anything to say?' I asked, looking directly at him for the first time since he'd turned up. Big mistake. The hurt in his eyes stabbed at my insides. He quickly covered it with a crooked smile.

'If you have to ask, then no. I don't suppose there is.' He turned up the collar of his dark-grey wool coat a little more as the wind picked up again and funnelled itself down the street. 'Come on, I'll walk you to the Tube.'

'That's all right. I ... um ... haven't quite finished here, and—'

'Izzy, for God's sake!'

I snapped my head up. I'd never once seen Rob angry. He was so laidback, normally being in his company was like a hit of Valium – in a good way. But not tonight. Tonight it seemed I had managed to push the right button.

'What's wrong with you?' he asked.

'Nothing's wrong with me!'

'Then why are you being like this?'

'Like what, exactly?'

'Ignoring my calls, my texts. Just generally refusing to speak to me at all and looking at me like you'd wish the ground would open up and swallow me whole! It wasn't me that left you at the

17

altar, Izz, and I'm damned if I'm going to take the blame for it!'

Silence settled between us. And then, to my utter horror – and apparently Rob's, judging by the look on his face – I started to cry.

'Oh no, no, no!' Within a moment, Rob had moved and wrapped his arms around me. 'Izzy, please don't cry. I'm so sorry. I didn't mean to upset you.'

I gave a reply to say that it wasn't his fault, I didn't mean to cry and that I wasn't even sure why I was crying. That's how the reply sounded in my head anyway. All that actually came out was a gurgly, mumbly sort of noise.

'Come on. Let's get you out of this cold.'

Rob scanned the street and saw a black cab with its light on. He curled his lips and emitted a loud whistle, sticking his hand out to signal the taxi. Seeing the cab turn towards us, he replaced his arm, the warmth of him flooding against me again.

'I don't need a cab to the station. It's not far,' I said. I knew money wasn't an issue for Rob, and there was no way he was going to let me pay, but I'd been brought up not to waste money. With the traffic crawling even more than usual thanks to the weather, I could probably walk there quicker to get my train anyway.

Rob didn't reply, merely opened the door for me as the taxi pulled up and stepped in behind me. He gave the driver an address I recognised as his apartment building.

'Rob,' I started.

'I know. You just want to go home.'

He had a knack of being able to do that. Suss out what I was thinking even before I knew I was thinking it.

I nodded.

'I understand,' he said, 'but the news alerts have been saying that a load of trains have been cancelled and stations closed. That was earlier, so goodness knows what it's like now. The snow's even heavier further out. It might be worth checking that your train is definitely running before you stand freezing on a station platform.'

'Oh. Umm –' I sniffed and rifled through my bag for a tissue – 'good idea. Thanks.'

'Not a problem. Maybe I should be thanking this weather. At least it's forced you to talk to me.' I looked down and studied our damp footprints mixing on the floor.

'Although I really didn't mean to make you cry. I sort of did want the ground to swallow me whole right at that moment.'

I glanced up, expecting to see one of his lazy smiles but his face showed nothing but remorse and honesty. I moved my head on his chest where it still lay after he'd got in the cab and pulled me back into the hug.

'That makes two of us,' I replied. And then realised how that sounded. I sat up, pulling away from him. 'I mean I wanted the ground to swallow me, not you! Standing there blubbering like an idiot at you for no good reason.'

I felt the warmth of embarrassment start to creep up my neck and pulled my scarf up in the hope of disguising it a little longer. Just as the silence was about to tick over into awkward, the taxi indicated and pulled in to the side of the road. We were in front of Rob's apartment complex. He tapped his card on the machine before following me out onto the snowy pavement.

As he was paying, I'd gathered myself, standing back from the edge of the road to avoid splashing from passing traffic. I waited, back straight, feeling resolutely British and foolish for my earlier unexpected outburst. Rob looked at me, his gaze becoming quizzical before he turned away to pull open the heavy door that led into the foyer of the swanky address. I hesitated before entering. Really I just wanted to go home but, if the trains were as he said they were, then it really would be best to find out which ones were still running rather than just blindly hoping mine was one of them. The taxi driver who'd dropped us off had mentioned he was glad we'd not asked him to take us further outside the city as his colleagues had been reporting the roads were getting a lot worse. Calling one as an alternative method to get me home was looking less and less likely. I could ring Mags and see if I could at least get to her flat. It was still a journey but less so than getting to my own place.

'I can see the cogs whirring.' Rob's words jolted me out of my thoughts.

'Sorry?'

Rob smiled as he stood aside for the occupants of the lift to exit before inviting me to enter first. 'I imagine your brain is currently working feverishly on how to get home?'

I blushed. It really was uncanny how well he could read me. If I spent an evening with him and Mags, I don't think I'd actually have to speak at all. They both had a knack of knowing what I was going to say anyway. Odd that Steven had never had a clue. Although, fair to say, that clearly went both ways as I'd had no idea he was going to ditch me at the altar either.

'I wouldn't say "feverishly" exactly,' I lied. 'But yes, I am considering what the best solution might be.'

Honestly, I was amazed my nose didn't grow. And from the amused look Rob gave me, so was he. 'Stop fretting, Izz. We'll get you home.'

The lift pinged and the doors swished open. I exited and stood aside, not knowing which way to go. I knew which building Rob lived in, but had never actually been there before. Rob followed me out. He turned left and walked down the hall to the end apartment and put his key in the lock. Turning it, he pushed open the door and stepped in, holding the door for me as I caught up.

'Wow, this is gorgeous!' I said, walking past him down the hall, pulling off my heels as I did so. Before me, from a huge picture window, the beauty of London shimmered under electric light. Snowflakes glittered past the window in a rush, and the roofs below now had a distinct covering of snow.

'Yes, I have to admit that the view really sold it to me.'

'I can see why.'

I turned to look around at the rest of the apartment. It felt welcoming and homely, but in a modern way. It certainly didn't have the macho, bachelor pad feel I'd been expecting. Rob even had scatter cushions on his sofas! It dawned on me that there was a definite hint of a woman's touch here. At the thought, a feeling I couldn't quite explain went through me. I shook it off and looked down at my feet, wiggling my toes. The floor was warm from the underfloor heating and felt lovely and soothing as it thawed my frozen toes. In the corner stood a perfectly decorated Christmas tree, with silver and white decorations twinkling in the glow from the accompanying warm white fairy lights. There were more lights across the mantelpiece and adorning the balustrade of the three steps that separated the kitchen from the main floor. Cards were starting to fill the hangers created for them. It was all elegantly beautiful, like living pages torn from an upmarket décor magazine. I'd seen Rob with girls during the time I'd been engaged to Steven but I'd never heard of him getting particularly serious with anyone. But then again I hadn't been in touch with him for months. Perhaps something had changed. I surreptitiously glanced around to see if I could spot any other signs of feminine presence. The last thing I needed right now was for a girlfriend to walk in and wonder why the hell her boyfriend had a strange woman, no doubt sporting spectacular panda eyes by this point, in their flat.

'Would you like something to drink?' Rob asked.

A hot drink sounded perfect right at that moment. The outside of me was thawing, but inside I still felt chilled to the bone after walking from the restaurant. But I really needed to get home. My hesitation told on me.

'I'm about to check the roads and weather but my ears are frozen and I'm pretty sure part of my brain is too. I also work better when I've got coffee inside me, so I'm making a drink anyway. You look half frozen and it won't do you any good if you go down with a chill, will it?'

I thought of my clients. Rob had a point. He saw me waver.

'One hot chocolate coming up. Take a seat, I'll fire up the laptop in a minute and we can plan your escape route.'

'Don't put it like that. I'm not looking to escape from you!'

Rob busied himself at the fancy drinks machine he had on his countertop. His mouth had an amused curve to it as he snagged a couple of the little pots that slid into the machine from a shelf just beside it.

'Actually I was referring to your escape from the city.'

'Oh. Of course! Exactly.'

From the corner of my eye I saw Rob almost imperceptibly shake his head as he continued to concentrate on the task in hand. I knew I'd hurt his feelings. He'd been nothing but kind to me from the day of the non-nuptials and I hadn't had the decency to act the same. It dawned on me that he was right with what he'd said earlier. I mean, he was wrong, but he was right. From where he stood, it probably did look like I was blaming him for the whole wedding debacle – even down to getting punched on the nose! And I didn't blame him at all – for any of it. In fact, I had been inordinately glad he'd been there that day, and not just because he'd indirectly saved me from getting arrested for decking a vicar. His presence, his calming demeanour and just the small squeeze of my hand he'd given during those horrible moments when he'd had to tell me Steven wasn't coming – it had meant so much. Firmly stuck right in the middle, he'd acted with absolute kindness and consideration towards me. I'd never thought about it from his perspective before. How would I have felt if I'd had to deliver a message like that? And all I'd done since was ignore any attempt at contact. I knew the reasons for it – at least some of them. But looking at it now, I could see how confusing it would have been for Rob. Oh God! I was a horrible human being!

Rob put the drinks down on the coffee table, a laptop tucked under his arm.

'One hot chocolate. Get that inside you and—' He stopped

as he caught a glance at my face. 'Are you all right? You've gone really pale. Look, take this.' He leant across, pulled a soft blanket from the other sofa and laid it around my shoulders. 'Do you feel sick, or feverish? I've got a mate who's a doctor. He only lives round the corner, I can give him—'

'Rob, I'm fine,' I said, although I didn't shrug off the blanket. It was so beautifully soft and snuggly.

The look on his face showed he doubted my self-diagnosis and he placed the back of his hand on my forehead.

'You don't seem to have a temperature,' he noted, his voice still sounding doubtful.

'I don't. I'm fine,' I said, picking up one of the mugs from the table.

'Then why do you look terrible?'

I looked up from my drink. 'Gee, thanks!' I laughed. 'You certainly know how to make a girl feel good!'

Rob tilted his head and pulled a face. 'You know what I mean. Although your colour does seem to be coming back a little now. Are you sure you're all right?'

I set my drink back on its coaster and turned to face him. 'Rob, I'm sorry.' Confusion clouded his face.

'For?' he asked.

I took a deep breath. 'Well, let's see. For punching you on the nose—'

'You already apologised for that at the time,' he interrupted.

'Yes, but I didn't apologise for actually breaking it.'

'To be fair, you didn't know you had broken it.'

'So it's true? I did break it?' I replied, a little horrified. I was still secretly hoping Mags had got her facts skewed on this. I don't know why I thought not breaking his nose was any better than breaking it. I'd still punched him, for goodness' sake. But in my own little twisted mess of logic, it made a semblance of sense.

'You did.'

'Oh my God.' I covered my face with my hands, shame and

23

embarrassment flooding over me again.

Rob laughed and gave me a quick squeeze around the shoulders. 'Don't even think about it, Izz. I've been playing rugby since I was six years old. It's not the first time it's been broken. I doubt it'll be the last, either.'

I dropped my hands down to my lap and slid my glance to him.

'Honestly. It's fine. Frankly, I was kind of impressed.'

'What? Why?'

Rob laughed. 'Izzy, look at you! You're this petite, waify, very feminine-looking little thing who looks like she'd blow over in a strong breeze and you knocked a six-foot-three, seventeen stone rugby-playing bloke on his arse and broke his nose.'

'And that's impressive? I'm more inclined to call it mortifying! And I'm not sure how I feel about being called a "waify little thing" either.'

'It wasn't meant in a derogatory way. A lot of men find it very attractive – look at Kylie! So don't knock it. And yes, it is impressive. I'm still getting jibes at the club about being decked by you. Either way, it certainly makes me worry less about you walking to the Tube!'

'Oh dear. I'm sorry you're getting teased. I didn't really think that whole thing through.'

'Don't worry. I give as good as I get.'

I grinned. 'That I believe.'

'That's the first real smile I've seen from you all evening.' At his words, the smile faded a little.

'Uh oh. Looks like I should have kept quiet.'

I rolled my eyes at him and he chuckled, sipping his coffee.

'Let's have a look at this weather,' he said, opening the laptop.

I put my hand on the lid and closed it again, gently. Rob looked up, the same expression of confusion on his face as he'd shown earlier. Poor Rob. I had a feeling he wished his meeting had been elsewhere this evening thereby avoiding bumping into me and inadvertently boarding the Isabel Emotional Rollercoaster.

'I need to apologise for some other things, and I need to do it now. I've already let it go on for far too long.'

Rob didn't say anything so I continued.

'I'm sorry I walked out at the church. I should have stayed until you came back in from making the announcement, not least to thank you for doing that.'

I could see Rob was about to say something. I put my hand on his arm to stall him.

'I never thought about the position that you were in. Having to come and tell me Steven wasn't coming. I know you and I weren't close but we were friends, and I'm pretty sure, from what I knew – know – of you, that it wasn't an easy thing for you to have to do. I'm sorry that you were put in that position and I'm sorry that I didn't handle it better.'

'Izzy.' Rob moved and took my hands in his. They practically disappeared within them. I never thought of myself as particularly petite. Mags was pretty dinky too so there was no big comparison usually. Now, sat next to Rob, my hands engulfed in his, I could see why he'd describe me as waif-like. And I realised that, from him, I didn't mind it. It wasn't the first time I'd heard a similar term, but from Rob it had seemed like a compliment. That was new. I looked up from our hands and into Rob's gentle brown eyes, surrounded by ridiculously long, thick and jealousy-inducing dark lashes.

'Izz?' His voice sounded unsure.

'Sorry, yes?' I came back from the lash envy.

'Please don't ever blame yourself for what happened. None of it was your fault. And I really don't like to think of you believing that any of it was.'

I pulled a face. 'I'm pretty sure some of it was down to me. I mean, it was me that he didn't want to marry, after all.'

'And he's a fool for that!' There was an edge to Rob's voice that I'd rarely heard. I tried to meet his eyes but he'd already turned away. Letting go of my hands, he pushed my mug towards me.

25

'This is getting cold.'

I leant forward and picked up the mug, cradling it in my hands, enjoying the warmth.

'I wanted to say sorry for ignoring all your calls and texts, too. I don't know why I did. Well, I do, I suppose.'

Rob still wasn't looking at me. I carried on.

'I was just embarrassed. At having been stood up. At having punched you. At having fled like an overly dramatic heroine in a Barbara Cartland novel. Just at everything. And I suppose I thought that having contact with you was too close to having contact with Steven.'

I felt Rob stiffen next to me.

'I understand.' His voice was tight. 'As I said, you shouldn't feel responsible for anything that happened that day. Everything that went wrong was down to Steven being a twat. It's as simple as that. And I can see now why you wouldn't want anything to do with me. What was supposed to be the best day of your life turned out to be one of the worst. And as the messenger, you're always going to associate me with that day, that moment. It's understandable. I guess I never thought about it like that. I just wanted to know that you were OK. Mags had assured me that you were – at least that you were putting on a brave face, which I knew you would. But I suppose I needed to see for myself. I realise now that I should have just taken Mags' word and not barrelled in.'

'Rob …'

He looked at me for the first time since he'd started his speech. 'There's something I do need you to know though. I am nothing like Steven. I would never, ever have done that to you – to anyone,' he corrected himself. 'I went to see him straight after and told him exactly what I thought of his actions and his cowardice. We haven't spoken since.'

'Oh Rob, no! I never meant for you to fall out with Steven over this. What happened between us shouldn't affect your friendship.

One has nothing to do with the other.'

'Yes, it does, Izzy. And of course it's going to affect it. How could it not? He ensured that it would by dumping me right in the middle of it all. And he lied to me. I was supposed to stay over the night before. We were going to go out and get breakfast in the morning then go back to the flat and get ready. Steven cancelled the night before and said he had a really bad headache.'

'He told me the same thing when I called to say goodnight. He does get bad headaches.' I obviously wasn't Steven's biggest fan right now, but I also had a streak of fair play running through me, which forced me to confirm his account and reasons. Annoyingly.

'Yeah I know. And I know that the nerves might have kicked it off, which is why I didn't think too much of it. But then he said that he wouldn't be able to do breakfast the next day either. I asked him why and he just said that he thought it would be better to have a lie in. When I asked him if everything was OK, he said it was. That he just wanted to make sure he wasn't going to feel bad at the wedding. I took him at his word because I never had reason to doubt him.'

'What is it that you're saying?'

'I'm saying that Steven knew the night before that he wasn't going to be at that church.'

I looked at Rob. 'You don't know that,' I said, my voice betraying my own uncertainty.

Rob ran a hand over his hair. 'Yeah, Izz. I do. He told me.'

I couldn't help the tears that pricked at my eyes, even though I willed them away. Rob noticed anyway.

'I'm sorry. I shouldn't have said anything.'

'Yes. You should. Please. Just tell me what else you know.'

'There isn't much else to tell. He said he'd meet me at the church instead. So, on the day it was getting later and later, and he wasn't answering his phone. I had all these visions that something awful had happened and was kicking myself for not going round. I was just about to drive over there when he finally picked up and told me that he couldn't do it. That he just didn't feel ready to get married.'

'I never pressured him into getting engaged or setting a date. You have to know that.'

'No. I know you didn't.' Rob took my hand. 'It wasn't your fault. None of it. Please don't ever forget that.'

I smiled at his sincerity.

'OK. But you still don't know that Steven didn't just panic at the last minute.' I had no idea whether I was trying to defend Steven – and if so, why. Or if it was that, somehow, being stood up at the last minute was better than the alternative Rob was hinting at.

'I asked him outright. When I went round there after you'd left.'

I shook my head.

'I'm sorry, Izz. I guess Steven had changed more than I thought over the years. The bloke I went to uni with would never have acted like that. He would have had the guts to sort it out earlier. And he would have had the guts to tell you himself.'

'Thereby reducing the chance that you'd be the one to get a fist in the face.'

Rob gave me half a crooked grin. 'I have to admit, I hadn't even considered that was a remote possibility until it happened. Perhaps Steven was more canny than I thought. Although he did look pretty shocked when I turned up at his place suitably bloody.'

'I can imagine.'

'He thought your dad might have done it.'

'Dad would never have hit you. He knew you had nothing to do with it. Though, I can't guarantee he wouldn't have floored Steven, given the opportunity.'

'Good to know. But, like I said, maybe I shouldn't have told you.'

'No. I'm glad you did. I know this can't have been easy for you, Rob. And I'm so sorry that it's caused you to lose a friend.'

28

'Yeah. Me too. But I asked him if everything was all right the night before. I gave him the opportunity to tell me then and there. If he had just told me then, I would have understood.' He pulled a face. 'Well, understood might be an overstatement. But dealt with it better, at least. There might have been a chance at salvaging the friendship. But not this way. He lied to me. He lied to you. He left you to face everyone. On your own.'

'I wasn't on my own,' I said softly, touching my shoulder against his for a moment, but keeping my face turned away, just until I regained my composure a little more.

'Izzy. I know it'll always be hard for you to dissociate me from that day, and I can understand that. I understand if you don't want to ever see me again but if you'll permit me to ask one thing of you, it's that you never lump me together with Steven just because, for one day, we were supposed to wear matching suits.'

I didn't really know what to say. My throat felt like it was closing up, so even if I'd known what to say, I'm not sure I would have been able to voice it. Instead I just shook my head. I swallowed hard.

'I promise,' I replied, eventually.

A brief smile flashed on Rob's face, not quite hitting his eyes. 'OK. Now that's all sorted, let's see about getting you home.'

I glanced up at the huge window. There were curtains hanging either side but I doubted Rob ever closed them. With a view like that, I certainly wouldn't. The snow was still falling and if anything, had only got heavier. When I looked back, Rob had the laptop open and was looking at a couple of different pages showing weather, roads and live traffic updates. His teeth worried his bottom lip as he concentrated.

'How's it looking?' I asked when I couldn't bear the suspense any longer.

'Yeah, umm, I think we can work something out.' He threw me a smile before going back to the computer.

I burst out laughing. Rob turned, his expression a mixture of surprise and confusion.

'What's so funny?' he asked, a smile forming on his face in response to mine.

'You.'

'I'm not sure I like the sound of that.'

I grinned again and bumped against his side in jest. 'You are absolutely the world's worst liar.'

He pulled a face. 'I am?'

'I'm afraid so. But don't worry. That's not a bad thing. Actually, it's a pretty good thing in my book.' I smiled, honestly. I'd had more than enough of being lied to. And I knew why Rob was trying to cover his fib in this case. He knew I wanted to get home but I was guessing from his terrible lie that the roads and weather were pretty bad.

'How do you ever win court cases?'

'What?' he asked, a completely bemused look on his face.

'You do have court cases sometimes, don't you?'

'Yes,' he answered slowly, clearly having no idea where this conversation was going.

'Well, don't you have to be able to fool people, and stuff? If your attempt at telling me the roads were fine is anything to go by, I – and don't take this the wrong way – I don't think you can be very good at it.'

'So what you're saying is, not only do you count me in the same low level of humanity as your ex, but you also think I'm terrible at my job? Is that what you're saying?'

I sat for a moment looking at him. His honest face had transformed into one with a completely unreadable expression. And put like that, it sort of did sound like that's what I was saying. But I wasn't! And then I caught it. The little smirk that was starting at the corner of his mouth.

'Oh, you!' I grabbed a scatter cushion and whacked him with it. 'That wasn't what I was saying at all. And you know it!'

30

'Fair enough' – he laughed – 'and for your information, lying isn't a part of my job. I have to go on what the facts say. And whilst I am apparently the "world's worst liar", I do have a pretty good poker face, which comes in far more handy in my job. Thank goodness.'

'You certainly do.' There was no denying that. Until I'd seen that grin start to sneak out, I'd had no idea of his true reaction to what he thought I was saying.

'So,' I started, replacing my weapon in the corner of the sofa, 'I'm guessing that the roads are pretty bad.'

Rob pulled an apologetic face. 'I'm afraid they're not looking the best.' He pulled the computer from the table onto his lap and pointed at the traffic page he had up. 'I've looked at all the possible routes we could try. They're all showing red at the moment.'

'And red's obviously not good.' I stated the obvious.

'No. Red means traffic's pretty much at a standstill. From what I can see, it looks like there's been an accident on the main route out and, of course, everyone else has tried to find other ways, which, with the weather and increased volume of traffic, has just bunged them up too.'

'Oh. That's not great, is it?'

'Not really. I mean, we can try—'

'We?'

'Yes, we.'

'You don't need to do all this for me, you know,' I said. 'Besides, I'm not sure I really deserve it with the way I've treated you.' I paused. 'And for the record, I'd hate it if I never saw you again.'

Rob looked up from the traffic website. 'Why don't we just forget all about that now? Start anew?' I returned the gentle smile he was giving me.

'That sounds really good.'

'Agreed. Now. Let's have another look at this weather.'

Chapter 4

Rob grabbed the remote control, pressed a button and his TV came on with a little welcome message.

He punched in some numbers with his thumb and BBC News 24 came up.

'... *with all main routes out of London currently extremely slow or blocked entirely.*' I looked at Rob and pulled a face. 'That doesn't sound too promising, does it?'

'Don't give up yet.' Rob smiled. 'Let's consult The Oracle.'

'The Oracle?'

He grinned. 'Twitter or X or whatever it is.'

He switched back to the main screen on his laptop and pressed the icon for the app. His timeline immediately filled the screen and I leant over a little to see what was trending. Sure enough #snow was right near the top. Rob tapped on it to see what opinions were being given out on the subject. Typically, there were various versions of 'America gets tonnes more of the stuff and things don't grind to a halt.' Rob and I glanced at each other and rolled our eyes. 'That old chestnut' the exchange said silently. The fact that America got tonnes of the stuff was exactly the reason why things didn't grind to a halt. I imagined that the same people who were moaning about the situation now would probably be the same ones moaning if a fleet of highly expensive snow ploughs were sat in a shed unused for ninety-nine per cent of the time because 'it's not like we get tonnes of the stuff very often.' Rob skimmed over those tweets and looked for something more constructive.

He found a tag labelled *#Londonsnow* and touched it. Another stream opened up. Silently we scanned over the comments. I glanced at Rob and could see that even his optimism was failing. From the television we heard the announcement that they were '… *now going live to our reporter, Beth Sanders.*' Beth thanked the anchor and began her report, advising that she was standing on one of the main arteries in and out of London to the south, which was now entirely blocked due to the snow. Behind her we could see lines of cars, some off at an angle, clearly abandoned. The reporter began an interview with one driver who had chosen to stick with his car. Looking completely fed up and frozen to the bone, the man relayed how, even though he'd left work early, he'd still now been stuck in his current position for over five hours.

I groaned audibly. 'Oh, that poor man.' I looked over at Rob and could see him weighing something up in his mind. 'What are you thinking?'

'OK, look.' He turned to me, reducing the volume on the TV a little. 'Obviously those roads are pretty blocked up, but I know you want to get home. The Range Rover will go pretty much anywhere and I know a couple of short cuts—'

'No! Absolutely not!' I cut in.

Rob looked slightly taken aback at my vehemence.

'I'm not getting home tonight and that's that. There's no way I'm going to ask you to put yourself at risk to get me there.'

'You didn't ask me and I wouldn't put either of us at risk. You know me better than that.'

'No. Final answer. I'll just ring round and find a hotel.'

'No! Absolutely not!' Rob returned my own words to me.

'Pardon?'

'There's no need for you to stay at a hotel. There's a perfectly good guest bedroom here.'

'Oh! No! I couldn't … I …'

Rob tilted his head at me, waiting for me to finish.

I sat up a little straighter and tried again. 'I couldn't possibly do that, Rob. I mean, it's very kind of you, but you've already done so much this evening, trying to get me home.'

'Izzy, I've looked up a couple of websites and put the news on. That's all.'

'No, that's not all. If it wasn't for you, I'd likely still be standing at the station freezing my backside off!'

'Well, then I'm glad I came along because that really would be a crime.' He gave me a cheeky wink, closed the laptop and put it aside. Then he rose and jogged up the three steps to the kitchen, heading for the fridge. 'Beer or wine?'

'Hang on, I don't think we finished discussing this,' I said, following him into the kitchen.

'Yes we did,' he said, his head now practically entirely inside the fridge as he rooted around at the back. He popped back out and shut the door, two ready meals in his hands, 'Which one of these do you want? Sorry it's nothing grander, but I wasn't expecting company tonight and I'd loath to try and ask anyone to deliver tonight in this weather, even if they were prepared to.'

I put aside the fact that Rob was bossing me about for a moment to reflect on the fact that he was showing such consideration to takeaway delivery people, and thought again how sweet he could be. But then I was straight back to the matter in hand.

I glanced down at the meals in his hands. They both looked delicious. But I wasn't used to being told when and where I was staying. Even though I knew it was all meant in the best and kindest way.

'Rob. I really do appreciate the offer but I think it's best if I just find a hotel. I've imposed on you enough. Besides, I've already eaten. Mags and I had dinner.'

'No imposition,' he stated, jiggling the boxes of food in his hands in question again, 'And you can just have a bit of one to keep me company. Any preference?'

I let out a huff. He was obviously sweet but, by God, he was also clearly stubborn as hell when he wanted to be.

'Thank you, but I'm not hungry,' I said. At which point my mutinous stomach let out the most enormous growl.

'No. I can tell.' Rob was wearing his poker face, but it didn't last long. I saw the corners of his eyes crinkle as my stomach rumbled again. He put the food on the counter and placed his hands on my upper arms.

'Izzy. Come on. Clearly you're hungry. I know I am.'

My traitorous body wasn't letting me out of this one so I conceded. 'OK, yes I'm hungry. Mags is on a pre-Christmas diet so we both just had antipasti. Which is fine, by the way! But I missed lunch. So, yes, I am a bit hungry.'

'And it would seem you get grouchy when you're hungry. Hangry.' Rob smiled, somehow softening the blow of the extremely accurate observation.

'Wow,' I said, flatly. 'You've really got this gracious host thing sussed.'

Rob laughed, letting go of me and poking holes with a knife in the plastic wrap coverings of the ready meals. He opened the microwave and shoved them both in, adjusting the timings so that they'd both be ready together. Pulling open the cutlery drawer, he handed me knives and forks, before going back to his original question.

'So, beer or wine?'

A few minutes later, we were sat next to one another on the sofa, ready meals tipped out onto plates, with red wine filling our glasses. The TV was still on the news channel, and showing reports of increasingly miserable looking drivers stuck on various routes, in and around the south-east. Reporter Beth was looking colder and colder by the minute. I knew that, but for the grace of Rob, there go I. Except I would have been in a far worse position because, unlike Beth, who was decked out from head to foot in North Face winter-ready clothing and boots, I had set out this morning in a knee-length wool coat and four-inch heels. Both of these looked fabulous but were definitely not up to the job of keeping me warm whilst I stood waiting for a train that was never going to come. But staying at Rob's tonight? Why was I having such a hard time with that? We were friends – again – that obstacle, at least, thankfully seemed to have been surmounted. I'd stayed over with Mags plenty of times when we'd been out on the town or had a movie night in with popcorn and jammies. Mags was a friend. Rob was a friend. So staying over here was just like staying over at Mags'. Wasn't it?

'Those cogs are whirring again.' Rob broke into my thoughts.

I took a sip of my wine, and hoped I didn't have Ribena smiles. Best to be honest. 'I just feel a little awkward about staying here tonight.'

'Why?'

Honestly, I had no idea.

'I don't really know. I suppose tonight's just sort of taken me by surprise – I mean, I haven't spoken to you in six months and then I bump into you, promptly cry all over you, and then you offer to risk life and limb to get me home, feed me and offer me a bed for the night because it turns out I actually have *zero* chance of getting home tonight. I just – I think it'd be better if I went to a hotel. It'd be less awkward.'

Rob nodded slowly, then looked directly at me with those eyes the colour of a melting Galaxy chocolate bar.

'Izzy. We're friends, right? We established that?'

'Yes. We are.'

'Good. So if you'd got to Mags' place and realised you couldn't get home, would you be saying that you should go and find a hotel?'

'No, of course not, but—'

'But what?'

'But …' I didn't actually know "but what". Rob had once again delved into what I was thinking and laid it out there for us both to see. I really was going to have to keep closer control of my thoughts.

'Is it because I'm a bloke and you're not?' He was grinning.

'Oh, I don't know!' I bumped my head down onto my knees, feeling just the tiniest bit idiotic.

Rob laughed and rubbed my back. 'Come on, Izz. We're friends. Nothing more. And no offence, I'm not looking for anything but friendship from you. If you were a great big hairy rugby player I'd still have fed you and offered you a room rather than letting you freeze on a station platform. The fact that you're …'

'Waify?' I filled in for him from my hunched over position.

'I was going to say "not"' – he laughed – 'just means that I at least got to eat one of those meals.'

'But I don't have any spare clothes – or my toothbrush!' I said, sitting up.

'I can stick your stuff in the washing machine, and put it in the dryer. You can borrow something to sleep in, and I have spare toothbrushes.'

I rolled my lips inwards at the plural. 'Toothbrushes, eh? That implies more than one.'

Rob waggled his eyebrows. 'Cheaper in bulk.'

I rolled my eyes and he laughed.

'OK. Fine. Then thank you. If you're sure I'm not imposing—'

'You're not imposing.'

'Or my being here isn't going to cause any …'

Rob frowned, but the smile remained on his lips. 'Any what?'

'Umm …'

'Izzy, just tell me what on earth you've thought of this time?'

'I just don't want you getting in trouble if your girlfriend walks in and you've got another female here. I mean, not that we're, you know … we're just friends, but if she walks in and there's another woman here and she doesn't know then she might—'

'She won't,' Rob said, shaking his head at me, a look of incredulousness fixing on his features. 'She won't because she doesn't exist. I don't have a girlfriend to walk in unsuspectingly. And before your crazy mind goes off on yet another tangent, I don't have a boyfriend either. Just for absolute clarification. Now that's taken care of, are there any other scenarios you need to tell me about that might possibly happen, or can we please just sit and relax?'

'No. I can't think of anything else,' I said.

'Thank goodness,' Rob said, with a little more feeling than I'd have liked.

'At the minute,' I added, just for that.

He looked at me for a long moment.

I pulled a face and half smiled. 'Don't tell me. Now you're beginning to think that Steven might have been on the right track leaving me.'

I saw a shadow flit across Rob's eyes, before he smiled. 'Nope. Not even close. I still think he's a twat. Now, switch that mind of yours to a slower speed, put your feet up and relax.'

I smiled back at him. 'I'm not sure it has a slower speed, but I can try.'

'Great!' Rob said happily as he let out a sigh and stretched his long legs out on the coffee table in front of us.

'Do you want to watch a film?' he asked.

'Yep, sure,' I answered. That actually sounded pretty nice. Wine, warmth, good company and something nice and inane on the telly. Although, oh dear, Rob was a really intelligent guy. I watched as he brought up the video streaming service and hoped he didn't head to the 'Foreign Films' section. I couldn't deal with subtitles tonight.

'What do you fancy?' he asked.

'Me?'

He laughed. 'Of course, you. You're my guest.'

'Oh! I really don't mind.' I snuggled into the sofa a little more, grabbing the blanket that Rob had put around my shoulders earlier. 'Although nothing with subtitles.' I decided to come clean because I knew he'd only fish out that thought from my brain anyway.

'Subtitles?'

'Yeah, you know. Something foreign with subtitles. Preferably not that. Although, of course, it is your house, so if you—'

'Oh God, please don't tell me you think I look like a hipster.'

I gave a hearty laugh. Hipster? Rob? Umm, that would be a no.

'Hardly! You look like you might have eaten a hipster, but you definitely don't look like one yourself.'

He laughed. 'I don't think there's much meat on them from what I've seen. So why do you think I would be watching foreign films?'

'Because you're intelligent and well-travelled and … stuff,' I explained, articulately.

'Well, thank you for the compliment. But whilst I'm sure there are plenty of very good foreign films out there, I'm afraid when it comes to movies, I don't like to have to think too hard. I want to just sit and watch, and shove popcorn in my mouth. That's about all I need from a film. Not very deep and meaningful I'm afraid but that's about the size of it.'

'I couldn't agree more!' I grinned at him.

He seemed happy with that revelation and looked back at the television. 'So, what'll it be? There's a "blow lots of stuff up" one here, or what about this one? I heard that's supposed to be good.'

'Rob?'

'Umhmm?' he asked, reading the description.

'That's a romantic comedy.'

'Yeah. So? Don't you like romantic comedies?'

'I do. But do you?'

'Sure. Some of them are pretty funny. And who doesn't like

39

a happy ending?'

'Are you taking the wotsit out of me?'

'Absolutely not. Ask my sister. I've watched enough with her. Actually she got me into them so if I've suddenly gone down in your estimation, then feel free to blame her.'

'Down?' I questioned, surprise that he would think that clearly evident in my tone, 'No, not at all. I just – I suppose I didn't expect that of you. But, it's a nice surprise. Don't get me wrong. A lot of blokes just moan the whole way through. Sort of takes the edge off the enjoyment.'

Rob leant back against the sofa cushions as he pressed play on the movie. 'By most blokes, you mean Steven?' He rolled his head to the side to look at me.

I rolled my head in a similar fashion. 'He wasn't exactly a fan, no.'

'Well, I like them. Blame my sister. And bonus for me, the women in them are usually pretty hot.'

'Aha! I knew there had to be another reason!'

'Oh' – Rob scoffed at me – 'and tell me you're not going to be drooling over him five minutes in,' he asked, pointing the remote at the admittedly suitably handsome male lead.

'Ha!' I said. 'You see, that shows how little you really know me.'

Rob raised a disbelieving eyebrow at me. 'Oh really?'

'Yes, really,' I said, leaning over to grab a handful of the popcorn he'd now tipped out into a bowl. 'It will be at least ten minutes.'

Chapter 5

The credits rolled on the film and I stretched my legs out under the fuzzy blanket. The wine was all gone and Rob had gradually slouched right down during the movie until his legs were now almost hanging off the other edge of the coffee table.

'Would you like some more wine?' he asked, as he wriggled back up into a semi seated position.

'Oh no, thanks! I've got some designs to work on tomorrow. Hangover Head would not be helpful.'

'Fair enough. Can I get you a coffee or anything?'

He really was a great host, despite my dig at him earlier. I smiled. 'No, really. I'm fine. Thank you.'

'OK.' He wriggled a bit more and pushed himself off the sofa. Leaning down he picked up the glasses and bottle in one hand and the popcorn bowl in the other. I made to help but he shook his head.

'It's all right. You look comfy. Stay there.'

I was comfy. I was beyond comfy. I picked up the remote and switched the TV off, then laid my head back on the sofa and looked out of the picture window. The lights in the room were low and offered little reflection on the glass. I sat and watched as London slowly covered with snow. Rob was scootling about in the kitchen, eventually coming to sit down on the table next to my feet, a coffee cup in his hands. We sat there in companionable silence for a while watching the snow fall on the city. Eventually I looked up at him, without lifting my head.

'Won't that keep you awake?' I indicated the coffee cup with my eyes.

'Nope.'

'Oh.'

'Sure you don't want one?'

I smiled. 'Yep. Thanks.'

We turned our attention back to the window and then both jumped when my phone let out a noise that I recognised as Mags' personal text tone.

I pushed myself up and pulled the phone off the table.

Just wanted to check you got home safe. Saw that trains being delayed/cancelled. Sorry I didn't call earlier. Met someone!!!!

I frowned at the phone. Met someone? How could she have met someone? I saw her get on the bus and the stop was about a five-minute walk from her front door.

Where did you meet them?

I waited.

On bus. Normally drives to work but car in garage today. Went for drink. Gorgeous!!!!

I was pleased for her. Obviously I'd have to check him out. That was our unwritten rule. But if he'd got past the hurdle of getting Mags to have a drink with him in the first place, he was doing pretty well. Mags wasn't one for wasting her time on people. I think it came as part of our peripatetic background. Moving around had meant we didn't get the chance to form a lot of long-term relationships. We got to sussing out pretty quickly whether people were worth us investing what would inevitably be our short time, or whether that time would be better spent with someone else. It sounded harsh but was really just a case of making the best of the situation. It was pretty clear I'd lost the knack over the years, having wasted four years of investment time with Steven. But Mags? She still had it.

'Mags met someone,' I said. For some reason, telling Rob seemed the most natural thing to be doing. 'When?'

'Tonight.'

'I thought you were together tonight?'

'She met him on the bus.'

Rob pulled a face that said 'hmm, interesting' and moved to the chair, putting his now empty cup on the table.

'So, what's she said about him?'

'Not much. That she met him on the bus and went for a drink.'

'Blimey. I've known you for four years and I still couldn't get you to go for a drink with me tonight.'

'Oh ha ha!' I stuck my tongue out at him. 'I'm here now, aren't I? And we had food and drink. Anyway. Different situation.' I stated.

'How so?'

'Because this bloke's obviously got different interests in Mags than you have in me.' Rob did a thing with his hand that indicated more explanation was required.

I gave him a look. 'He asked her for a drink because he wanted to check her out, not check up on her.' Rob did a small nod. My phone made its little noise again. I looked down at the screen.

So you got home OK?

Hmm.

Sort of. Train cancelled. Tree and a shedload of snow on line.

What does 'sort of' mean??? Are you OK? Where are you???

Mags loved a punctuation mark. Here we go.

At Rob's.

I pressed 'Send' and looked at Rob who was now peacefully resting his head on the back of the chair and watching the snow. He looked relaxed. And for some reason that made me smile. He turned his head and caught me watching him. Oh shit. That looked weird. I jumped in.

43

'My phone is going to ring in a moment.'

A slow smile spread from one corner of his mouth. 'Did you get psychic when I wasn't looking?'

I raised an eyebrow. 'Nope. But Mags just asked if I was home. Which I'm not. So she asked where I was.'

'And you've said here … which for some reason is going to make your phone ring?'

As if on cue, my phone lit up, and Mags' ringtone jingled out, a cute picture of her appearing on the screen as it did so.

I flipped my hand out as if to say 'Ta dah!'

Rob looked confused, laughed and went back to watching the snow as I picked up my phone. Unwillingly I unwrapped myself and got up from the sofa as I answered, touching Rob's arm as I did so, handing him the blanket and pointing to indicate he should sit there instead of folding his huge frame into the armchair. He smiled at me, and nodded, his hand brushing mine as he took the blanket.

'Hi,' I answered, walking over towards the other side of the room.

'Hi?' Mags repeated. 'You can't just tell me that you're at Rob's flat in the middle of the night and then just say "hi" when you answer the phone!'

'What?' I laughed. Apparently, Gorgeous Bus Boy had bought my friend more than one drink. She sounded positively tipsy. 'Then how am I supposed to answer the phone?'

'What happened? How come you're there? Did you kiss him yet? Oh my God! Are you in bed? Oh! I'm so sorry! I'll call you—'

'Mags! Mags!' I raised my voice and jumped in front of her train of thought.

'What?'

'What are you on? It's Rob! Of course I haven't kissed him and oh my God, no! We're not in bed! Why on earth would you think that?'

'I … just thought …'

44

'No. Definitely not. It's not like that.' I was doing my best to try and keep the very awkward conversation as low in volume as possible without it seeming obvious that I was bothered about Rob hearing. I had a feeling I was failing miserably.

'I bumped into him outside my studio. They were cancelling trains all over the place, including mine, so I ended up coming back to his place so that we could take a look at the traffic and the weather. All the roads are blocked solid. We had a microwave meal and watched a film.' I thought I may as well tell her everything in case something came up later and she read more into it because I hadn't mentioned it.

'And now?' she asked.

'And now what?'

She let out a sigh. 'What. Happens. Now.'

'Nothing. Happens. Now,' I said. 'I'm going to bed shortly.'

A squeak of excitement came from Mags' end of the line.

'On my own,' I clarified, but couldn't help laughing. 'What's got into you tonight?'

'Nothing,' she replied. 'It's just that Rob is nice. Really nice. He's been so concerned about you, and now he's shown up on your doorstep, like a white knight—'

'Oh, blimey! Bus Boy really sprinkled the love dust on you tonight, didn't he?'

'He did not!' Mags said, but there wasn't as much indignation in her voice as I would have expected.

Wow. Bus Boy really *had* made an impression.

'Well, I'm going to go to bed. I'll talk to you tomorrow. Hopefully the snow will have gone then and I can get home.'

'OK. Sleep well!' Mags said, her voice indicating that she thought that sleeping should be the last thing on my mind.

'You're potty. Love you. Night night,' I said, and hung up.

I walked back to the sofa, put the phone on the table and plopped back down next to Rob. He shooshed the blanket out so that it covered both of our legs. And for some reason, it didn't feel awkward. It felt natural. I was just about to start wondering if that should worry me when Rob spoke.

'Is Mags all right?'

'Yep. I think Bus Boy got her a bit drunk. But yeah, she's OK. I think she might actually really like this guy. She was acting a bit lovey-dovey.'

Rob didn't look at me but out of the corner of my eye, I saw him raise his eyebrows. He'd known Mags long enough to know that was an unusual state of affairs for her.

'I know.' I agreed with his silent statement.

'So, she knows you're here then.'

'Yes.'

'She all right with that?'

I looked at him. 'Why wouldn't she be?'

'I don't know. I just didn't want her thinking that I was, I don't know, taking advantage of you, or something.'

A giggle burst up. 'You're frightened of her!'

'I am not!' Rob defended himself. 'I'm just saying that I didn't want her getting the wrong idea about us. About this.'

'Afraid of another broken nose?'

Rob pulled a face. 'Somehow I don't think Mags would be that generous.'

He probably had a point. His nose would be the last of his worries.

'She won't get the wrong idea, Rob. I promise. I put her straight on that.'

He looked at me. 'So, she did suggest something?'

'Why do I suddenly feel as if I'm in the witness box?'

He smiled at me.

'You look like a shark about to attack.' I laughed. 'Is that what you do? Get people to relax with your easy manner and gorgeous smile before going straight for the jugular!'

Now it was his turn to laugh. 'You've been watching too much

46

Law and Order.'

I wobbled my head in a 'maybe yes, maybe no' sort of way.

'And you didn't answer my question.'

'Oh my God!' I laughed, resting my head on the back of the sofa, 'You are not going to let this go, are you?'

'I just don't want Mags thinking I'm—'

'Rob. She doesn't. Don't worry about it. She knows you're just being a friend.' I bumped against him in a gesture of reassurance. He smiled and nodded without looking at me.

'Good,' he said. 'Yep, that's good. Right. I'd better find you a toothbrush, hadn't I?' With that, he got up and headed off towards the bathroom.

Half an hour later I was sitting ready for bed in Rob's guest room. I stood up and looked at the image in the mirror. Rob had lent me a pyjama top that was still in its packet.

'I only ever wear the bottoms,' he'd explained, handing it over to me.

To say it was a little big was a mild understatement. Let's just say, I probably didn't actually need to stay in Rob's flat – I could camp out in this shirt. The top covered most of my thighs, the sleeves brushed my knees and there was about a mile of fabric each side of my body. Sweetly, he'd also included a pair of socks which again, although miles too big, were lovely and cosy.

Ever since I'd pulled an all-nighter at the studio a couple of years ago – a bride had come in for a final fitting having spent the previous three weeks on a clearly very effective crash diet – I now always made sure I was prepared for another. The remote, yet still possible, chance that someone looking for something in my drawer may unwittingly plonk my spare undies out into full view gave me a twitch, which is why they lived in a securely zipped pocket of my carry-everywhere tote. Thankfully. Rob might be sweet enough to lend me pyjamas and socks but I was pretty sure I'd be out of luck in the underwear department and there

47

was no way on earth I was going 'commando' in this weather.

Rob said he'd left a new toothbrush out in the bathroom for me, so I stuck my head out of the door and peered round. It had actually turned into a really lovely evening just sitting and relaxing together. But I wasn't quite ready to face up to him in my – or rather his – pyjamas just yet. I looked around. I could hear movement in his bedroom so I took the opportunity to scoot along to the bathroom and get my ablutions taken care of while he was otherwise occupied. I went in, locked the door and picked up the toothbrush. As I peeled the packaging away, I thought back to what he'd said about buying in bulk, and wondered just how much of that was true. And then I wondered why it bothered me if it was.

I finished cleaning my teeth and, upturning one of the glasses on the counter, popped my toothbrush in it. I stared at the glass for a moment, it being there was yet more evidence at the hint that this place definitely had a woman's touch to it. I mean, who has two glasses in their bathroom – unless you own a hotel. Or – the other thought barrelled back at me – you're used to having people stay over. A lot. We were back to the bulk buying of toothbrushes and I was too tired to think about it all. Or think about why I was even thinking about it all. I unlocked the door and cracked it open a smidge, checking to see if I could make it back to the guest room undetected. All clear. I did a half walk, half run thing towards the bedroom door. Except the momentum from the 'run' part of the manoeuvre kept me going, and my cosy socks offered no purchase on the wood floor and I kept right *on* going straight into the door. I grabbed at the handle in an attempt to stop the inevitable but it happened anyway and I landed hard on my backside in the hallway.

'Izzy?'

Rob's door flew open and he stood there in the matching bottoms to my enormous top. After a split second of just staring at me, he rushed over but I was already batting him away, embarrassed.

'Are you all right?'

'I'm fine,' I said, trying to decide the best way to make an elegant recovery from the prone position I was now in. I decided there wasn't one. I sat up and winced. Rob caught it. He bent down, hooked his arms underneath mine and stood me up.

'Thanks.'

'Are you all right?' he asked again.

I did my best to erase the mortifying picture I had in my head of me sliding down the corridor that must have greeted Rob as he pulled open his door, and instead put on a big smile.

'Absolutely.' Not true. My backside was killing me. 'Socks. Floor. Slippy,' I explained. 'But I'm fine. Really. Just a bit of a sore bum.'

A smirk fluttered across his mouth, albeit briefly.

'And don't think I didn't see that.'

'Sorry,' he said. 'I'd offer to rub it better for you, but that'd be such a cliché.'

'It would.'

'So I won't.'

'I'm so glad.'

He grinned at me, and I couldn't help but return it. He took a couple of steps back towards his own room.

'Sure you're OK?'

'I'm sure, Rob. Really.'

'All right, but just let me know if anything hurts later, or tomorrow. As I said earlier, my mate's only round the corner.'

'If I'm not going to let you rub anything better, what makes you think I'm going to let anyone else have a go?'

Rob looked happily puzzled. 'My mate's a doctor.'

'Ohhhhh! Yes. Right. You did say that.'

Rob took a couple of steps back towards me again, leant over and opened the door. As it had apparently become clear I wasn't to be trusted with these things myself.

'Night, Izz.'

'Night, Rob.'

He bent down and kissed me on the cheek.

'Sleep well,' he said before turning and heading towards the bathroom. I watched him go. It was kind of hard not to. He looked pretty gorgeous in a suit. In pyjama bottoms and a T-shirt he looked … I stopped myself. What on earth was I doing? This was Rob. We were friends. And he'd even said earlier he wasn't looking for anything from me, other than friendship. And I wasn't looking for anything other than that right now either. If I was, I'd have jumped on the hot Italian from earlier. But I didn't. Because I wasn't ready for anything like that in my life right now. But I still couldn't help watching Rob walk away. My gaze slid to his feet. No socks. Ha! I knew it. Sabotage.

Chapter 6

I was sitting on the floor of Rob's living room the next morning, my papers spread all around me, when he wandered in still dressed in his pyjama bottoms and T-shirt. His face had a sleepy look to it and his jaw showed a distinct hint of scruff.

'Morning.'

'Morning!' I replied, my eyes going back to my work.

'How's your bum?'

'Absolutely fine, thank you. Yours?'

He laughed and shoved a coffee pod in the machine and pressed a button. Leaving it to run, he came over and crouched down to where I was sitting with his lovely warm blanket around me. He pulled it back and peered around it, and the acres of pyjama top, to where I was sitting on a large and, more importantly, soft cushion. He brought his gaze up to where I was purposefully avoiding meeting it.

'So I bruised it a bit.'

He let the blanket fall back and stood up. 'Did you get yourself coffee?'

'No, I thought I'd wait for you.' I glanced up.

He smiled at me and a few minutes later placed two cups of coffee and a pile of toast on the breakfast bar. I climbed up from my perch atop the cushion and padded over to one of the seats facing the window. Rob took the one next to me. I picked up one of the coffees. Wrapping my hands around it, I looked out at the snow.

'Doesn't look like it's stopped all night.'

He shook his head. 'Nope,' he said, simply, snagging a piece of toast and leaning back in his chair to reach for a knife for the marmalade out of the drawer. I watched him for a moment and pictured the scene ending badly. Hopping up, I walked over the few steps to the cutlery drawer, pulled it out, took a knife and handed it to Rob.

'Thanks,' he said, oblivious to the scenario I'd run in my head.

I returned to my chair and hoisted myself back up onto it. It occurred to me that this was the perfect situation in which to find myself feeling self-conscious. I was sitting in someone else's kitchen, wearing someone else's pyjamas and little else. But I didn't. And it wasn't just the fact that Rob's top was about three times bigger than some of my dresses. It just felt comfortable with him. Talking. Not talking. Getting up to get cutlery for him so that we didn't end up with matching bruised bums.

'What are you working on?' he asked, nodding his head to the side at the pile of stuff I'd left on the floor.

'I have a bride who's getting married in a castle over in Ireland, and she wants a dress that reflects the history, but doesn't look like a costume.'

Rob took another bite of toast and swallowed. 'Can you do that?'

I nodded. 'Of course.'

We sat for a few more moments.

'Rob, I think I need to try and get over to Mags' place today. It's obvious I'm still not going to get home but I can't stay here again—'

'Why not?' He wasn't tetchy. He was just asking.

'Well, because I'm sure you've got plenty of things to do and

52

I …' *have no idea what I'm trying to say.*

'Look out there, Izz. I don't think anyone's going to be doing much of anything today apart from staying in and keeping warm. Which sounds pretty damn good to me. I know you'd probably prefer to be at Mags' place right now, and if that's what you really want, I'll do my best to help you get there – but I can pretty much guarantee that those shoes you love so much will be completely ruined by the time you do.'

Oh yes. Right. Snow plus gorgeous shoes which were certainly not made for navigating snowy pavements. Yep, he had a point. That was a bit of an issue.

'This "Castle Bride", is that something you have to get done this weekend?'

I nodded. 'Yes, ideally. I said I'd send her something over, just some basic ideas to start with, by the end of tomorrow.'

'OK. I've got some papers to look at too, so if you're happy that you have everything you need to get on with things here, why don't we just get our work done and reassess the situation later?'

'OK.' I nodded.

'Great! Oh, your dress should be dry. I put it in the machine last night.'

'Oh, thanks!' I hopped up from my seat and moved over to dishwasher where I began loading the breakfast plates in.

'I'm just going to take a shower. Unless you want to eat first?' Rob hesitated at the doorway. 'No, it's fine,' I said, now reaching into the dryer to pull out my clothes. 'We can– oh no!'

'What's wrong?' He frowned, padding back in slowly.

I pulled my dress out of the dryer and laid it over the back of the seat. Rob glanced at it. 'Am I missing something because it looks – oh!'

I was holding up my beautiful designer cashmere cardigan. The colour of cornflowers in summer, I'd spent ages deciding whether to buy it and had finally splashed out in celebration when my very first bride walked down the aisle. As soft and gorgeous as I'd imagined, adding style and elegance to my outfit, it had been perfect. And it was still perfect. Assuming you were the size of a three-year-old.

I still hadn't said anything and Rob still hadn't moved any closer.

'I'm guessing that label must say "Do Not Tumble",' he eventually volunteered.

A nod and a strangulated noise came from me as I laid my gorgeous, now tiny, cardi on the counter.

There really was no rectifying this. It was gone.

'I'm so sorry, Izzy. I'll get you another one.'

I shook my head and finally looked at him. 'It's all right. Really. It's just a jumper.' Which was true. It was only a jumper. Just some wool all knitted up. And I knew that Rob would want to replace it, whatever I said. It's just that this one had such special memories attached to it – that first dress, all the way from design to completion. The bride had been so insistent on having me there on the day because she was so happy with her dress and wanted to share that joy with me. And now I wouldn't wear it again. I felt stupid at being upset over a bunch of wool.

'It's not just a jumper though, is it?' Rob asked.

I looked back up and shoved all the silliness aside. 'Of course it is. Don't worry about it! Thank you for drying the rest of my clothes, anyway,' I hurried over in my head the fact that my underwear was also in there, and Rob would have had a good eyeful of that.

He held my gaze a moment then turned and headed back towards the bedrooms. 'I'll have a shower in a bit. I'm going for a run.'

'What, now?' I called to him.

'Yes,' came the reply from behind the now closed bedroom door.

'But it's feet deep in snow! You'll break your bloody neck!'

There was no reply. A few minutes later, Rob appeared wearing running leggings, thankfully with shorts over them. Lovely as any man in good shape looks, leggings are not a good look. He was zipping up a breathable jacket and a hat was pulled down over his ears. He finished lacing his shoes then pulled on his gloves. All the time I was stood just watching. I knew this was something to do with me, and I didn't like it.

'Rob, this is ridiculous.'

'What is?'

'You, doing this.'

'Izz, I go running most weekends.'

'Yes, but five minutes ago, you weren't going. Then we go have Cardi-Gate and the next minute you're heading out in several feet of snow for a run.'

'It's nothing to do with that, Izzy. Yes, I feel bad that I ruined your top. But as you said, it's just a jumper, so I'll replace it and we'll be all square. This? This is just about me feeling like going for a run.'

I didn't believe it for a moment. And he knew I didn't. We both knew that the jumper wasn't just a jumper either. It was all raging out of control, and yet neither of us were prepared to say anything, pretending everything was all absolutely fine. When clearly it wasn't. I was upset and pretending I wasn't. He was upset that I was upset but pretending that he didn't know I was upset, so that we could both go on with this ridiculous charade. This was exactly why I should have gone to a hotel last night. Complications like this don't happen at hotels. Yes, they might still have shrunk my cardigan but I could have happily yelled at them and asked them why they didn't read the labels. Rob, on the other hand, I couldn't even begin to be angry with because he'd merely tried to be helpful and had done so much to make the evening relaxed and pleasant. Oh God! Why hadn't I just stood my ground and gone to a hotel!

Rob's movements brought me back out of my trance. 'Rob,

really. This is just silly. Look at it out there!' I pointed to the window where the snow was coming down again. 'You'll freeze!'

'Thermals,' was all he said.

I didn't have a reply for that one.

'Rob, please. Come on, it's horrid out there.'

'Izzy, stop worrying. I've been out in far worse conditions than this on manoeuvres in the past.' He turned to fish his keys out of the bowl on the side.

'Yes, but that was only because there was someone telling you you had to go! Probably someone quite short and shouty!'

He looked at me meaningfully but said nothing.

I threw my head back. 'Argh! You're impossible!'

'Not the first time that's been said,' he replied, pulling open the door.

'Apparently, you haven't improved.'

'Doesn't look like it,' he agreed. 'See you in a bit.' With that, he closed the door behind him and left me in the silence of the flat.

I felt a little better after a shower and hair wash but not a lot. Rob still wasn't back and my mind kept racing off into scenarios where he was spread eagled on the pavement with his limbs pointing in directions they really shouldn't. I needed to focus my mind. I stepped into my dress and pulled on the socks that Rob had lent me last night instead of the lace topped stockings I'd had on in the day. Which also would have been in the washing machine. Oh flip. Oh well. He'd seen it all now. I was mostly warm but without my cardi, my arms were definitely on the chilly side. Wandering out into the main area, I noticed some laundry folded next to the dryer. Nosing through it, I found a Help For Heroes sweatshirt. I pulled it over my head and waited for it to settle under my bum before heading over to where I'd spread out my work this morning. I sat down gently on my cushion and began looking at the drawings.

An hour later I was putting the last finishing strokes of colour to a design when I heard a key turn in the lock. I pushed myself up from where I had sprawled and watched as Rob walked through the door. His nose was shining as red and bright as the festive lights at Covent Garden Apple Market and he was rubbing his hands together in an effort to boost circulation.

'Good run?' I asked.

'Yep,' he replied, bending down to undo his laces.

'How many times did you fall?'

'Just the once.'

'Are you all right?'

'Yep.'

I shook my head and got up, padding across to where he was still bent over fighting with his laces. I watched for a second before bending down to the same level. I could see his frozen hands were struggling with the soaking laces.

'Here.' I pushed his hands out of the way.

'No, it's fine. Really, I can—' He attempted to move my hands.

I didn't reply. Just pushed his own back out of the way again and slid down on the floor so that my feet were either side of my hips. He'd made a right mess of the ties and I peered at them, before focusing in on the right end to start with.

Rob leant back and sat his bum on the floor, finally accepting he wasn't going to win this one.

'How do you even sit like that?' he asked after a moment, a hint of amusement in his voice.

'It's comfy,' I replied, concentration creasing my face. 'I'm really quite bendy.'

'Good to know.' He laughed, softly.

I pulled a lace and it came free! 'Ta dah!'

Rob pulled at the other one and I could see his hands were turning a bit more of a normal colour. 'Thanks.'

'You're welcome.'

He quickly pushed himself up from the floor and held down a hand for me to grab on to. I did so and was propelled upward into a standing position far quicker than I expected.

'Ooh!' I wobbled. 'Headrush.'

'Sorry.' Rob was apologetic as he steadied me. 'I'm used to heaving blokes up off the rugby field. You're a bit lighter.'

I acknowledged the likelihood of that.

'I'm going to take a shower. I picked up some lunch on the way back.'

'OK. Yes, go and warm up, for goodness' sake. I'll make us some drinks.'

I was just dishing up the soup and warm bread Rob had brought back with him when he walked back into the kitchen. He was dressed in a pair of well-worn cargo trousers with a loose T-shirt over the top. Rummaging in the same laundry pile I'd gone through earlier, he pulled out a hoody and slipped it on. He took the dishes, put them in place on the breakfast bar, and turned to take the plate of bread.

'I like this look,' he said, smiling at the eclectic style I'd ended up with today.

'Do you?' I laughed. I was pretty sure I looked ridiculous but I didn't really mind. It was only Rob, after all. It's not like I was trying to impress anyone.

'I do.'

'I hope you don't mind me borrowing your sweatshirt. It was a bit chilly.'

'Of course not. Looks good on you.' He winked at me in a jokey way. 'I can turn the heating up more if you want.'

'No! I'm fine now. Really.'

We tucked into the nourishing fresh soup and delicious bread. 'This is lovely!' I said, tasting it for the first time.

'Glad you like it. I didn't know what you'd want, but I know you're not picky so thought you'd probably be happy with what I chose.'

'You know me well.' I laughed. It was true. I pretty much ate anything.

'Not that well,' he replied, keeping his head down and soaking up the last drops of his soup with a hunk of bread, before popping it in his mouth.

I moved around on the bar chair to face him. 'What's that supposed to mean?'

He didn't look at me for a while. I waited, watching him watching the snow. I could wait. I would wait him out. Like they always said on TV. Let them fill the space. Oh God, who was I kidding? I couldn't wait.

'I said, what's that supposed to mean?'

'I rang Mags when I was out.'

'OK,' I said. I had no idea where this was going.

'I could see I'd messed up big time with your jumper this morning—'

'Rob, please! Forget about—'

'No, Izzy. You should have told me what it meant to you. Why it was a big deal. Not just said that it didn't matter. Because it does. And if it matters to you, then it matters to me.'

'Oh, Rob! It was an accident. Yes, I was upset! Ok? Does that make you feel better? I was upset that the beautiful cardigan I'd splashed out on in celebration for my first wedding gown is now the size of baby clothes! I am not happy about that – but neither you, nor I, can do anything to change it so I'm not going to get into a state about it. It's not like you did it on purpose! You were being kind. I can't get angry at you for that.'

He sat up straighter at the counter, forcing me to tilt my head up to look at him.

'I'm really sorry, Izzy. I will buy you another. I know it won't be the same, but at least you won't have to wear that anymore.'

He pointed to the sweatshirt. It was actually pretty comfy. 'Well, no, not in public …'

He grinned and unexpectedly kissed me quickly on my cheek before standing and scooping up the dishes.

'Rob?' I asked, pulling out two hot chocolate pots for his

drinks machine. 'Umhmm?'

'Why did you ring Mags?'

He stood up from stacking the dishwasher. 'Because I could tell there was more to this than you were telling me. You're not generally prone to drama. You love your clothes but you were really upset over this' – he held up my tiny cardigan – 'so I knew there was something special about it but you wouldn't tell me what. So I had to go to the next best source.'

'I see. And you got your answer, obviously.'

'Well I got the idea that I was on the right track when I told Mags what I'd done and she asked whether I was calling her from beyond the grave.'

I tried to keep the smile off my face. 'Really?'

'Yes. I believe her exact words were "You did what?" shortly followed by "Is there currently a large carving knife sticking out of your chest?"'

A smile broke through. Mags was right. Ordinarily, I would have been wanting to reach for the biggest, sharpest implement I could lay my hands on. But this time? The look on Rob's face had been enough. It really was just a jumper after all. I handed him one of the mugs of hot chocolate and he followed me into the living area where we sank down onto the sofa. He ripped open the bakery bag he'd picked up and revealed two apple turnovers.

'I'll need to go out for one of your ridiculous runs if I eat that too.'

Rob ignored my protest and handed me a plate before beginning demolition proceedings on the other confection.

'What's ridiculous about running?' he asked, four bites later when he'd finished.

'Not with the running itself. Just you choosing to go out and do it when there's several feet of snow on the ground just because you're in a huff!'

'I wasn't in a huff.'

'Oh, pffft! You were totally in a huff.'

Rob leant forward and put his drink down.

'And you say I'm impossible.'

'You are,' I confirmed, sipping at my hot chocolate. 'Especially when you're in a huff.' I added quietly.

I saw him turn and look at me, his expression a mix of amusement and disbelief. I peered over the top of my cup, and raised one eyebrow at him, daring him to challenge my declaration. He leant over and took my cup away, placing it on the coffee table next to his. I sat where I was, not quite sure what was happening. Rob turned back and looking down at my hands, took them in his own.

'I'm sorry that I went out earlier. I know that it worried you but I really have been in worse situations.'

'You did fall over though,' I pointed out.

'Yes. I did. And if it makes you feel better it bloody hurt, so it serves me right, eh?'

'No. Of course not.'

He squeezed my hands gently. Not that I could see my own hands, swamped as they were within his.

'I was just frustrated that we couldn't talk about what was really quite a simple problem. It didn't give me much hope for anything else.'

'I didn't want to talk about it. I could see you already felt bad about it so what was the point of me getting all uppity about it? It wasn't going to change anything.'

'Fair enough.' He smiled at me. 'Thank you. Although I've been screamed at for a lot less, so just for future reference ...'

'Did you just give me permission to yell at you?'

'I ... no, I don't think so. At least that certainly wasn't my intention.'

'Wait, what did you mean about "didn't give much hope for anything else"?' I frowned at him, casting my mind back to what he'd just said. 'Anything else of what?'

He let go of my hands and turned back to our drinks, passing mine over to me.

'Nothing, really. I didn't mean anything specific. I just meant … that I … that it would be good to be able to talk about things, whatever things.'

I pulled a face over my mug. For an articulate solicitor, that didn't sound like a great argument. Mind you, he was practically as blue as a Smurf when he'd come back from that run, so perhaps his brain was still thawing out. I let it go. He was right. I should have just told him that the jumper had been bought to celebrate something.

'I'm sorry, Rob. I promise that next time you ruin something I will tell you exactly why I'm so upset. I could even throw some screaming and shouting in there too, if you'd like?'

'Sounds perfect,' he said with a grin and finished off his drink.

I scooped up my stuff and began to pile it back into my bag. I'd made some really good progress on the designs and had a couple that I was sure this bride was going to like. I'd emailed the sketches and notes over to her and said I'd call her in a couple of days to give her a bit of time to think over things and come up with any questions or extra ideas. From his position on the sofa, Rob saw me finish clearing up.

'All done?' he asked.

'For the moment,' I replied, tucking the laptop sleeve into my big shoulder bag, along with the portfolio file. 'What are you up to?'

He was sitting at an angle on the sofa, with his legs stretched out along the length of it. He had some files resting on his stomach and one in his hand.

'Just a couple of briefs I needed to look at. I'm pretty much done now though.'

'Uh-huh.'

I went back to my bag and fiddled about for a few seconds. 'Izz?'

'Yes?'

'Are you sniggering because I said I was looking at briefs?'

'No! Of course not!' I said, completely lying my face off.

I heard the papers land on the floor and a second later, Rob's arm was round my waist, pulling me up off the floor and placing me next to him on the sofa. He sat back and looked at me. I raised my eyes cautiously. I couldn't help having a childish sense of humour. It was a family trait. And it amused me, which was the whole point of a sense of humour, I thought. It didn't hurt anyone so I wasn't about to defend it. I'd ended up stifling it so much with Steven because, although he never actually said anything, it was clear he often didn't approve of me and Mags falling around at something inane and ridiculous. I realised that I missed it. I missed laughing at what I wanted to. I wasn't about to expect others to find all the same things funny, but I wasn't going to be judged for what I deemed to be amusing. So, if Rob was about to tell me I shouldn't be sniggering at him and his briefs, well, he was in for a disappointment.

'You're hilarious,' he stated simply, his brown eyes dancing with laughter.

'I am?' This was a surprise.

'Yes.' He gave me a squeeze then got up and went into the kitchen. I scooted round on my knees to watch as he began pulling items out of the fridge and placed a chopping board on the counter.

'What are you doing?'

'Dinner.' He smiled.

'What's for dinner?'

'Vietnamese chicken and sweet potato curry.'

'Oh, that sounds delicious!' I said, pushing myself off the sofa and going over to where there was now a whole line up of yummy-looking ingredients, awaiting preparation.

'Can I help with anything?' I moved out of Rob's way as he placed some chicken breasts down on the counter. Tripping slightly, I glanced down and noticed one of my socks was working its way off my foot and now sat several inches beyond my toes. I leant on Rob's arm and lifted my foot up, wiggling it back into the capacious sock. He in turn stood patiently waiting as I rearranged my hosiery.

'Better?'

'Much. So, what can I do?'

Rob was a really good cook. I decided this on the first mouthful of the curry. It was wonderful. 'Good?' he asked, smiling as I suddenly realised I was making 'yum' noises.

I nodded.

'Good,' he said again and set about his own plate.

'How did you learn to do all this?' I asked a little later as we started on another bottle of wine, empty plates long since cleared away.

'What? Cook? It's not that difficult. It's just a case of reading and practice.'

'Not just that. I mean, this whole flat. It's perfectly styled.' I stood up, wobbled, sat down, and then stood up again. Rob remained seated. 'I mean, this tree. It's gorgeous! It's like something out of a magazine. And the lights here – just so – it's all, so … lovely!' I had a feeling I might have had a little too much wine. We'd opened a bottle when we began preparing dinner, and another cork had just gone pop. Perhaps I should sit down again. I turned back towards the sofa, and scooted my sock-encased feet along the floor.

'Ha! Who needs to pay for Somerset House ice skating when you can do this?' I pushed off and slid along.

'Dumdumadah, dadadadadadumdumadah …' I recreated the Bolero music with what I deemed to be absolute accuracy and slid past the back of the sofa. Rob watched with an odd look on his face, which for the most part looked like amusement.

'You're bloody nuts, woman.'

'Charming!' I said, sliding back past him.

'You do remember they both end up on the floor at the end of that routine, don't you?'

'I'm putting my own spin on it.'

'Oh, for God's sake, please don't.' He laughed, getting up and coming across to where I was now happily humming Ravel and taking small scooty steps. The warning about falling over hadn't been entirely lost on me and I wasn't yet drunk enough to forget that my backside still hurt from the tumble yesterday. However, I soon forgot all of it as the next moment I was flipped over Rob's shoulder, where he then spun me round again until I was in the air, and face to face with him. Gently he let me slide down until my toes once again thankfully found the floor. He laughed before wandering up into the kitchen, where he then began looking through cupboards.

'What was that?' I asked, when I got my breath back.

Having apparently found what he was looking for, he walked back past me and headed for the sofa.

Seeing I was yet to move, he grabbed my hand and pulled me in the same direction.

'What? You're the only one allowed to put your own spin on things?' He tugged me gently. 'Come on, Queen of the Ice, come and sit down before you fall down.'

'Totally blaming you now if that happens, by the way!'

'All right.' Rob wasn't fazed.

'Do you always fling your girlfriends about?'

Rob tilted his head and gave me a look. I suddenly realised what I'd said.

'I didn't mean "girlfriends" girlfriends! Obviously! I meant your friends who are girls. Hence Girl. Friends. Girlfriends.'

I also realised that I was doing the air quotes thing again. Definitely too much wine.

'Obviously,' he repeated. 'And no. Not generally. Whether they are actually girlfriends or friends who are girls.'

'So?' I waggled my head at him, indicating I was looking for an explanation.

He shrugged. 'You're easy to fling about.'

My mouth dropped open. 'Seriously!'

'Oh, come on. I saw you smiling! Don't tell me you didn't enjoy it.'

He was right. It had been fun. Unexpected and silly and fun. Oh! It was so annoying when he was right.

'So, if this isn't your usual evening routine, how did you know you wouldn't drop me on my head?'

'Because, one, are you joking? You seriously think I can't pick you up without dropping you? You've noticed the size difference between us, right?'

'Ha ha! I've seen all those wedding videos where the poor bride gets dropped by some groom trying to show off.'

Rob laughed and closed his eyes. 'Isabel Bryant, I swear that if you ever marry me, I promise not to drop you during our wedding dance.' When he opened them, they were shining with merriment. 'Happy now?'

I nodded. Although happiness wasn't all I was feeling. There was suddenly a big old dollop of confusion added in because the thought of being in such a position with Rob didn't sound all that bad. Yep. Definitely too much wine.

Chapter 7

I pushed my wine glass away and put all rogue thoughts of a wedding dance with Rob to the very far corners of my mind. Where no one, not even Rob or Mags, went. It was just an off-the-cuff remark that he hadn't even thought about when he said it, so I shouldn't either. I glared at the wine glass for getting me into all this.

'What's it ever done to you?'

'Huh?' I jumped as Rob's voice broke into my thoughts.

He nodded at the glass as he tipped cashew nuts into a bowl. 'You're glaring at that glass like it ran over your cat.'

'I don't have a cat.'

He raised an eyebrow at me. I took the remote control from his hands and changed the subject.

'What are we watching?'

I'd really wanted to see the film but comfort got the best of me and next thing I knew, Rob's voice was drifting down softly into my sleep. Slowly I opened my eyes. He was standing with his back to me and my phone to his ear.

'Of course. No, I'll tell her. Yep, speak to you soon. Have a good time. Bye.'

By the time he'd turned around, I was sitting up and running my hands through my hair, trying to get it into some semblance of order.

'Did I wake you?' He looked concerned.

'No, not really.' I pointed at my phone, 'Who was that?'

'Mags,' he said, handing me the phone.

I scrolled through the texts which had started out with a general '*Hi Hon, hope you're OK. Let me know*' but after no replies over a couple of hours, had ended with '*Where are you?????*'. I assumed it was at this point she had decided to ring and Rob had answered the phone so as not to wake me.

'She said she'd texted you but got worried when you didn't reply because it wasn't like you.'

'No. I reply to her pretty quickly generally, unless I'm at work. Same with her.'

'I didn't like to wake you. But you should call her back.'

My phone pinged with Mags' text alert. I read the message.

'No, it's fine. She knows I'm all right.'

Not to mention the fact that asking her why the hell she'd just sent me big grin and kissy face emoticons might be a little awkward right now.

'OK.' He sat back down next to me and I quickly switched the phone's screen off. 'You missed the film.'

'Yes, I'm sorry about that.'

'That's all right. It wasn't that good anyway. Nice sleep?'

I nodded and felt that sleep reaching out to claim me again. Rob stood up and gently pulled me from where I was starting to get comfortable again.

'Come on you, go to bed.' I made a bit of a huffy whining noise but knew he was right. I shoved off and headed for the bathroom. Managing to make it back to my room this evening without ending up on my backside, I quickly stuck my head back around the door to the living room which was now lit only by one lamp and the TV. The sound on it was down low, probably in deference to me, which I thought was sweet.

'Night.'

Rob turned his head. 'Night, Izz. They've just said that they're clearing some of the roads tomorrow morning, and the snow's stopped – so looks like we'll be able to get you home.'

'Oh right! That's great!' I replied, sounding a lot more enthusiastic than I felt.

'Thought you'd be pleased.' Rob returned, now facing the screen.

I said goodnight again and headed off to the guest room.

Rob was just coming through the front door when I walked out from the bathroom, having showered and dressed, pulling his sweatshirt on back over my dress and wearing the clean socks that he'd kindly provided for me. He didn't look quite so Smurf-like as he had done yesterday after his run, but it was obviously still pretty cold out there.

'Good run?'

'Yes. And I didn't even fall over once today!'

'That's because you can actually see the pavements today, by the looks of it,' I said, peering down out of the window as I took the bag of groceries he was carrying off him and placed it in the kitchen.

'That always helps.'

'So, what's all this for?' I asked, partly because I needed to distract myself from looking at Rob's extremely fit body and partly because I was just being nosy.

'Sunday lunch. It's my turn to cook it today.'

'Oh! Right. I'll get out of your hair. I saw some cabs starting to move about down—'

'Oh, no you don't! You're on spud peeling duty.'

'I am?'

'Do you mind?' he asked, suddenly sounding a little unsure.

'Of course not! How many?'

69

'Enough for four. There's a big pan in that drawer in front of you.'

He pulled at his laces, which were less stubborn this time, and yanked off his running shoes, before padding off down the hallway in his socks. A few minutes later I heard the shower start so I pressed the power button on Rob's digital radio in the kitchen, relaxed into the sounds of Classic FM and piled up peeled potatoes in the pan.

By the time Rob came back. I'd also prepared the carrots and the broccoli that were in the bag, hoping that they were actually for Sunday lunch. I'd got a bit carried away, and just prepared everything in sight. Assured that they were indeed for today, I felt better and started work on the strawberries Rob had now brought out of the fridge, along with some meringue nests and cream.

'So when you said it was your turn to cook lunch today, is this some sort of tradition?'

'Well, it's not a strict thing. Just my family like to get together and we tend to alternate who cooks. Today ended up being me.'

'This is a family dinner?' I was suddenly back to feeling awkward. 'Oh, Rob, I should go. I really shouldn't be—'

'It's fine. It's nothing formal, Izzy. Don't worry about it. My parents can't get up because of the snow anyway, so it's just going to be my sister and her fiancé, and you and me.' He glanced at me as he picked up two of the meringues and squished them into pieces in one scrunch. 'Assuming you're staying.'

Silence hung over us. I didn't want to intrude on a family dinner. I'd never even met any of Rob's family and then there'd be the whole thing of having to explain what I was doing there, and, well, it wasn't like I was his girlfriend, but I had just spent the weekend with him. But then, weren't there probably a lot of people in London this weekend who hadn't planned to stay? Of course there were. But most of them would be in hotels. Oh!

'You'll really like her.'

'Sorry?'

'My sister, Jenny. I'd love you to meet her. I think you'll really like her.'

I couldn't say no now, could I?

'This is the same sister who introduced you to the wonderful world of the rom-com?'

'The one and only.'

'Then I'll be honoured to meet her.'

Rob didn't say anything but the smile he gave me said it all. I was definitely staying for Sunday lunch. If any awkward questions came up, I'd deal with them. Or he would. I was pretty sure about that. I turned back to the counter, picked up the knife and finished preparing the strawberries, ready for Eton Mess.

The doorbell chimed and I looked at Rob in surprise.

'I thought people had to be buzzed up to these swanky heights?' I was teasing but it did make me wonder about just how strict their security levels were.

'Jenny lived here for a while. They know her down at the desk.' He smiled at me as he passed to go to the door. 'Don't worry. No need to raise the Threat Level.'

I mentally stamped my foot. Was every single thought I had really that clear for him to read on my face? I sincerely hoped not.

'Hi, Jen. Hello, mate,' I heard Rob greeting his guests, as I stood in the kitchen, desperately trying to find something to do to in order to look useful. Nope. Nothing. He had everything under control. Typical.

'Izzy?' I turned to find Rob standing there holding his hand out towards me. 'Let me introduce you.'

I took hold of his hand and let him lead me gently towards his guests. A woman – whose eyes and jet-black hair were too much like Rob's not to be related – watched me with interest and a smile from her wheelchair. The man with her was a similar build to Rob but not quite as tall. His hair was short, tidy and fair and his blue eyes crinkled at the edges, ever poised for the possibility of laughter.

'Izzy. I'd like you to meet Jenny, my sister, and this is her fiancé, Mike. Mike, Jenny, this is my friend Isabel. She got stuck in town with the snow. I thought it would be nice if she joined us for lunch before I take her home later.'

'Hi,' Jenny said, holding out her hand. 'Very pleased to meet you! What a gorgeous dress.'

'Lovely to meet you too.' I shook her hand, and thanked her for the compliment, smoothing the skirt a couple of times a little nervously as I did so.

'Hello!' Mike shook my hand enthusiastically.

'Hello.' I replied.

'Mike's the doctor round the corner I mentioned the other day. We served together in the Army.'

'Oh, right.'

'You've been stuck here a few days then?' Jenny asked, casually, looking up at her brother with the most innocent of expressions. I'd already guessed that the question was far more loaded than it first seemed and from the warning look he gave her, at the same time as trying to hide it from me, he knew she was fishing. I smiled. It was entirely understandable. If I'd had a brother, I was pretty sure I'd have been inclined to be just as nosy.

'I'm afraid he's been stuck with me since Friday night.' I laughed, and gently touched the hand he had resting on the back of the chair behind him to let him know it was OK. I could handle this. Out of sight of his guests, he turned his hand and held mine briefly.

'You're not the Isabel that punched our Rob here and broke his nose, are you?' Mike laughed, clearly not expecting an answer in the positive. Almost immediately, Mike made an 'Oof' sound, then began rubbing his ribs, a slightly confused expression now clouding his features. Jenny was smiling, and behind our backs, I'd quickly slipped my hand out of Rob's as he once again tried to take it.

72

I gave them all a little glance and nervously smoothed my skirt again. The elephant was already in the room, trumpeting merrily, so we may as well address it. Jenny clearly knew who I was and poor Mike was now obviously feeling awkward at having apparently put his foot in something – but quite what, he wasn't sure. Rob just looked pained.

'I'm afraid I am that woman, yes. And I would like to take the opportunity to apologise for what was a very unprovoked attack on your poor brother, which he really didn't deserve. I can't tell you how mortified I was immediately afterwards. He's never been anything but kind to me! So I can completely understand any animosity you might feel towards me.'

'Me?'

'Yes. I mean, he's your brother–'

'Izzy – can I call you Izzy?'

'Of course.'

'Please don't give it another thought. Rob's clearly forgiven you, and he's the only one that matters. Besides, there are plenty of times I'd have liked to punch him myself so I can completely understand how it might have happened.' Jenny reached out and squeezed my hand, just as her brother had done all those months ago. She smiled up at me in reassurance.

I nodded back, unable to form any words for the moment. Suddenly, stupidly, I felt overly emotional and had the horrible feeling I was about to cry!

'Izz, can you give me a hand to check on the chicken?' Rob steered me out and we headed back into the kitchen area. From the corner of my eye, I could see Mike helping Jenny from her chair onto the sofa, which also involved a whispered conversation. I had a feeling he was getting his ear bent for stepping in it, but I was also sort of glad it had happened. At least it got it all out of the way.

'Sorry about all that.' Rob turned to me, shutting the oven door on the delicious smelling roast chicken, 'Are you OK?' He

73

brought his hand up to my face where my eyes were still welling.

I stepped back and nodded, which dislodged a tear. Quickly I brushed it away with the back of my hand and took a few deep breaths to help regain my composure. Rob was still looking at me, his hand now resting on the countertop.

'I don't know what's wrong with me this weekend! Sorry. I suppose I still feel bad about what happened and I just didn't want to spoil things by having your sister angry at me, even though it's absolutely understandable if she is.'

'She's not.' Rob shook his head slowly, smiling softly at me, 'And I'm not. It's long forgotten.' He prodded his nose. 'Well, not necessarily forgotten but most definitely forgiven. The only person you're awaiting forgiveness from now is yourself.'

'But you're all so nice to me.'

'Because you make people want to be nice to you.'

I pulled a face at him showing that I appreciated the sentiment, even if I didn't quite believe it. 'Right.' He took hold of my waist, turned me around and pointed me towards the cabinets. 'Moving on as we are, if you can grab some glasses, I have a very nice bottle of wine and some Shloer chilling in the fridge.'

It was absolutely the best Sunday lunch I'd had in years; I could happily have eaten it all over again. Once the ice had been broken by Mike's hammer-like conversation blooper, we all relaxed and I laughed more than I had in what seemed like a very long time. Of course, I laughed with Mags, but I couldn't remember the last time I'd relaxed and laughed like this. Most of the time, half my mind was on what needed to get done next in the studio, what the next part of my business plan was, how I should perhaps just take another look at that email. But right now, I was completely comfortable, full to the brim with delicious food and happy in the company I was surrounded with. Rob was in the middle of a story, which Mike kept interrupting and correcting, until Rob eventually made a rude gesture at his friend showing him exactly what he thought of his corrections, which set everyone laughing again. And Rob had been right about Jenny. I did like her very much. We'd had a lovely time chatting all about her upcoming wedding and her plans to start her own beauty business whilst the boys got stuck into sports talk.

'Who's for coffee?' Rob asked.

I followed him into the kitchen, bringing the last of the plates with me as Mike and Jenny got settled back on the sofa.

'Thanks.' He nodded, as he worked on the coffees.

Smiling, I picked up the plates and began rinsing them ready to put in the dishwasher.

'You don't have to do that. Just leave it. It'll give me something to do when you've left.' As he said it, I glanced up at him and for the briefest of moments, I thought I saw something in his eyes, a question, maybe.

'I'm sure you have much more thrilling things to be doing later,' I said, ignoring his instructions and stacking the dishwasher anyway.

'Do I?'

'Probably.'

'Such as?'

I stood up from the appliance and looked across at him. He was leaning back against the counter, his sock-covered feet were crossed at the ankles and his arms were crossed loosely over the vast expanse of chest. Suddenly I had an urgent need to check that I'd stacked everything correctly and, after fiddling with the cutlery holder, I pushed the tray back in and shut the door. Standing up, I looked back over. He hadn't moved and had an expression that I couldn't quite make out on his face. I knew he wasn't drunk as he'd only had the non-alcoholic stuff due to the fact that he'd promised to drive me home later.

'What?' I asked, a little smile threatening my lips. I didn't know what I was smiling at, but it felt good anyway.

'I'm waiting to hear what thrilling things you think I have

lined up for later. Because I'm thinking it's going to be quite dull without you here after this weekend.'

I didn't take him seriously for one minute. 'Oh I'm sure you'll find some more briefs to look at,' I threw back.

Rob's bark of laughter made his guests look round and I noticed the brief exchange that took place between them as they did.

'As I said before,' he stated, walking towards me until I had nowhere else to go and bumped back into the drawer, 'hilarious.' Chuckling, he scooped his arm around me, moved me out of the way and fished some teaspoons out of the drawer.

'Glad you think so,' I forced out, hoping that the flush of heat I was feeling wasn't showing on my chest and neck.

What the heck was wrong with me? Perhaps I should I have hooked up with Italian Restaurant Man if just having a man pin me against a kitchen cabinet before wrapping his arm around me so that he could get silverware out of a drawer was sending me into hot flushes. But I knew I'd made the right decision with Italian Man. And that it wasn't a basic lust I was feeling. I was seriously beginning to worry that I might actually be developing a crush on Rob.

He turned his back and went over to the coffees, placing them on a tray with all the condiments. He really was unbelievably domesticated. The jeans he was wearing were well washed and getting threadbare on the knee, and they made his backside look really, really good. Oh God! I did have a crush! I had the hots for Rob! I stood up straight. Don't be ridiculous, Izzy. You do not have a crush on Rob. You are just feeling warm, and enjoying good food, wine and company. For the first time in a long time. Even before everything ended with Steven, I couldn't remember the last time I'd felt this … Oh my God, happy. That's what this was. I was just happy. For the first time in ages, I was actually happy! Oh thank goodness for that. Lusting after Rob would make things so complicated, and I really didn't need complicated in my life right now. Not now that I'd found 'happy'.

'Uh oh, the cogs are whirring again.' Rob nudged me as he picked up the tray.

I rolled my eyes at him. 'I am allowed to think, you know.'

He chuckled, 'Come on, you.'

We said goodbye to Jenny and Mike and waited as Jenny tucked her hat down over her ears. 'So, are you heading off home now?' she asked.

'Shortly, I think,' I replied, turning to Rob for some confirmation. He was leaning on the doorframe and he straightened up as he saw his sister was ready to go.

'Yep, in a little while. But apparently Izzy's got some briefs she wants me to look at, so I guess it depends how long that takes.'

I felt my mouth fall open. 'I do – what I said, I meant … that's not what I meant.' My skin felt glowing from my toes to my ears, and not in a good way.

Jenny and Mike kissed us both goodbye, heading for the lift. Rob shut the door and grinned at me.

'I can't believe you just said that in front of them!' I started. 'What will they think?'

'It was a joke. Which they knew. It's fine.'

'Rob! I just met them and I'm staying at your house! They already think there's something going on and now you've said I'm going to show you my knickers!'

He began laughing harder.

'Rob, it's not funny—'

'Oh it is! And for the record, I never said that you were planning to show me your knickers, although if you're offering …'

'Argh!' I picked up a cushion from the sofa and threw it at him. Of course he caught it. 'I'm going to get my stuff,' I said and stalked off.

'It doesn't really matter, though. I already saw them in the washing machine anyway,' he called after me.

I returned to the living room, threw all of the cushions I could get my hands on, then spun on my heel and went to grab my stuff from the guest room. At least I knew for certain now though. I most certainly did not have a crush on Rob.

I wasn't really cross with him. I was just embarrassed. From what his sister and her fiancé could see, I was a woman prone to violent tendencies who chose to sleep with a man just because she couldn't get a train. At least that's how it felt to me. Explaining it to Rob on the way home, comfortable and cosy in the front seat of his Range Rover, it did have a slight ring of the ridiculous, which is what he accused me of being if that was what I thought his sister would think. When I made to protest again, he cut his eyes to me from the road momentarily and I let it go.

Rob pulled the car into the parking space in front of the old house. It had probably once been a beautiful place but converting it into flats in the seventies had done it no favours, and now it sat looking sad and a little neglected, despite three out of the four flats being occupied. I saw Rob sweep his eyes over the place but there was nothing in his expression to read. I could only guess that it was much the same as mine had been when I came to look. Unimpressed. Fortunately for Rob, he wasn't in the position of having to hurriedly find somewhere to live because his relationship had just gone badly down the tubes, thereby leaving him without a home. I'd stayed with Mags for a few weeks but my back could only take so much of a pull-out bed and although this place was far from perfect, it had been available to move into straightaway and was on the main line. Those were really the only two things going for it, but I'd been so sick of flat hunting by then plus all the time it was sucking out of my day when I had work to do, I just took it. The lease was coming up soon and I really needed to find somewhere better to live. I hated it here, and tended to spend as much time as possible at the studio.

'You don't have to come in. All joking aside, I'm sure you do

78

have better things to be getting on with.'

'Not really. I'll see you to your door,' Rob replied, still looking around with that blank expression on his face.

I fished a bunch of keys out of my bag, and plugged one in the main door. Jiggling it a little, I finally got it to turn. The door creaked like something out of bad film when I pushed it and then stuck partway, requiring me to give it a big heft in order to actually walk through.

'Sorry.' I apologised as Rob gave it another shove in order to make enough space to get his bulk through. 'I've mentioned it to the landlord a few times but not a lot seems to happen.'

Rob said nothing.

'I'm just going to check my post. Hang on a tick,' I said, and did a quick walk-run thing to the middle of the corridor where a rack stood, with four cubbyholes, one for each of the flats. A peeling sticker with a faded number denoted which space belonged to which flat. I peered at the gap for my number, and pulled out what was more than likely junk mail. I shoved it in my bag to read later on the off chance that it wasn't. As I turned back towards the front, and the stairs up to my own flat, the door of the one below me opened and a man stepped out.

'Hi, Isabel.'

Oh great. Pervy Peter. Just what I needed.

'Hello, Peter,' I said, doing my best not to look at him too much and encourage a conversation. He'd positioned himself in front of the stairs which meant I had to go right past him in order to get to my own place. Another reason for getting out of here.

'Haven't seen you all weekend. I was a bit worried.'

I doubt it, I thought. The waft of wacky baccy that floated out of that flat every time a door opened was intense. I doubt Peter and whoever he'd brought home this time would've even seen the weekend, let alone me if I'd been here.

'All fine!' I put on a bright smile, still not looking at him as I made to go past, doing my absolute best not to notice that one hand had been moving in Pervy Peter's pocket the whole time he'd been watching me. Peter didn't move.

'I believe the lady would like to get by,' Rob's voice said close to Peter's head. My neighbour jumped about three feet in the air. Until this point, he'd been completely unaware of the presence of another person which gave an idea as to quite how spaced he was, given the fact that it was generally quite hard to miss anyone of Rob's size. Peter turned around and found himself looking at the lapel of Rob's charcoal wool coat. He tipped his head back until it met a face. The statement had been made in a voice that was quiet, calm and matter-of-fact but there was no mistaking the meaning in his eyes. *Do Not Fuck With Me.* Even in his stoned-out state, recognition of that message flashed in Peter's brain. Standing back from the stairs, he quickly returned to his own flat, stopping for a moment to glare at me, then slammed the door.

'Excellent,' I said, pretending I was irritated rather than a little freaked out by the glare I'd just received.

Rob said nothing but followed me up the stairs to where I shoved another badly cut key into my own door and stepped inside.

It wasn't great. I admit that. But I'd done what I could with it when I'd moved in. I was pretty sure the young lad at the local DIY superstore had thought I was off to destroy evidence of a heinous crime as he'd scanned my trolley full of bleach, scrubbing brushes, gloves, overalls and protective eye wear. Admittedly I probably didn't help myself by promising that I hadn't actually just committed a murder, and then laughing. His previous look of 'slightly suspicious but still bored' was immediately replaced by a more alert one, which apparently also included the mental instructions never to look me in the eye. Poor boy. I should have really explained that I'd just let a really manky flat. Although, to be honest, I think by that point, all my credibility had long since gone.

'Would you like a drink? Tea, coffee?'

'Come back to my place,' Rob replied.

'What?'

He crossed the room, assessing, and seeing movement, glanced out of the window. Plumes of cigarette smoke were floating out across the garden from Peter's flat downstairs.

'Come back to my place. Please.'

I looked up into his eyes and saw that although the look he'd given Peter had long since gone, he was still absolutely serious. Not one hint of the laughter that usually lingered there remained.

'Why?'

'Because I don't like the thought of you here. On your own. That guy is stoned out of his head, for a start. You know that all the time he was looking at you, he was—'

'Yes! Thank you!' I cut him off.

'Come on, Izz. Please! I hate the thought of leaving you here. I can't go back to town, knowing you're … here.' His face wrinkled on the last words as the unmistakable sound of squeaky bedsprings began a refrain from Peter's flat.

I rolled my eyes and put the television on to help mask the noise. Handing Rob a mug of the coffee I'd made without waiting for a reply, I sat next to him on the sofa and together we watched *Antiques Roadshow*, both doing our best to ignore the assortment of sounds now drifting up through the floorboards.

Mags was on my studio doorstep as I turned the corner the following morning. Her eyes were shining, and I had a feeling it wasn't just from the cold. I hurried towards her, gave her a big hug and let us into the studio, which was, thanks to the thermostat and timer, wonderfully warm and inviting.

Mags handed me one of the Costa takeaway mugs she'd been holding and we sat on the Chesterfield ready to exchange our news.

'What time do you have to be in?' I checked the vintage-looking clock, as Mags checked her phone.

'Soon.' She pulled a face.

Mags loved her job in PR, but I had the feeling, after what she'd been telling me about just how well the weekend had gone, that she'd much rather be spending time with Martin, otherwise known as Gorgeous Bus Boy. He'd dropped her off at my studio this morning, which when she mentioned it told me much more than she thought it did.

'We're going ice skating at Somerset House tomorrow night. Can you come? I want you to meet him, and he wants to meet you. He knows this doesn't go anywhere without your approval.'

I laughed. 'Oh, Mags!' From what I'd seen it was going along at its own speed quite happily already. Again, pretty unlike Mags, who normally took things quite slowly, so this guy was obviously something special. At least, he'd better be. 'Oh no! I can't!'

'What? Why not?'

'I have to go to Paris tomorrow.' I pointed a finger at her in warning, as I could hear for myself exactly how pretentious that sounded. 'I've got to meet with a client there tomorrow afternoon. It could be a really good networking opportunity. I wouldn't be going otherwise. Can we do it some other time?'

Mags creased her brow. 'Are you free for lunch?'

We arranged a lunchtime meeting, and then Mags started grilling me about Rob. After assuring her many times over that absolutely nothing happened between us the whole weekend, Mags finally gave up on that particular line of questioning.

'I don't know why not, though.'

'What do you mean?'

Mags turned her head and gave me a look, 'Oh, come on, Izz. You can't tell me you haven't noticed he's totally gorgeous. Plus he's sweet, funny, intelligent, and has a good job. Hon, he's got the whole, shall we say, package!'

'We're friends. That's all. So, I'll thank you to leave any mention of his package at the door!'

'Spoilsport.'

'Izzy? There's someone here to see you.' My assistant, Tash, poked her head around the screen. It wasn't a huge studio but I had a thing about people calling across the room. It didn't seem to go with the whole ambience of elegance and class I was going for if someone bellowed across the floor.

'Thanks, Tash,' I said, looking up from the table where I'd just finished cutting out a toile for the 'Castle Bride'. She'd come back to me on Sunday night, declaring that the first design I'd sent her was "absolutely what she had in her head", even though she "didn't even know it was in there". Her email wording had made me laugh. Perhaps Rob was rubbing off on me – that whole mind-reading thing might be catching.

I smoothed down the skirt to my dress, grabbed my heels from where I'd taken them off earlier and checked my hair in the mirror. After my flying visit to Paris, I had a whole French thing going on today. I patted my chignon, checking no stray curl had made its way out. Satisfied that I was now prepared to meet my client, I stepped out into the main salon to find Rob looking at the display of black-and-white photographs. Whilst Rob was concentrating on the images, I noticed that he in turn was being ogled not only by my assistant, but also by the bride and mother who had been going over designs and thoughts with Tash moments earlier.

My heels clicked on the polished wood floor as I entered, and the noise caught Rob's attention. 'Hi!' he said, his face breaking into a huge smile. 'Wow! You look stunning!'

I was already returning the smile, but at his words, it spread further over my face until it almost hurt.

'Thank you!' I said, coming up to him, where he bent a little and kissed me on the cheek. He met my eyes for a moment and then peered down. Sussing that he hadn't bent anywhere near as much as he usually did, he checked out my shoes. They were ridiculously high but they looked amazing. I wore other ones to walk in so really they were just for show. But what a show.

83

'How do you even stand up in them, let alone walk?' he asked.

I slid my glance to Tash who was now staring at us both. She saw me looking and quickly got back to work, at the same time distracting our other spectators.

'I thought you said I look stunning?'

'You do! I'm just …' he looked down again '… intrigued.'

I smiled and shook my head. 'What are you doing here, anyway?'

'I had a meeting with a client not far away so I thought I'd just drop in and say hello.'

'Oh! How nice! I'm so glad you did.'

And I was glad. Rob seemed pretty happy with the reaction too. It wasn't hard to understand why, bearing in mind the initial greeting his previous visit had induced last Friday.

'How was Paris?'

Twenty minutes later, I'd told him about Paris and about Mags' new man, whom I did thoroughly approve of, and explained that they were now planning a post-Christmas getaway. Rob had told me how his week had gone, questioned me yet again about Pervy Pete and then reluctantly said he needed to get back to the office. I was surprised at how disappointed I was to have to let him go. He kissed me goodbye on the cheek and I walked to the door with him. The weather was absolutely bitter as I opened the door and stepped outside with him.

'Get back in there! You'll freeze!'

'I think I'll last a couple of minutes.' Something within me wanted to have a moment with Rob to myself, without an audience, however discreet.

He smiled. 'Do you ever do what you're told?'

'Depends on whether I'd already planned on doing it anyway.' I grinned back at him. Although, bloody hell, he was right. I was freezing.

'Get back inside, woman.' He pushed open the door and waited for me to step back inside.

He pulled the door closed and waved through the glass at me. I stood watching him hurry away, collar turned up against the cold. Over the street noise, I heard a shrill whistle that I recognised and a taxi heaved itself across to where Rob had stuck his hand up to signal it. He pulled open the door, and stepped in quickly, closing it behind him. Within seconds, it was lost among the many others filling the streets and he was out of sight. I walked back on my skyscraper heels and settled myself in front of the toile, refreshed by the unexpected, and surprisingly welcome, distraction that had come my way.

Chapter 8

I knew I probably ought to be heading back home by now. I'd been in the studio since eight o'clock that morning which wasn't unusual but bearing in mind it was a Saturday shortly before Christmas, it might have been a little sad. I was going to leave earlier, but then I'd thought what 'home' was right at the moment, and decided to spend another hour or two in my cosy, friendly studio. An hour later it had started to rain heavily and I wished I'd actually stuck to my guns and gone home earlier after all. I was going to get soaked walking from the station back to the flat.

I hurried along the street, keeping my head down under my umbrella, whilst at the same time desperately trying not to maim any of the Christmas shoppers that were solidly filling the pavements of the capital. I could see the sign for the Tube station just up ahead and carved out a pathway to get there. Just as I was about to turn in, my mobile rang. I debated about just letting it go to voicemail but as my parents were currently away on the other side of the world, I knew there was no way that was going to happen. My dad had a penchant for trying new things and although Mum and I had done our best to talk him out of some of the more extreme things, bungee jumping was still on his list. To be fair, I could see his point when he told us that he'd completed plenty of jumps during his time in the army when he wasn't attached to anything whatsoever, so the bungee thing probably did seem like playtime to him. And it probably would be. But Mum and I still weren't keen. Although he kept himself super fit, he wasn't twenty-five anymore, and I didn't want something to happen to him on the end of a bloody great elastic band. I had to answer, just to check.

I forced myself through the pack of people surrounding me and tucked myself against the wall. Digging into my bag, I pulled out my phone. Rob. I didn't yet have a picture to accompany it.

'Hi!'

'Izzy? Are you at home?' His voice sounded tense, completely opposite to the relaxed, easy-going state he'd been in when he'd dropped in to my studio a couple of days ago.

'No. No, I'm not. Why? Rob, what's wrong?'

My stomach turned over. I wasn't used to hearing this strain in Rob's voice and I didn't like it. I knew him well enough to know that whatever was causing it must be pretty major.

'Rob?' I tried again. I could hear voices in the background which suddenly became muffled. 'Where are you?'

'I'm at home. Where did you say you were?'

'I'm in town. I had some things to do at the studio but I've just got to the Tube. Rob, tell me what's going on? Are you OK?'

'Yes, sweetheart,' he answered, the familiarity of the term confirming to me he was definitely distracted. 'I'm all right. It's Jenny.'

'What's happened?' I burst out, almost before he'd finished. 'Is she all right?'

'Look, I know it's Saturday and you probably have plans, but do you think you could come round, just for a little bit?'

'Of course I can,' I replied, having now given up on trying to get any information out of him. The only plans I'd had for today involved getting home and avoiding Pervy Peter (although, since his encounter with Rob last week, the happenstance meetings that seemed a little too frequent to actually qualify as happenstance, had miraculously dropped off). Past that, it was likely a case of watching something off Netflix with the volume inevitably increased as nocturnal activities downstairs got busier. Of course, I wasn't about to tell Rob that this was the extent of my Saturday night plans. Although, at the moment, I think I could have said I had a trip booked to the moon for eight p.m. and he wouldn't really have blinked. His mind was definitely on other things.

'I'll come and get you,' he said.

'No,' I said, stepping back into the throng of the crowd and doing my best not to get swept upstream by the current of people, 'I'll get a cab. It's fine. There's one here, I can be there quicker this way.'

With one hand still holding the phone to my ear, I pulled open the taxi door and climbed in, giving the driver the address for Rob's apartment building as I did so. The cabbie nodded and we pulled back into the late afternoon traffic.

'I'm in the cab now, so I'll see you soon.' I reported back to Rob, as I rummaged underneath my skirt and pulled out the seatbelt.

'Right. Look, Izzy, thanks.'

'You're welcome, Rob.' I replied, although as I still had absolutely no idea what the heck was going on, I wasn't sure if I'd be able to help but if there was anything I could do I wanted to do it, and that he really was completely welcome.

I hung up and mentally hurried the traffic along. We were still several hundred yards away when the traffic slowed. And then stopped. I heard the cabbie talk to someone else on his mobile, via the Bluetooth earpiece that stuck out against his shaved head.

'Think we might be here for a while, love. Traffic's all backed up from some accident earlier.'

'Oh, I see.' I peered out. The rain was still coming down hard but this cab was clearly going nowhere for some time to come.

'Can I get out here then, please?'

''Course,' he said, and told me the fare off the meter. I tapped my card and pushed open the door, unfolding myself out into the sharp air and drenching rain. I stood well back as the cab pulled off and then hurried across the road, telling myself that I really ought to put a pair of trainers in my bag for walking to and from work. Rushing along in the rain, in the run-up to Christmas, along the streets of one of the busiest cities in the world, whilst wearing five-inch platform heels, really wasn't one of my most brilliant ideas. But this was an emergency. And desperate times called for desperate measures. Anyway, who was I kidding? Me in trainers? The only time those got anywhere near my feet was when I was engineered into taking part in a charity walk (I refuse to lie and say that I ran). I certainly wasn't about to make them part of my day-to-day style, however sensible the idea was. Right now though, I could see the logic.

I finally got to the apartment building and hung on the huge brass door handle for a moment as I caught my breath and found some energy to haul it open. Stepping inside, I huffed out Rob's apartment number and my name to the concierge. He nodded at me and then asked me to wait. A few moments later, after making a call, he gave me permission to go up and directed me to the lifts. I thanked him and hurried over, pressing the button a couple of times to call one. It seemed to take forever but finally a car arrived and I stepped aside as an elegant and rather snooty couple, judging by the look they threw me, exited. I ignored it and stepped in, pressed Rob's floor number and then quickly pressed the "close doors" button in case anyone else appeared.

As I was silently transported upwards, I pushed my hair back with my hands. It was more than damp, as was the rest of me. I turned round and leant on the handrail, then jumped as I saw myself in the mirror opposite.

'Oh no!' I groaned. My hair had absolutely no memory of the straighteners that morning, and was competing with my eye makeup for 'worst feature'. The lift dinged its arrival. I had no time for repairs so I quickly ran my fingers under my eyes to catch the worst of the eye makeup debacle and pulled a hair clip from the outside pocket of my bag to twist my hair up into. I stuck the clip in my mouth and grabbed a handful of unruly locks as I stepped out of the lift into the corridor.

Rob was waiting.

'Oh my—' I jumped for the second time and the clip fell to the ground.

'Sorry,' he said, picking it up and handing it to me, before enveloping me in one of his amazing hugs. 'Thank you so much for coming.'

'That's—'

'Oh my God, you're soaked!' he said, cutting off my gracious acceptance, 'Why are you wet? I thought you were going to get a cab?'

'I did!' I explained. 'But the traffic backed up, so I got out and ran the last bit.'

Then he saw my shoes. 'In those? Izzy! You should have called me!'

'For a few hundred yards? Don't be daft!'

'Come on, let's get you dry.' He took hold of my hand and we walked up the corridor, me taking several steps to each one of his, thanks to a skirt that definitely wasn't made for taking large strides. As we approached the door to his apartment, I tugged on his hand.

'Rob?'

He stopped quickly and turned. Quicker than I could stop at any rate. Bouncing off his chest, I stepped back. He placed one hand on my shoulder, checking I'd got my balance. The other still held tightly to my own. His gaze was soft, but distracted.

'Can you tell me what's going on before we go in please?'

He seemed to be weighing up what to say. My insides were getting more and more knotted. 'Is Jenny all right?' I prompted.

Rob let out a sigh and slumped a little against the wall, still holding on to my hand. I looked up and tilted my head.

'Oh, Izz,' he sighed, his tone more dejected than I'd ever heard it. 'I don't know. I didn't know what to do. She's so upset and I don't know how to fix it for her. I can't stand seeing her like this, not after everything she's been through. I should be able to help.' He ran his hand over his face, hiding it from me momentarily, but he couldn't hide the pain that showed in his eyes as he looked back at me. 'I don't know if you can even do anything.'

'Well, I can't if you don't tell me what the problem is.'

He looked down at me, gave a little nod and took a deep breath. 'I think it's probably just better if you see for yourself.'

Turning, he took the few extra steps to his door and pulled out a key from the back pocket of his jeans. Unlocking the door, he stood back so that I could enter. Coming in close behind me, Rob helped me off with my coat, hung it up on the coat hook then took my hand again and began to lead me into the living area.

'Wait!' I said, reaching down to pull off my heels. As much as I liked being closer in height to him, my feet were soaked and I wasn't about to add mass scarring of his beautiful wooden floor to whatever other catastrophe had taken place. He waited, retaining my hand, holding it up a little to help me balance as I quickly pulled off the shoes.

Rob began to move.

'Hang on a tick,' I said, stopping again. I felt my feet. Sopping. I knew Rob was in a hurry to show me whatever it was he had to show me, but I didn't want to leave puddles with every step – or get trench foot, for that matter. I knew this wasn't going to be elegant but I didn't have much of a choice. Definitely not the best day to choose to wear a pencil skirt. I let go of his hand, leant back, put my bum against the wall and hoiked my skirt up a bit. Quickly, I grabbed hold of the lace top of my hold-ups, and speedily peeled them off, one after another. I hadn't dared look at Rob, and I hoped that, like a gentleman, he'd had the good manners to look away.

'OK. Better,' I said, dropping my soggy stockings into my shoes and straightening away from the wall, 'Sorry about that, they were a bit—'

I stopped as I looked up and saw Rob's face. OK then. Pretty sure he didn't look away after all. 'Not very gallant of you not to turn your back, but at least I made you smile which is something.'

'Sorry,' he said.

I tipped my head at him. 'As I said before, "World's Worst Liar".'

He gave me the briefest of apologetic smiles then led me from the entrance way into the living room.

'Izzy?' Jenny seemed surprised, and confused, to see me. Obviously Rob hadn't included his sister on the plan to get me round. Her eyes were red and puffy from crying. Another woman, older but just as dark and elegant, sat next to her with one arm around Jenny and the other holding her hand.

'Hi,' I said, feeling unbelievably intrusive.

I was glad that Rob still held my hand as the silence and awkwardness that had now descended on the group of people in the room was palpable. Rob must have felt me tensing because he suddenly broke into action.

'Mum, Dad, this is my friend Izzy.' I let go of Rob's hand as my manners automatically kicked in and I stepped forward to shake hands. Rob's dad stood to the side of his wife and daughter. Mike was sitting in the armchair next to him, a look of uncertainty on his face. He stood when the introductions were finished and leant over, giving me a kiss on the cheek.

'Hello. It's nice to see you again.'

I smiled and nodded, more because I didn't know what else to do.

'I'm sorry, Izzy. I didn't know you and Rob had plans tonight. We'll get out of your hair.'

Jenny leant down and began grabbing at the volumes of tissue paper that covered a good proportion of the living-room floor.

'No! No, it's fine. We don't. I mean, Rob … um …' I looked at Rob, hoping that he was going to step in.

He didn't say anything and Jenny looked from one of us to the other. She frowned, and then threw her hands up in the air.

'Oh my God! Rob! You called her here?'

'I thought she might be able to help!'

'Look, Izzy' – she turned to me – 'I'm really, really sorry about this. My brother has completely wasted your time. I can only apologise—'

'Why don't you let her see before you dismiss the idea?' Rob's voice was raised but a glance at his face showed it was more frustration than anger.

'Oh, for pity's sake, Rob. Don't be ridiculous! No offence to Izzy, but she's not a miracle worker. And you should have asked me before you called her anyway!'

'I tried asking you, but you were too busy having a bloody meltdown to give me any sort of answer!'

'Rob!' his mother warned.

'Oh! Excuse me for being upset that my wedding dress is a total disaster!' Jenny was screaming at Rob now, tears flowing down her face.

'Jenny,' her dad started.

'It's probably nowhere near as bad as you think—'

Rob! No! I kicked him to shut him up but the damage was done.

Jenny was red in the face. 'Not as bad as I think? Rob, I'm getting married! People are supposed to look at the bride and say things like "beautiful" and "stunning", not "it's not that bad"!'

'Jenny, just calm down—'

'No! Rob, stop! You have no idea how I feel, so don't try and pretend that you do. I know that you think you're trying to help but dragging Izzy out here is not helping. All it's done is get her soaked, and embarrassed me.'

I looked down at my feet, not quite knowing what to say or do.

'Mike, I'd like to go home please.' Jenny looked at Mike and

93

it was clear that she felt the discussion was over.

Rob, it would seem though, wasn't done.

'Right, so what exactly are you going to do then?'

'What?' Jenny snapped at her brother.

'About your wedding dress?'

'Rob, darling. I think perhaps it's best if—'

Jenny cut her mum off. 'I don't know yet.'

'Well, I assume you're going to need one and as you already spent months trying to find something before you ordered this one, it's obviously not going to be that easy. Especially with Christmas coming up and your wedding being New Year's Day.'

'No shit, Sherlock,' she bit back at him, grabbing the edge of her wheelchair to pull it closer, ready to hoist herself across from the sofa into it. 'Thanks for pointing that out!'

'So why don't—'

'Why don't I what, Rob?' The tears had started again now, and her hand was gripping the side of the chair, her knuckles showing white. 'Just leave me alone! You don't understand!'

'Then tell me!'

I looked between them. Both their faces showed such pain and hurt. I'd seen the other day just how close Rob was to his sister. It was evident to anyone who spent time with them, but I also knew the background. About the accident, about her staying with him during recovery, about him giving her free rein to redesign his flat because she wanted something to do, hence the woman's touch I'd sensed, as well as encouraging her in her dreams for her own beauty business. I knew that behind all the screaming and yelling currently raining down, there was absolute love.

Rob was a man used to being in control. He was used to assessing a situation, finding the best plan to deal with it and getting it done. Jenny would always be his little sister, however old she was. As big brother he felt it was his job, his duty, to take care of her when she needed it and to fix things for her when they went wrong. I'd seen the pain in his face the moment I stepped out of the lift and I could see it now – it was killing him that he didn't know how to fix this for her. He was trying, I knew that. And she knew that.

But Jenny also had a point. He didn't understand. He couldn't. A man couldn't understand just how special That Dress had to be for a bride. Because it was more than just *a* dress. It was The Dress. No man, no matter how empathetic they were, really got that. For the vast majority of women, their wedding day was *the* day in their lives when they would look their absolute best, at their most glamorous and beautiful. And having the Perfect Dress was part of all that. It had to be right, absolutely right. And the phrase 'not that bad' should have no part to play in the conversation.

And for Jenny, there was so much more. She'd been told she'd never walk again – but she was going to walk down that aisle. Only the bridal party knew. And me. It had come out when she'd been explaining how difficult it had been to find a dress – it had to be beautiful but practical for walking in. Jenny had been training so hard, working with physios as well as with Mike and been so determined to gain the strength to wear those leg braces and walk down that aisle to Mike. She deserved to be walking it in the most beautiful dress she could imagine. She should be wearing it right now, never wanting to take it off after that first try because it made her feel so damn wonderful. Instead, she was sitting there with red eyes and tears streaking down her face, in a shouting match with the brother she loved so very much.

'Just leave me alone!' Jenny yelled back. 'Leave me alone and stop butting into my life!'

The shock on Rob's face said it all. Everyone saw it. Including Jenny. She flicked her eyes away and yanked the wheelchair up close to the couch, manoeuvring it into the best position for her transfer.

The air was so thick with tension, I was surprised anyone could actually move at all. Jenny knew she'd gone too far, and I was pretty sure, from their previous interactions and from the look on her own face when the words tumbled out that she hadn't meant what she said. But now she didn't know how to unsay it. I surreptitiously looked around the room. Mr and Mrs Winchester looked distraught, and Mike looked bewildered, his cheery features now clouded and sad. I felt so sorry for him. He and Rob were obviously extremely close, more like brothers than many blood relations. And now he was caught right in the middle. Nobody spoke.

'Right!' I piped up. 'Here's what's going to happen.'

Chapter 9

I was completely aware of the five incredulous looks I was now getting as I stood there, drawing myself up to my full height, which at a smidgen over five feet one, probably wasn't all that impressive, but I had to work with what I'd got.

'Jenny. First of all, you're going to show me this dress.'

'Izzy,' she sighed, 'it's really not worth it.'

'Jenny. It wasn't a request. Now, where is it?' I turned around, looking through the acres of tissue paper that littered the floor. I had no idea where my boldness had come from, or what exactly was 'going to happen'. I just knew I had to do something.

She paused, then pointed to the left-hand side. 'Over there.'

I followed the line of her finger and bent down, feeling about in the paper until I felt fabric under my hand. Nasty fabric. Oh dear. This didn't bode well.

'Here we are!' I stood up, bringing the dress with me. I shook it out and held it up, before clamping my lips together tightly to stop the cry of horror escaping. Jenny was spot on. The dress was a disaster.

'Hmm,' I said, buying myself time in which to think of what the heck to do next. I was very good at what I did. It was the one thing in my life where I had absolute confidence. But I knew

97

immediately that there was no hope for this monstrosity. The fabric was cheap, the seams were twisted and the "diamantes" were falling off even as I moved it.

'Do you have the picture of what you ordered?'

'It's on the table.'

Rob walked across the room and picked up the sheets of paper lying on his dining table. Returning to the rest of us, he handed them over to me silently. He looked at me as he did so and I could tell that, for once, he had no clue as to what I was thinking. Which made two of us.

'Thank you,' I said, taking the print-outs from him.

I placed the dress back down on the floor, and took a look at the paperwork. One of the sheets was an invoice. It was for hundreds of pounds. These people made me so mad! Hadn't they heard of W B Yeats and his warning 'Tread softly because you tread on my dreams'? Con artists like this weren't just treading on people's dreams, they were stamping all over them with bloody great hobnail boots!

I turned over the page and saw the picture Jenny had printed out from the website. The image showed the model looking beautiful, stunning, and all the other words that Jenny had said she wanted people to think when they saw her walking down that aisle. I peered at the design, then down at the dress now lying abandoned on the floor, then back at the design. At the most, it bore a passing resemblance to that shown in the picture, but there was no way it was from the same fabric. I knew fabric and it was hard, if not impossible, to change its properties. The dress on the floor was a slinky nylon, and there was no way on earth to make it fall like the skirt on the dress in the picture was doing. I glanced up and saw several pairs of eyes watching me, everyone on tenterhooks. I had to do something. I could see in those looks that I'd given them all a glimmer of hope, the possibility that this was fixable. Taking that away now would just make them all feel even worse than before. Turning round and saying, 'Yep.

You know what? There really is no hope for this. Sorry about that,' just wasn't an option. Except that was exactly what I was going to have to say.

'I'm sorry, Jenny. You're right. There really is nothing that I can do with this.' I lifted up the dress with my toe.

Jenny let out the breath she'd been holding and swallowed. 'No, that's fine. I know. It's bad. I would have told Rob that if he'd given me the chance and saved wasting your time.'

'Look, it was worth a shot,' Rob interjected.

'I'm not finished,' I said.

Everyone looked at me. After all this was done, I really needed to sit them down and explain I'm not normally this bossy. In fact, I'd never been this bossy in my life. Great time to start. God knew what Rob's parents thought of me. Although I wasn't sure why that suddenly bothered me. I pushed it out of my mind and turned my attention back to the matter in hand.

'Have you spoken to the company you ordered it from regarding return?'

Jenny shook her head. 'I thought it was better if I calmed down a bit first.'

'Yes, that was probably a good thought. OK, so Monday morning you give them a call and explain that as it's nothing like the image you chose so you are returning it for a full refund.'

'I have to say, I don't have a lot of faith in their returns procedure if they're happy to deceive people with rubbish like this in the first place.' Jenny looked so dejected, it broke my heart. I took a seat next to her.

'You're probably right, which is why, once you've spoken to them, you're going to call Rob who, if they've refused the refund, is going to write a very clever, very scary legal letter threatening them with all sorts unless they return your money in full.'

Jenny looked at her brother warily. I imagined the words she'd thrown at him earlier were resonating in her head but I was going on the assumption that Rob planned to forgive his sister. I just hoped that I was right. I looked up, and met his eyes.

'Yep, absolutely,' he agreed, sounding almost relieved to have some sort of purpose in this situation at last. 'Let me know what they say. Just don't agree to anything they offer, until you get it in writing from them.'

'No, of course not,' Jenny replied softly, not quite meeting his eyes.

'Right, next.' Jumping up from the sofa, I stood in the middle of the sea of tissue paper and began kicking it around like a child with autumn leaves.

'The dress might be no good, but their packaging is certainly thorough! Boys, I need you to clear all this out of the way.'

Without hesitation, Rob, Mike and Mr Winchester all started grabbing bits of tissue and shoving it back in the large box that the dress had been shipped in. Within a couple of minutes, the floor was clear once again and I was giving my next set of instructions.

'Good. Now, Mike, if you could pass your lovely fiancée her leg braces?'

Mike jumped in to action straightaway, grabbing the braces I'd seen as I came in. I'm not sure whether it was the ex-soldier in him automatically responding to the command, or whether he sensed a woman on a mission when he saw one, and knew better than to ask questions in such circumstances. I had a sneaking suspicion it might be the latter.

Jenny took the braces off him but didn't make an attempt to put them on. 'Izzy?'

'Come on.' I chivvied her up, 'You're walking up that aisle so I need to take some measurements of you standing.'

'Why would you need measurements?' Jenny said slowly.

'Because I need measurements to make a dress.'

Jenny's eyes suddenly brimmed. 'Oh, Izzy. That's so kind of you but I couldn't ask you to do that.'

'You didn't ask,' I reminded her.

'No, but I know how gorgeous your dresses are and how

much time goes into each one. As beautiful as I know it would be, it's much more than I can justify spending on a dress, what with saving up for a house and trying to start the business. We can't guarantee that Rob's going to be able to get me the money back for that thing' – she flapped her hand towards the box now tucked in the corner of the room – 'and I know that you mean well and I really, really do appreciate it. I just can't accept it.'

'OK, one, I'm pretty sure Rob is going to be able to get you the money back. This is child's play to what he's used to dealing with. Isn't that right, Rob?' I asked, turning to him for confirmation and hoping that he was just going to go with it.

'Child's play.' Rob nodded, not missing a beat.

'Right, and two, Jenny, I'm not asking you to pay for this. Think of it as a wedding gift.'

'Oh, Izzy, no! I couldn't.'

'You can. And you will. So long as you let me put a picture of you looking unbelievably beautiful on your day up on the wall in my studio, that's all the payment I need.'

This wasn't strictly true. My profits would definitely be taking a hit doing this pro bono, but I'd had a few good months so I was pretty sure I'd be able to cover it. And right now, it wasn't about the money. I could afford to do it. Just about. And the tiny bit of hope that had glinted in the eyes of Jenny, and her mum, when I said I had a plan was more than enough payment for me right now. I'd worry about the rest of it all later. As much as he wanted to, Rob couldn't fix this for his sister. But I could. And I was going to.

'Of course you could! But I would feel terrible not paying you and then we're back to square one.' she looked at Mike. 'I mean, that was the whole point of making this a small wedding, so that we could put our money to better use.'

Mike stepped forward from where he'd been standing next to Rob and took a seat on the floor opposite his fiancée. Gently, he took hold of her hands and held them. He looked into Jenny's face and I could see his eyes shining with unshed tears.

'Jenny. When I first met you, I knew that one day I was going to marry you. I was head over heels in love with you by the end of our first date. You're beautiful and clever and you never let anything beat you. The determination you've shown in training with those braces is incredible. I know it's been hard work but not once have you complained. You've just got on with the job. I think you look gorgeous in everything you wear and you know I'm not much up on things when it comes to clothes and fashion. I generally just take your advice.' He smiled and Jenny touched his face softly, tears now running down her own. 'I'd have got married in a pigsty so long as it meant I got to be married to you. Now I know that wouldn't exactly have gone down well with you.'

'No, not really,' she agreed, laughing through her tears.

'What I'm trying to say is that I think you should let Izzy make you a dress. We know then that it will be right for you and you'll feel as beautiful as I know you're going to look. It doesn't matter what it costs. I saved my deployment pay separately and I've not touched that. We can put that towards it. I know you said that you want to use our money for "better purposes" but, Jen, there's really no better purpose in the world to me than making you happy. It doesn't matter how much money we have if you're not happy because that's all that matters.'

By now, I don't think anyone in the room had entirely dry eyes. Certainly I didn't. You'd have thought that over the last few years of being immersed in weddings, plus having my own personal disaster, I'd have developed a thicker skin when it came to such things. But I hadn't. Not in the slightest. I still loved a wedding. I still loved romance and I still blubbed every time. Something that I was trying desperately not to do right now – and failing miserably. I turned slightly so that I was no longer facing the others and quickly swiped at my face with the back of my hand. Turning back, I caught Rob watching me. It was pretty clear that nobody had been left unmoved by Mike's declarations of love.

I expected him to turn away but he didn't. He kept on looking at me and then mouthed the words, 'Thank you'. I smiled and shook my head, before looking away, forcing the eye contact to be broken. I was pretty sure that it was just because we were all being swept up in this extremely emotional moment, but for those few seconds, I had a feeling that I might want Rob looking at me like that for a long time to come.

'I'm not sure, Mike,' Jenny said, eventually.

I knew how much she wanted her own home and business. She was willing to make sacrifices. But I couldn't let her sacrifice the chance to have what she really wanted, and deserved – a beautiful dress for her special day.

'Right, how about this?' I began. 'We'll make a compromise. I make you the dress of your dreams but you pay for the fabric. Wholesale price.'

'But, Izzy. This is your business. You can't go giving your time away.'

'And I don't but these are extenuating circumstances. And this is happening.' I'd apparently found my bossy boots again and strapped them back on. 'Now you, Missy, need to get those braces on so that we can make a start.'

I saw a smile start to form on Jenny's face which was immediately reflected in her fiancé's. 'Are you sure?' she asked.

'Absolutely.'

'Oh, Izzy' – she held out her hands to me and I bent down next to Mike – 'Thank you so much,' she whispered.

I leant forward and hugged her. 'It's my pleasure.'

Half an hour later, Jenny was getting out of the braces and I had all the measurements I needed.

'OK, chaps. This is girls' time now. Why don't you three go and have a beer somewhere and let us get on with the fun stuff for a while.'

'Yes, ma'am.' Rob saluted me, did a proper soldier pivot thing on his feet and headed off to grab a coat from his bedroom. A couple of minutes later he was back.

'Right. We'll make ourselves scarce then. How long do you need?' Rob asked as he finished tying the lace on his shoe. 'We could get some takeaway on the way back.'

'That sounds lovely, darling!' his mum said, holding out her arms to him for a hug before he left.

He stepped over and duly hugged her, enveloping her almost as much as he did me. Although she did have the advantage of extra height on me. Like most people. Straightening back up, he looked at me for an answer.

'Umm, I don't know,' I said, glancing at the clock on his mantelpiece. 'Give us a couple of hours or so.'

He nodded. 'We can do that.'

'Great,' I said, and noticed he was turning to go. I caught his eye and then shifted my glance to his sister and then back to him. Confusion was the only look I got back. Once again, I shifted my glance to Jenny, and then back to him, adding a tiny sideways nod of my head this time for emphasis.

I'd noticed that since Jenny's outburst at Rob, she'd not looked at him directly. It was obvious to all of us that she'd regretted her words the moment they were out, especially when she'd seen the look on his face. She knew that everything he'd done, and continued to do, for her was because he loved her and no way did she really think he was butting in to her business. It had come out in the heat of the moment and she hadn't been able to take it back. And now she didn't know how to try.

I knew that Rob would forgive her, had probably already done so, but his feelings had been hurt. However, to get this to work I needed Jenny in the best place she could be. I wanted her to enjoy everything now and not be niggled by the upset of earlier. I needed Rob to be the bigger man and make the first move. On my third attempt, I added raised eyebrows to the nod and the eye glance. I saw a flicker of understanding on his face but also

104

hesitation. I mouthed the word, 'Please?' Almost imperceptibly, he shook his head at me, and then stepped over to where Jenny sat.

'Have fun, sis,' he said, giving her a hug as though nothing had happened. 'Any preference on the takeaway?'

Jenny's arms tightened around him. 'I'm so sorry. I didn't mean any of it.'

'It's fine. I know.'

From my vantage point at the edge of the living room, I could see relief flood through everyone in the room. The last bit of tension dissipated away into nothing and Mike gave me the biggest smile. The happiness in that smile alone would have been more than enough payment for me. This couple had both been through tough times. Mike had served his country, seen battle, things that once seen could never be forgotten. Jen had been in the wrong place at the wrong time and had her life changed forever. I couldn't take away the horrors Mike had seen, or give Jenny back the use of her legs, but I could do something to make them both smile. And that felt pretty good to me. Mr Winchester and Mike both went over to the sofa to say goodbye to their respective partners and I made a point of studying the measurements I'd just taken. All of a sudden I felt the outsider. This was clearly a very close family. Understandably, with what they'd been through, and it looked as if Mike was treated as another son already which I thought was wonderful. But I didn't really fit in anywhere, and as the emotions of earlier fuelled the temporary goodbyes of the moment, I suddenly felt very intrusive.

'Thank you so much.' Rob's deep voice was soft in my ear. I turned quickly and looked up at him.

'It's nothing. Really.'

'It's not nothing, Izz. Right now, it's everything. Just look at her.' Jenny was laughing with her parents and Mike. He was right. She did look a whole lot happier than she'd done earlier. I smiled at the scene.

'Well, hopefully it'll go some way to making up for breaking your nose.'

Rob laughed. 'I already told you I'd forgiven you for that.'

I waggled my head in a manner that suggested I wasn't entirely satisfied with that in my own mind.

'So, do you have any preference on takeaway?'

'Oh, Rob, that's really kind but I think I'll probably just shoot off once I've got everything I need from your sister.'

His face fell. 'You did have plans. I'm sorry, Izz. You should have told me you had a date.'

'I don't have a date!' I said, tripping over the words in my attempt to get them out as fast as possible. For reasons I wasn't sure of, it seemed important to make it absolutely clear to Rob that I most definitely did not have a date.

'OK.' He smiled. 'So what's the rush? Why not stay for dinner?'

I threw a glance at the others, and dropped my voice even lower. 'Rob, I'm intruding here. I've bossed my way into making a dress for Jenny because I can't bear to see her, or you, upset like this, but I'm not about to barge in on your family time.'

'Listen to me,' he said, his large, warm hands resting either side of my waist. 'You're not barging in. I want you here. And I know Jenny will. She'd hate to think that you were going to leave afterwards. I know she would.'

'I don't know. I—'

'Oi,' he said, causing me to look back up from his chest, 'don't even begin to think that you're the only one who can take a swig from the bossy fountain. You're staying for dinner.'

I wavered right up until the moment he kissed my cheek and then wrapped me up in one of those incredible hugs. I guess I was staying for dinner.

Mike and his soon-to-be father-in-law approached us and began putting on their shoes. I stepped aside from Rob and leant over to get my bag. Rob watched, and then took the bag off me, preparing to carry it over to the sitting room.

'Bloody hell! What have you got in here?'

I took it back off him and rolled my eyes. 'I thought you lot carried fifty-kilo rucksacks in the army?'

'We did. And we had everything we needed to live off in them. You're in the middle of a city and are only out for the day.'

I tipped my chin up. 'I believe I gave you instructions to buzz off.'

Rob grinned and dipped down for another swift kiss on the cheek. I couldn't help but smile when he did. I knew I shouldn't. They didn't mean anything. Not really.

'Buzzing as we speak,' he said, and hustled the other two men to the door. The catch closed behind them and I was left with Jenny and her mum. I turned back to them and gave a wide smile.

'Right! Jenny, didn't you tell me that you'd created a Pinterest board for wedding dress ideas? Do you want to pull that up?' I lifted my laptop out of the oversized tote I'd taken back off Rob and unzipped the case before handing the machine over to Jen. 'And we have these, for some extra inspiration.' I delved in the bag again and pulled out a stack of the latest bridal magazines and put them on the coffee table. I'd taken them from the studio earlier to sit down with tonight and pore over. They plopped down with a heavy thud and I thought briefly that maybe Rob did have a point about the weight of my bag.

'And one more thing,' I said, running into the kitchen and helping myself to the bottle of champagne I knew I'd find in Rob's fridge. I'd commented on it last week, asking about the special occasion whereupon I'd been informed that he always kept one in there, just in case. Right now, his attention to detail was coming in extremely handy. I collected a corkscrew and glasses and took everything into the living room. 'Bubbles!' I announced, theatrically.

'Oh, how lovely!' Eleanor Winchester clapped her hands together as I extracted the cork with a pop and a flourish. I'd lost count of how many of these things I'd opened over the last few years, and I was now on first name terms with the wine warehouse's delivery driver. It had taken me months to stop feeling like I had to explain it "wasn't all for me", usually followed up by a slightly maniacal laugh, which probably hadn't helped my case. I filled two glasses and handed them to my, now, clients. I poured the tiniest drop into another glass for myself and made a toast.

'To Jenny.'

'To Jenny!' her mum chorused.

'To me!' Jenny cheered and laughed, before downing a good proportion of her glass.

'Steady on, darling. Let's get you a dress designed before you get smashed!' Eleanor cautioned.

'But after that,' I said, 'feel free to get completely smashed. Now, tell me every idea you had, no matter how big or small, or how crazy it might sound. I want to hear them all.'

Chapter 10

A little over two hours later, we heard the men come back and the tantalising aroma of food drifted in from the corridor where they were shedding coats and shoes.

'Lebanese!' Rob announced as he came into view, holding up three bags bursting with takeaway containers.

'Ooh, yum!' we all cheered together.

I got up and followed Rob to the kitchen. 'Hi.'

'Hello.' He grinned down. Clearly he'd had a drink or two.

'I just wanted to say that I owe you a bottle of champagne. I borrowed yours for Jenny and your mum.'

'Borrowed?'

'Well. Used. Obviously. Hence the reason I owe you one. I have a nearly full box at the studio so I'll get one to you as soon as possible to replace it.'

'Don't be daft, Izz,' he said, moving me bodily out of the way of the cutlery drawer so that he could get to it, 'that's why I keep a bottle in there. I couldn't think of a better reason to open it. No replacement required.' He moved me again as I was now in the way of the crockery cupboard.

'Oh. If you're sure.'

'I'm sure. Here, can you take these?' He loaded six plates

into my arms and I headed off towards the table where Mike was already laying out table mats. These boys were well trained. Everyone took their places and started digging into the food, which tasted just as delicious as it smelled. I watched and listened as banter was exchanged and stories were told. They were wonderful at including me and I couldn't remember the last time I'd enjoyed a Saturday night quite as much. Although, thinking about it, the previous week sat watching a rom-com with Rob had been pretty nice too.

As we sat after our meal, letting it all settle, Jenny tapped a spoon against the edge of her glass, the crystal ringing out over the conversations still going on.

'I'd like to propose a toast.'

We all looked at her expectantly.

'To Izzy, for coming to the rescue today and for preventing me from becoming a complete Bridezilla.' I flushed bright red and began to protest but my words were drowned out by a hearty round of 'To Izzy!'

I'd love to say I accepted it graciously but that depends if grinning like a loon counts as gracious. Probably not. But they were happy. And that made me happy. I couldn't help smiling.

'And,' Jenny continued.

'Oh crikey, she's on a roll,' her brother teased.

'To Rob. For being the best brother a girl could wish for. And for knowing exactly when to butt in.' She inclined her head at him and he winked at her.

'To Rob,' I cheered along with the others as I looked over at him. He'd bowed his head a little, ostensibly in jest, but I had a feeling he was showing a little more emotion than he felt comfortable with in company.

'And of course, to Jenny and Mike!' I chinked my glass against the others as we all drank to my toast.

Rob glanced across the table at me. He knew exactly what I was up to with my distraction tactics. The quickest of winks came my way before he turned back to say something to his dad.

'I'm assuming that as you polished off all my champagne, you have a dress?' Rob asked a few minutes later.

I laughed. 'We don't have a dress yet – I'm good, but I'm not that good – but what we do have is a design. I'm going to get started on it tomorrow whilst your mum and Jenny head off to Rigby & Peller to get the required foundation garments. It's all in hand.'

'It's Sunday tomorrow, Izz.'

'That's all right. I didn't have anything planned anyway so it's fine.'

'You do seem to work very hard, dear,' Eleanor said. 'Rob's told me that you're often in your studio until very late at night.'

'Oh,' I said, wondering what to do with the information that Rob had been discussing me with his parents.

Evidently, Rob read the look on my face.

'Mum was giving me a hard time about working late,' he explained. 'I said that anyone with their own business often spends an awful lot of time at work these days.'

'Oh!' I said, again, then engaged my brain some more. 'Yes. It's pretty competitive out there. And the truth is I love what I do so whilst yes, I am at work a lot, it's also my passion so most of the time it doesn't feel like work. I know I'm very lucky to be able to say that.'

'Do you ever work from home?' John Winchester asked.

'Yes, a little. I do the odd bit, research and some sketching. A bit of social media, that sort of thing – but generally I prefer to be in the studio.'

'She doesn't like her flat,' Rob added, helpfully.

I glared at him. He looked back at me, an innocent look on his face.

'Oh dear!' Eleanor turned to me.

'It's not that bad!' I laughed. 'Rob's exaggerating. He dropped me off the other week after the snow and he didn't like it, so in

111

his mind, it's unlikeable. I can't blame him though, it's nothing like as nice as this place.' *Or the place I had to move out of when my fiancé dumped me, for that matter.*

'I didn't like it because you're not comfortable there and you have a leering pothead for a neighbour.' Rob had that calm but decisive tone back in his voice.

Like a tennis match, all eyes turned to me. I wasn't about to spoil what, up until now, had been a very nice evening by getting into an argument with Rob about my living arrangements. Of course I'd love something as gorgeous as this flat but I couldn't afford it. He seemed to have forgotten that minor detail. Unlike him, we weren't all anal enough to start saving for a deposit at three years old, although with the way house prices were in London these days, that might not be a bad idea to start implementing.

'He is a little odd' – I laughed it off – 'but it's not like I'm there long term. I'm looking for something else so that I can move when my lease runs out.'

'How long have you been there, Izzy?' his dad asked. I'd noticed his face cloud when Rob had mentioned the 'leering pothead'. Like father, like son.

'Coming up to six months.'

'And where did you live before, dear?'

From the corner of my eye, I saw Rob shift in his chair.

'Down towards Canary Wharf.'

'Didn't you like it there?'

Ha! I bloody loved it there. And frankly, after I'd finished redesigning and redecorating it, it was perfect – not to mention being worth a whole bunch more than when my ex had bought it – but, because my name was never put on the paperwork, I was out of a home. Steven had always said it would be easier just to get it done once with my married name, rather than paying to have it done again once my name changed. And I trusted him. More fool me. Another mistake I wasn't going to make twice.

'Yes, it was very nice. It's just that I was living there with someone else and to all intents and purposes, it was his flat. Things ended quite suddenly and I needed somewhere to live. Hence the current place. But, as I say, I'm looking around.'

Eleanor smiled. 'I hope you find something you like soon.'

'I'm sure I will,' I replied, still not looking at Rob. I was a bit cross with him for bringing my living arrangements into the conversation. Of course, he'd had no idea which way the conversation would turn and I knew he'd never choose to make me feel awkward. But the fact was that, because of him, I now did and I needed to stew on that for a bit.

'Shall I clear the plates?' I ensured the subject was changed by doing it myself. Getting up from the table, I gathered all the dirty crockery. His mum started to help but I said I could manage and took the used plates into the kitchen and put them down carefully next to the dishwasher.

'I'll make some coffee.' I heard Rob's chair scrape and moments later felt him near me as I loaded up the machine.

'Just leave them, Izzy, I'll do it in a minute.'

'I'm nearly done,' I said without turning around. There was a pause before I heard him getting mugs out of the cupboard and the coffee machine burst into life. I stood up and closed the door to the dishwasher. Turning around to leave the kitchen, I came face to chest with Rob.

'Whoops! 'Scuse me,' I said, making to step around him. He moved ever so slightly with me. Nothing so much as would attract attention from the others across the room. But enough for me to notice and get the point. I sighed and looked up.

'I'm sorry about the questions. I didn't realise Mum would ask for more intel.'

'She was just making conversation. She doesn't know about … me staying, does she?'

'No.'

'Right. Good. It's just that when she said how you'd told her I

113

worked late … I was just … Well. I didn't know what else you'd told her about me.'

'Nothing. As I said, she was giving me a bit of grief, in a worried-Mum way, about nights I'd been doing in the office. I explained that, one, a few of my clients are in the Asia Pacific region which means if I have to speak to them, it's going to be a weird time here, and two, that I had various friends who were also often late at their jobs, especially when it was their own business. You were one of about four people I named.'

'Fair enough.' I nodded. So he hadn't been talking to his mum about me, specifically. That was good. I mean, of course he hadn't. And why would he? Oh dear, maybe I did work too much. My brain certainly felt extremely tired right at this moment. The line of cups on the counter caught my eye.

'No coffee for me, thanks. I was just about to make a move.'

'Now?'

'Yeah. I know. Shocking, eh? I'm actually heading off to my horrid flat before ten p.m.'

'Can't you stay?'

'No, I don't think so.'

'Are you mad at me because of what I said about your flat?'

I wasn't about to lie. 'Yes, a little. But I know that you mean well, so I'm getting over it.' I gave him a little look to show he was pretty much forgiven. Lucky for him, he had that whole gorgeous thing going on which I'm sure got him pardoned for things a lot quicker by a lot of people.

'At least stay for coffee,' he countered.

Honestly, I was tired and really should have gone home but my brain just couldn't be bothered to argue with him. And he was right. As much as I protested, I didn't like my flat. The more I was out of it, the happier I was. And I'd enjoyed my time here today, with Rob's family. It made me feel a part of something whilst my own parents were away.

'OK. You win.'

He gave me a grin that had I been so inclined, and/or wearing any, would have knocked my socks off.

I leant around him and took a couple of the drinks already prepared through to the living room, and placed them on the coffee table. Rob followed shortly after with the rest of them, and the condiments, on a tray.

'I can hardly believe it will be Christmas in a week,' Eleanor mused, glancing at the rain that was now throwing itself against the picture window.

'It does seem to have gone fast this year,' her husband agreed.

'What time do you think you'll be able to get to us next week, Rob darling?' his mum asked.

Rob raised his eyebrows in thought. 'I'm not sure. Hopefully by about eight-ish, depending on traffic. I can get something to eat on the way down though, so don't worry about waiting for me.'

'Nonsense. I'll have something for you. I can always warm it up if you get delayed.'

'Thanks. I can just give you a call when I'm leaving and let you know during the journey if there's any big hold-ups.'

'Make sure you pull over if you're going to call me.'

'Mum, the car has hands free. Stop worrying.' Rob smiled and took a sip of his coffee.

I stood up. 'I'm sorry. Would you excuse me a moment? I just have to make a quick call.'

Delving into my bag, I retrieved my phone and walked down the hallway. Unlocking the front door, I went out into the public corridor and pulled the door to behind me, taking care not to latch it so that I didn't have to bother the others when I returned. I pressed 'Search' on my phone and googled what the current time was in Sydney, where my parents were staying with friends for the week. Five a.m. Oh. Probably not the best idea to give them a Skype call right now then.

I leant back against the wall and let out a sigh. I was happy they were finally doing this trip but right now, I was really, really missing them. I clicked on another icon on my phone's home screen and WhatsApp popped up. I pressed the thread I already had going with Mum and Dad and typed a message, wishing them a good day and asking what they'd been up to. I mentioned that the rain was lashing down here and that I'd just got a new commission. I didn't mention it was for New Year's Day. Or for free. They already worried about the amount of hours I put in, so I knew that knowledge would only cause them to worry more. 'Love and miss you lots,' I typed at the end and sent it off, ready for them to collect when they got on the Wi-Fi the next day. Silly as it seemed, sending that message off made me feel that little bit closer to them so I composed myself and headed back towards the door to Rob's apartment. Just as I got there, Rob stuck his head out.

'Everything OK?' he asked.

'Of course!' I gave him a bright smile.

He stepped out into the corridor and pulled the door to as I'd done a short time earlier. 'You are such a fibber,' he stated.

'I am not! Everything is fine.'

'Sure?'

'Absolutely sure.'

He looked at me without saying anything more, but he made no move to go back into the apartment either. I held my nerve. I knew his tactics. Waiting for me to fill the space. Two could play at that game. I looked back at him evenly. I could do this too. See? For about ten seconds.

'Oh! God, you're annoying!'

'Thanks,' he said.

'I was really missing my parents. I was going to ring them but as it turns out it's five a.m. their time that's not really an option. I sent them a message instead.'

'Oh, Izz!' He moved a step closer to me. I moved back. I didn't want comforting right now.

Sometimes when you're low, and people are really sweet to

116

you, it can be just enough of a tipping point. I had an awful feeling that if I let him in right now, I might just burst into tears. And having done that to him on one occasion already, I had no intention of doing it again. Especially not with his family in the next room!

'I'm fine, really,' I confirmed. 'Come on, let's go back in. I don't think I'd quite finished my coffee anyway.'

We walked back in, Rob following me, and I dropped my phone into my bag as I passed it. I was never one for having it on me all of the time. So long as I could hear it if needs be, that was more than enough for me. Unlike Mags, who practically had the thing glued to her hand. I retook my seat and finished my coffee, tucking into a couple of delicious biscotti the men had picked up at a local Italian deli on their trip out earlier.

'So, Izzy, what are you doing for Christmas? Are you going to family?'

'No, not this year. My parents are actually travelling in Australia and New Zealand for six weeks at the moment. They won't be back until mid-January.'

'No brothers or sisters?'

'Nope. Just me. They decided I was quite enough to deal with!' I laughed. No need for strangers, even lovely ones like the Winchesters to know that my mum very nearly died having me and that the doctors had advised her not to try having any more children as it could well be fatal.

The others smiled at my joke but I could see my revelation about my parents jetting off wasn't sitting well with them. I wasn't about to have them thinking bad of my parents, even though explaining meant revealing a little more than I would have hoped to. But, to me, it was the lesser of two evils so I dived in.

'Their trip was booked ages ago. I wasn't supposed to be here for Christmas either, you see, so when they discussed going, I told them they should definitely go.'

'Oh. I see.' Eleanor smiled brightly, clearly not really seeing

117

but being delightful about pretending to.

Rob smiled at her, then shook his head very gently at me. I knew he was telling me I didn't have to do this, didn't have to go on with the explanation but I was halfway there now and I had nothing to be ashamed of. It was humiliating at the time but I'd done nothing wrong and, as Rob, a week ago, had refused to take the blame for Steven's actions, I didn't see why I should either.

'My fiancé and I had planned to go to Barbados for Christmas,' I explained, looking at Eleanor. From the corner of my eye, I saw Rob tense and his expression cloud. In for a penny, in for a pound I thought, and continued on, 'Except he was actually supposed to be my husband by that point. We'd planned to get married in May but he backed out at the last minute.'

I realised that this was the first time I'd said this out loud to anyone since it happened. Normally I changed the subject if a conversation was veering towards me and marriage, which wasn't uncommon in my line of work, but I felt that it was time to stand up and accept it, at last. And accept that it wasn't my fault.

'Oh dear. You poor thing! I am sorry. I hope he at least had the decency to give you a little notice! There's so much planning involved.'

'Mum,' Rob cautioned.

'What? I'm sorry, Izzy, have I said something wrong?' She looked worried.

'No,' I said, smiling in reassurance, 'not at all. It's absolutely fine. But no, he didn't. He waited until I was at the church. And then sent Rob here to give me the message that he wasn't coming.'

Eleanor and John looked aghast, first at me, and then at Rob who was now staring at the coffee cup in front of him.

'Really?'

'Yes, afraid so,' I said, when it was obvious that Rob wasn't going to respond at all. 'I don't know if you remember but Rob had a broken nose back in May.'

'I do remember, some incident on the rugby field,' Eleanor

said, although her tone suggested she was beginning to wonder if she had all the facts.

'Not exactly. More like an incident in a church. Actually me in a church.' Two pairs of eyebrows shot up in surprise.

'I can only apologise to you for doing that to your son. It was very much a case of me shooting the messenger, so to speak. I would like you to know that I've never ever hit anyone prior to that, or since.'

Nobody said anything. I wondered if, in retrospect, telling Rob's parents that I'd punched out their firstborn was the best idea. But when I'd finally said it, I'd felt good. It felt right. Whatever the consequences, I was fed up with tiptoeing around everything to do with my nuptial non-event.

'You must have a hell of a hook!' His dad broke the silence, a grin that looked a lot like Rob's spreading across his face.

'You know she knocked him on his backside?' Mike added, resulting in a sharp look from me, which he shrugged off, smiling.

'Really? Good Lord!' John laughed.

I noticed that Eleanor wasn't laughing. It was clear she didn't find me being violent towards her son in the least bit amusing.

'I am sorry, Mrs Winchester.' I reverted back to her full name. 'It all happened so fast, I couldn't believe I'd done it.'

'Oh, my dear,' she said, leaning over and taking my hands in her own. 'I hope you don't think I'm upset about that?'

My face confirmed that was exactly what I thought.

'No, no, no. Not at all! I'd likely have done the same thing.'

'Wow. Thanks, Mum!'

Eleanor let go of my hands briefly to wave away Rob's comment, 'You know what I mean.' She took my hands again and held them. 'I obviously don't know you very well, but from what I've heard from Rob, you're hard-working and, from what I've seen today, you have a very kind heart. I know what it's going to take for you to get this dress done for Jenny, and yet you offered to do it without hesitation, because you knew it would not only help her, but all of us. Whoever the man is that chose not to turn up at that church on that day made a very big mistake. He let a wonderful girl slip through his fingers. And I hope that the next man has the good sense to appreciate just what he has.'

I didn't say anything. I couldn't right at that moment. A lump had formed in my throat and was resolutely refusing to shift.

'Thank you,' I squeaked out, eventually.

Eleanor smiled and patted my hands. Suddenly she looked at Rob, then back at me. 'You said this was all back in May?'

'Yes. That's right.'

She looked back at Rob. 'Wasn't that when you were supposed to be best man for Steven? You told us it got called off at the last moment.'

Rob didn't answer and I looked between them. 'You know Steven?'

'Yes. Rob and he were quite close at university so we saw him a certain amount. They drifted apart a bit when their lives took different paths for a while, what with Rob joining the army, but I was pleased to hear they had reconnected. I can't believe that the Steven we knew would do something like that.'

I shrugged my shoulders and gave a resigned smile.

'People change, Mum,' Rob said.

'And was this what you fell out over?' Eleanor said, turning to him.

'I never said I fell out with him.'

'You didn't need to say so. I'm your mother. I know these things. But you have, haven't you?'

Rob took a deep breath. 'Yes.'

'Right. So, was this the reason?'

'It's not quite that black and white, but yes.'

'I see.'

'I'm sorry, Eleanor. I never realised you knew Steven, but of course you would. I'm so sorry if all this has made you feel awkward.'

120

'Me? Oh, Izzy. Not at all! I'm not one to take sides generally but I do know that my son is very laid-back with people and whilst he won't be made a fool of, he will give people the benefit of the doubt, if there's any opportunity. So the fact that he hasn't been able to rectify whatever happened between them leads me to believe that Steven really didn't behave in a way that I would have expected him to. He left you waiting and Rob to break the news? Rob's right. People do change, and clearly not always for the better. But I stand by my earlier comment. Steven made a very big mistake letting you go.'

'Thank you, Eleanor. That's very nice of you to say. Although, with some perspective, it might have been the best thing for both of us, if not the best way of doing it. But it's all in the past now, and I'm OK.'

'That's very good to hear, Izzy. I'm so glad. And now I'd like to invite you to come and spend Christmas with us.'

Opposite, I saw Rob freeze, his coffee cup halfway to his mouth.

'Oh no, Eleanor! I really couldn't. Honestly, I'm over the whole thing now, I promise.'

'I know, I know,' she said, patting my hands, 'but I hate to think of you alone in that flat, even if it's not as bad as Rob says. And we'd love to have you! You already said you'd need to do a couple of final fittings for Jenny – that way she'd be on hand whenever you needed her. Of course, you could bring anything you needed to work on it. We can give the conservatory over entirely to you as your "studio away from home".'

'It's really kind of you to ask, Eleanor.'

'Aren't you going to Mags'?' Rob asked. We all looked over. He was the one person in the room at that moment who really didn't look thrilled with his mum's suggestion for my holiday arrangements. I had to admit at being a little bit confused by his reaction. One minute he was asking me to stay, but the next it seemed he was attempting to find options for me at Christmas that didn't involve me being with him, or his family.

121

'Um, no,' I replied, a little unnerved, and if I admitted, the tiniest bit upset by his complete lack of enthusiasm. 'Mags' whole family is getting together this year. They did invite me but I just fancied a bit of a quieter one this year.'

This was true. Mags' family were just as much family to me as my own. We had the bond of having shared the same lifestyle and continued to build upon it. My dad and hers were as close as Mags and I. And whilst I loved her and her brothers dearly, and all the little ones, I'd only recently returned from spending the weekend with them for her twin nephews' birthday bash. This involved spending far too much time than was good for me, or my stomach, on an indoor bouncy castle, followed by a week and a half of daily hair washing to remove smooshed-up jelly beans that had ended up there during the many, apparently sticky, cuddles I'd indulged in. I was also fairly sure that my latest vintage bag acquisition was never going to be the same again after a helpful five-year-old overheard my declaration that I was going to save my piece of cake to take home with me, and promptly put a slice direct from the gateau straight into my bag. Something I hadn't discovered until later when I got home and reached in for my keys.

'But Rob's right. I'll probably head up to see them at some point.' I hadn't actually had any plans to do this. Mags and I would speak on the phone and text every day anyway, but I wasn't going to let Rob Winchester know that I was a little hurt, not to mention confused, by his attitude. 'Really, don't worry about me. What with seeing Mags, watching Christmas TV, and finishing anything I need to on Jenny's dress, I'm sure that the time is going to fly by!' I beamed at Eleanor.

'Please come, Izzy.' Jenny now joined in.

'It'd be lovely to have you.' Rob's dad added his voice.

To my right, Mike was nodding heartily, agreeing with his fiancée and soon-to-be in-laws. The only person who hadn't added anything in the way of encouragement was the one person who, ever since I'd known him, and certainly in the last couple of weeks, was the one person I'd thought I could count on to offer it.

'And I'm sure your parents would be much happier if they knew you were somewhere safe, and with friends,' Eleanor added.

'Please say you'll come!' Jenny repeated her plea.

I chewed the inside of my cheek in thought. Mrs W had hit a weak spot. I'd had to, almost literally, wrestle my parents into not cancelling their holiday, hiding their laptop until they promised me they wouldn't. They'd waited such a long time for this trip, and had planned it so carefully, catching up with friends and finally seeing places they'd dreamed of for years. But I knew that they hated the thought of me staying at home, alone, especially in that flat. They, unfortunately, held the same opinion of the place as Rob did. Spending the week with the Winchesters down in the beautiful New Forest certainly would take a weight off their mind. But I knew I couldn't accept the invitation if there was going to be an atmosphere thanks to Rob's attitude.

Eleanor took advantage of my hesitation. 'That's settled then! Oh, wonderful!' she said, clapping her hands in joy again as she seemed wont to do. I couldn't help smiling at the others, as pleased as they seemed with the news. Rob, however, had his eyes down, his expression hidden by the coffee cup he'd now refilled.

I'd really enjoyed my afternoon, once the drama had been got out of the way, spending time with Jenny and Eleanor and then later, laughing over dinner with the whole group. Why shouldn't I accept their invitation if they'd been kind enough to extend it? I knew I'd still have some final work to do on Jenny's dress but I was planning to pull in every single favour I had from my seamstress in order to get as much as we could done between us before I left for Dorset. Wrangling a wedding dress and associated gubbins onto a busy festive period train definitely wasn't a viable option but if Mike and Jenny didn't mind coming over and collecting the dress and everything else I might possibly need and taking it down to her parents in their car, then I could just hop on the train after work the day before Christmas Eve, and meet them all down there. I stole a glance at Rob, but he was now talking to his dad about something and I couldn't catch his eye. I really wanted to ask him if he was comfortable with the whole deal. As it was, he soon made his position a bit more clear without me asking.

'Mum. You know Isabel and I aren't a couple, right?'

'Of course I do, dear. We all know your tastes run a little more towards the … obvious. I'd already planned to put Izzy in the guest room. Don't worry. I shan't be making any accommodation faux pas!'

I was intently studying my fuchsia pink painted toenails. Of course we weren't a couple. That much was obvious. We were friends, or at least so I thought. So why bring it up like that, in front of everybody. If he'd thought I was mad with him before, then boy was he in for a shocker now!

'I really do need to be going.' I stood, gathering my things quickly. 'Thank you so much for the invitation, Eleanor, John, I think it would be lovely and I very much look forward to it!'

Jenny beamed.

'I'll be seeing Jenny a few times in the week anyway and we can make arrangements then about getting everything to you and I'll get a train down on the evening of the twenty-third if that's all right? If you could let me know the name of a local taxi firm I can call from the station, that'd be great.'

'Oh, John can pick you up from the station. It's not far at all, don't worry about that.'

'I'll drive you down.' Rob entered the conversation. His tone was, like that expression he wore sometimes, completely indecipherable. 'I can't get away until the day before Christmas Eve either, so it makes sense if I'm already going down.'

'Oh!' I said brightly, covering the agitation and confusion I felt towards him right at the moment. 'It's no bother. I quite like the train. It'll give me a chance to read the book I've been wanting to start for ages.'

I knew I was rambling but he'd thrown me with his attitude change once the subject of me spending Christmas with his family had been raised. In fact, he hadn't just been unenthusiastic, he'd been positively determined to find an alternative option for me. And what was with him suddenly calling me Isabel? Hardly anyone called me that and certainly Rob didn't.

'Don't be silly. It's a waste of your money. I'm driving down anyway. I'll just pick you up after work. You can put everything you need in the boot and we'll head down.'

Did he just accuse me of being 'silly'? I sent him a glare. He saw it but made no apology or alteration to the expression on his face. This was very far from over, but I wasn't about to make a scene in front of everyone, so I let it go, for the moment.

'All right then,' I said, smiling sweetly at him to cover up the fact I was gritting my teeth. If he thought he was going to get a thank you, he had another think coming.

'Perfect!' his mum said, seemingly completely unaware of the undercurrent of the conversation. 'I'll expect you both around eight-ish then. Oh, it's going to be so lovely!'

I couldn't help but smile at her enthusiasm and really hoped that she was right.

I said my goodbyes, complete with hugs, and Rob said that he would walk me to the lift. I told him it wasn't necessary but, as seemed to be his inclination this evening, he did it anyway. He grabbed the keys to his flat from the bowl on the console table and stood waiting as I forced my feet into my still very damp shoes. I picked up the stockings I'd shed earlier and tucked them in a side pocket of my bag so that they wouldn't dampen anything else. As I did so, I thought back to previously when I'd leant against the wall and taken them off, and the cheeky look on Rob's face at the time. It couldn't have been more different to the impassive one he wore now. I wasn't generally one for taking the blame when I knew I hadn't done wrong. I was more than willing to hold my hand up when I'd cocked up but I couldn't for the life of me think of what I'd done here so I wasn't about to apologise for anything! For God's sake, I'd come running, quite literally, in five-inch heels that were now probably entirely ruined to help Rob out and this was the thanks I got? I took my coat from him silently and rammed my arms down the sleeves, becoming more and more annoyed as I replayed things in my head.

Chapter 11

Stepping out into the main hallway, I threw a glance back.

'I'm pretty sure I can make it from here without getting lost, thanks,' I said, a little snarkily, and began walking down the corridor.

'What's up with you?'

I spun on my damp heeled shoe. 'Seriously?'

He shrugged his shoulders. 'Yes. Seriously.'

'You! You're what's wrong with me! I dropped everything and came round here because you asked me to, without having any idea as to what I was stepping into.'

'Which I appreciate.'

'Good. And then, when the drama is over, we all appear to have a very pleasant evening, and you even ask me to stay a little longer, which I do. But right now I really wish I'd just left, because first off, I'm now going to be home much later and secondly, ever since your mum invited me to spend Christmas at their home, you've been acting like a total arse.'

'Excuse me?'

'You heard me,' I said, punching the lift call button several more times – my fingertip going white under the shell pink nail varnish from the effort I was putting into it.

'I've not been acting like an arse, as you so delicately put it.'

'Really? You're going to start criticising the way I talk now?'

'No. I'm saying that I wasn't acting in that way. I thought you'd have other plans. I have to say that I was a little surprised that you'd want to spend the week with strangers anyway.'

I opened my mouth to reply but nothing came out. I closed it and tried again. 'Strangers?'

'Well, it's not like you know them all that well. You only just met my sister last week, and my parents today.'

'Well, lucky for me your mum doesn't seem to abide by the same rules as you in terms of length of association when it comes to being hospitable.'

'Mum loves having guests.'

'And you don't. Apparently. Or perhaps you'd just have preferred them to have been someone more "obvious"?' I said, remembering the description Eleanor had used when describing Rob's taste in women. And now I thought about it, she had a point. Whenever I'd seen him with a woman, said woman pretty much always looked like a model – and often actually was. But what the hell did that have to do with me being at their house for Christmas? I was hardly going to cramp his style!

'There's nothing wrong with my taste in women.'

'I don't believe anybody said that there was. You just might not have been in quite such a rush to clarify that we aren't a couple!'

'Why not? You don't want to be part of a couple. You always make that perfectly clear to everyone, what with your five-year business plan. And I wanted to make sure that there were no embarrassing mix-ups with the sleeping arrangements. I'm not keen on sleeping on the floor when there's a perfectly good bed in the room.'

'What the hell is wrong with these lifts?' I pressed the button again.

'There's nothing wrong with them. You're just being impatient.'

'Well, I tell you what,' I said, rounding on him. 'Why don't you add that to the list of why you don't want me spending the holidays at your parents' house and give it to your mum. Then she can decide what she wants to do. Perhaps you could tell her to let me know.'

The lift arrived and I stepped in. I could feel my face glowing from anger with Rob, but mostly, I was just hurt. I didn't understand his behaviour. All I knew is that he wanted me nowhere near him this Christmas. The door started to close and I breathed a sigh of relief. Just then a hand clamped on one side and they slid noiselessly open again.

'I'll pick you up on the twenty-third. What time will you be ready?'

'Thanks but I think I'm going to get the train after all.'

'Don't be childish.'

'Childish? Me? This from the man who's sat sulking ever since I got invited.'

'I wasn't sulking. I was just considering whether this was the best option for you.'

'Oh, give me a break, Rob. Look, tell you what. I'll make it easy for you. Just go back in and tell your mum I changed my mind. OK? I'll speak to your sister in the week when she comes to the studio, even though we're "practically strangers", and work out the best plan for her final fitting. Now, if you'd be kind enough to get your bloody great hand off the door, I'd really, really like to go home.'

Rob gave me a look, said nothing and let the door go. Having stood to attention the whole time I'd been ranting at him, I suddenly felt bone tired. I slumped against the rail in the car and leant there until it slowed to the gentlest of stops at lobby level. The doors slid open. I grabbed my bag, lighter now that I'd given my copies of all the wedding magazines I had to Jenny. My heels echoed as I made the walk from the lifts to the door where a liveried doorman opened one for me. I thanked him and turned back towards the nearest Tube station. It wasn't on my line but I couldn't be bothered with getting a taxi. I needed the anonymity of the Tube right now, banking on the almost cast-iron guarantee that no one was going to speak to me.

I changed lines and caught a train that would lead me in the direction of the overground station where I could then make my last connection home. The Tube train pulled off and sped up, its familiar rhythm soothing me, the occasional jolts as we got to a steeper corner assuring me that I was moving away from the city and from the day that had gone from bad to good and then plunged right back into the heart of bad again.

The overground train trundled through the rain, the droplets making streams along the window as we moved through the darkness. Eventually the announcement came for my station and I got up and headed towards the door. It was quiet here now around this time, so I was the only one to exit. Stepping off, I began to walk down the platform as the train doors beeped to signal their closure and the engine noise spun up once again and powered off down the line. I shoved my bag up onto my shoulder, aware of an ache in my neck, probably caused by said bag. But I had a feeling that the confrontation with Rob, if I could call it that, bearing in mind he'd made little effort to become too involved, was probably contributing.

I reached the front door of the flats just as Peter was heading out with a bag of rubbish to put in the bins. Part of me was interested to see which one he'd pick, bearing in mind the possibility of what 'organic' remnants might be in his bag. But most of me just wanted to run a hot bath, and lie in it for a long time. He froze for a moment when he saw me. I saw his eyes dart about. Probably I ought to have put him out of his misery and told him that the big scary guy wasn't there but unfortunately he'd caught me in a shitty mood and I wasn't feeling generous, so I let him squirm. God knew he'd made me feel uncomfortable on enough occasions. I carried on walking.

'Peter,' I said.

'Isabel. All right?' He was heading towards the bins but in a strange sort of crablike motion, his gaze still darting around.

I didn't reply, just carried on inside, kicking the door closed behind me. I heard the shout of 'hey' outside, but ignored it. I wandered to the post cubbies, pulled out a bill – perfect – and then went back towards the stairs. As I put my soaking foot on the bottom stair, Peter began hammering on the stained-glass panel of the front door. All I needed now was for him to put his hand through that. I muttered something unladylike under my breath and stepped back down, returned to the door and flicked the latch to open it. Peter shoved himself in out of the heavy rain, bumping into me. I stumbled back and managed to catch myself on the banister before I nearly fell straight on my backside. Peter stood there, looking at me, a strange expression on his face, which for him was really saying something. He'd unnerved me before but he'd never frightened me. Until now.

'Watch it!' I said, my Army brat side shoving itself to the fore to cover up anything else I was feeling.

'You shut that door on me on purpose.'

'I assumed you had your key. The rain was blowing in. Anyway, you're in now so what's the problem?'

I fought to keep my breathing even and turned my back on him, effectively ending the conversation. I took a step up the stairs. A hefty tug on my coat brought me stumbling down backwards. My hand shot out, making a grab for the banister, I missed, whacking my forearm on it hard instead. Quickly, I tried again, this time getting a purchase and managed to steady myself, remaining on the step, but turning quickly and meeting my neighbour at eye level.

'Get away from me!' I screamed at him, the fear now coming out, mixed with emotions from earlier that were already bubbling way too near the surface.

'No boyfriend here to defend you this time, I see.' Peter sneered and made pantomime gestures of looking around for someone.

'I don't need anyone to defend me, you little turd. Now I suggest you get lost before I show you exactly why I don't need a man here to beat the shit out of you!'

Bearing in mind the only punch I'd ever thrown was that one on my wedding day, I was, to a large extent, bluffing. But so long as I talked the talked, I was pretty hopeful that I wouldn't have to walk the walk. Although, if it came to it, I'd managed to knock a massive bloke like Rob on his arse, so I was pretty sure I could do the same to the wiry-framed Peter. Or at least stun him long enough for me to get the hell out of there, which was all I wanted to do right now.

He looked me up and down again. I glared at him in response and waited for him to make the first move. Finally he stepped back and headed off to his flat, a colourful trail of descriptive language, presumably aimed at me, in his wake.

I picked up my bag that had fallen off my arm when Peter had yanked me back and slipped it back over my shoulder before mounting the steps and finally reaching my front door. Rob was right. It wasn't a good place to live. I'd thought my neighbour was harmless but the look in his eyes tonight chilled me. And now I'd pissed him off. I was hoping that, with a bit of luck and some pot by tomorrow he'd have forgotten it all, but there was no guarantee. I kicked off my shoes and padded into the bathroom, emptying the last of the bubble bath into the tub as water gushed out of the taps. I needed to start looking seriously for a new place to live. Tonight. Wearily, I pulled my laptop out my bag and unzipped the case. My hands were shaking from the encounter with Peter but I was refusing to acknowledge any of it right now. Really I should just call Mags, blurt out the whole thing – Rob's weird behaviour, the horrible moment with Peter, everything – and just unload it. But I didn't. Mags would worry and want to come round. Or more likely want me to come round to hers so that I was out of the flat, but I was exhausted. I'd not left the studio before ten once this week, as I worked to get the Castle Bride's toile finished for her first fitting. Heading out into that filthy weather again would take energy I just didn't have. Besides, the last overground train left in a few minutes and there was no way I'd make it now. I'd locked my door with every single key turn and bolt there was on it and a chair was wedged up against the handle for good measure. I didn't really think Peter would make another attempt to try and intimidate me, or anything else, but I wasn't taking chances either.

I checked on the bath level and slid down the side of my bed to sit on the thick rug I'd put there which did a twofold job of making it look pretty and hiding a particularly unpleasant stain. Lifting the lid of my laptop, I let a loud and heartfelt groan. A large crack ran across the screen from left to right. Trying the power button, I held my breath. I was good about backing up my machine to the Cloud, thank goodness, but this was a hassle I really didn't need right now. It had been fine at Rob's so could only have got broken when it fell on the stairs after Peter yanked me back down. They were uncarpeted, wooden stairs. Not exactly laptop friendly, even when it was in a case. The insides made a grinding noise, followed by an apologetic whirr, then went silent.

I closed the lid, and stood up. Putting the machine on my dresser, I pulled out a drawer, rummaged underneath some French knickers and pulled out a huge bar of chocolate I kept there for emergencies. Taking it, I grabbed a towel from the shelf, stripped off my clothes and made my way to the bathroom.

The next morning I headed back into the city and straight for the electronics department in John Lewis on Oxford Street. I showed the assistant my laptop. He pulled a face and I pulled out my credit card. I called Mags' eldest brother who was our go-to guy for anything computer-y. It went to voicemail which didn't surprise me. Brett didn't really do Sunday mornings. I left a message explaining what had happened and asked him to call me back. To cheer myself up, I stopped off at the haberdashery floor and spent time stroking the fabrics and flicking through pattern books. Just as I was heading towards the escalator, my phone, which luckily had survived the drop last night, began to chirp its little tune. I slipped my hand into the much smaller handbag I'd brought out today and pulled it out.

'Hello?'

'Izzy? It's Jenny.'

Oh no. What's happened now? 'Hi, Jenny. Is everything OK?'

'Yes, it's fine. I'm just wondering if I could ask you for a bit of advice?'

'Of course. Fire away.'

'Mum and I are at Rigby's and I've found some undies I really like. I'm just not entirely sure as to whether they're going to work with the dress. I'm a little worried the back might be a bit too high. I was wondering if Mum took a photo and sent it to you if you'd be able to tell from that whether you think it'll be all right with the design?'

'You can do that, but I'm actually in town anyway. If you want I can just come over there. It'll be easier for me to know for certain then. They're not cheap and I'd hate to say yes when it turned out to be no, all because I'd misjudged something. At least this way we could be sure.'

'Oh, that would be fantastic! Are you sure you don't mind?'

'No, of course not. Give me ten minutes.'

We hung up and I headed down the escalators, and out of the store. Taking a shortcut across Hanover Square, I was soon at the boutique on Conduit Street. Entering, I saw Rob's mum waiting for me up the end of the shop, looking elegant perched on one of the chairs.

'Izzy, darling. You are so sweet to do this. Are you sure we're not putting you out? Were you at your studio?'

'No. I was buying a new laptop actually. Mine met a bit of a sticky end last night and I can't afford to be without one. Anyway, that's all very boring! How are things going here?'

The excitement flooded back onto Eleanor's face. 'We found the most beautiful basque set. I mean, really!' She lowered her voice. 'Seriously, I think once Mike sees this, I may well be a grandmother this time next year!'

'Mother!' Jenny's horrified voice came from a nearby cubicle.

Eleanor pulled an 'Oops! Caught me!' face but her manner and expression still showed that if the circumstance were to occur, she would be more than happy.

'Can we come in, Jen?' I called back.

'If it'll help stop my mother's imagination racing forward several years, then please do!'

I laughed and stepped in. Eleanor was right though, the basque was beautiful, not to mention probably well in line with not only Mike's, but a lot of men's, ideas as to what women wear. Or at least what they'd like them to!

'It's gorgeous!' I said.

'It is, isn't it?' Jenny was beaming. After the tears of yesterday, I was so happy to see her enjoying the process once more.

'We just weren't sure if it would work with the dress.'

'Can I see the back?'

Jenny duly obliged, leaning forward in her chair so that I could see where the top of the underwear came to. I ran through the design in my head again.

'Right now, it would show a little.' I saw Jenny's face fall.

'OK. That's all right. I'm sure there will be something else.'

'There probably is, but if this is the one you want, we can work with it. As the dress isn't made yet we can just adjust the design to make it work with this. It's no problem. It would only mean lifting the back of the dress a little, if you were happy with that, just so that it comes to a level above this. That gives it space to not peek out every time you move. It won't change the design of the dress very much at all. You'll barely notice it. I can just take a couple of measurements now and then we can make any other adjustments to the toile when you come in next week.'

'Really? Are you sure it'll be all right? I mean, I love this, but I love your design for the dress more.'

I grinned and gave myself a moment to enjoy the warm fuzzies from that statement, and then reassured Jen it would be just fine.

'Ok. Then I'll take it!' she said to the assistant who had now joined us.

'Wonderful! Just pass it out when you're ready and I'll get it wrapped for you.'

I took the couple of measurements I needed to be getting on with and then left them to it. 'I'll wait out here.' I pointed to the chairs and went and took a seat, flicking through the current issue of *Vogue* whilst I waited for Jenny and her mum to finish. They were soon out and paying for the items.

'We were going to go and have a coffee whilst we wait for the boys. Have you got to rush off?'

I pondered a moment. I didn't have to rush off anywhere. Brett obviously hadn't risen from his beauty sleep yet so I was kind of in limbo until he did. Spending a while with Eleanor and Jenny was a nice way to pass the time until he called, but if I was honest, right now I wasn't all that keen on seeing Rob. The fact that neither woman had questioned me as to why I was no longer coming to them for Christmas suggested that Rob hadn't told them I'd changed my mind – which left me wondering what I was supposed to do now. And then I decided. Sod him.

'No, not at all. I'm waiting for a friend to call to help me with this thing' – I hoisted aloft the John Lewis bag, that now contained two laptops, – 'but until then …'

'Oh, good!'

We left the shop and walked back up the road towards a coffee shop. Finding some free seats, we got our drinks and made ourselves comfortable and were soon chatting away. For all Rob's accusations of his family being strangers to me, I'd never felt so comfortable, so quickly, with anyone before. It felt good. I felt just as relaxed with them as I did with Rob. Or at least, as relaxed as I'd felt with him until he'd gone all weird last night. The three of us were so engrossed with our conversation that none of us noticed the men walk up.

'You got something then?' Mike folded his large frame into the chair next to his fiancée, lifted the Rigby & Peller bag up onto his lap and was about to dive into it when Jenny snatched it off him.

'What do you think you're doing?'

Mike shifted his eyes. 'Is that a trick question?'

'No.'

'All right, then I was going to look and see what you'd bought.'

'Exactly!'

'Umm …'

'You're not allowed to see what I've bought!' Jenny exclaimed.

'Why not? You always show me normally.'

'The key word there being normally. This is for the wedding! You can't see it yet.'

'I thought that just applied to the dress.' Poor Mike seemed thoroughly bemused. I glanced up at John and Rob who were laughing. John patted him on the back.

'Don't worry. Just follow instructions and you'll survive. It's worked for me all these years.'

Mike nodded, clearly taking the words under advisement.

Jenny leant over and pulled Mike closer. 'It'll be worth the wait, believe me.'

Mike's grin got wide and he shifted himself and whispered something in his fiancée's ear that made her blush and giggle. I smiled and concentrated on finishing my coffee.

'Hello, Izz! I didn't know we were seeing you today.' John Winchester stepped around the chairs and came over to give me a hug and kiss, which I returned warmly.

'We weren't sure about something with the undies and darling Izzy came to the rescue again.' Eleanor rubbed my arm.

'Well, I was close by anyway, so it wasn't a big deal.'

'I don't know what we would do without you.' John's smile

was warm. 'Can I get you another drink?'

'No, I'm fine. Thanks.'

'I'll go and get the rest in then.' He headed off to the barista and began giving his order.

Rob had taken a call on his mobile as his dad and I began talking, but was now finished and caught my eye.

'Hi.'

'Hello.'

He took the seat next to me. 'Looks like you've saved the day again.'

I gave the briefest of smiles. I still wasn't sure what had got into Rob last night and I wasn't about to pretend that everything was fine just yet.

'Not really. Just a quick bit of advice.'

'It's more than that to them.' He nodded to where his mum and Jenny were looking at a wedding magazine.

'It's my job.'

'I didn't realise you did call-outs.'

'I was already out.'

'So I understand. I didn't know you were due back into town today. I'd have offered you the guest room, to save you to-ing and fro-ing.'

I'd avoided looking at him whilst we'd been talking but I now turned and gave him a look of incredulity. 'Really?'

'Of course.'

I held his gaze a little longer and then just rolled my eyes.

'I deserved that,' he said, leaning closer, his voice quiet beside me.

I didn't look at him.

'Can we get past this? Please?'

Now I turned my head. 'I've no idea, Rob. Can we? The problem seemed to lie entirely with you last night, so I'm thinking that's probably your call to make, not mine.'

'Can I talk to you outside for a minute?'

138

I thought about it.

'Come on, Izzy. Please. At least give me a chance to explain.' He took a look at the expression on my face. 'Try to explain.'

Grabbing my coat, I stepped over my new purchase and headed to the door, Rob following close behind. The rain had stopped overnight and strong winter sunshine had taken its place. But it was all show. There was no heat to it and the wind charging down the street was bitter. I shivered and pulled my coat around me more, folding my hands into it to keep them warm. Rob shifted position and the wind stopped. He was like a human windbreak.

'Better?' he asked.

I was grateful for the momentary protection from the weather but I was still cross with him.

'I'm all right. Considering I'm standing on the street instead of inside a nice warm coffee shop.' I looked longingly at the steamed-up windows we were now standing outside. 'What is it you wanted to say?'

'You were right last night.'

'About what?'

'About me being an arse. You're right. I was.'

'I know. I was there.' If he thought he was going to get off easy, he had another think coming.

He nodded and smiled.

'And don't smile like that at me either. It might work on a lot of women but not me, and definitely not today.'

The smile faded on his face, replaced by concern.

'Did something happen?'

I hesitated. If I was honest, I wanted nothing more than to tell Rob about what had happened with Peter last night. Not because I wanted him to do anything about it – I didn't want him involved at all like that. Somehow, I just knew that telling him would make it better. It always did. At least it had, until now.

'No. Apart from you beaming down from Planet Weird last night.'

He looked at me for a long while. I knew he didn't believe me but, to my relief, he let it go.

'Yeah. About that. I'm sorry. I felt bad about leading you to get questioned on where you lived and how you came to be there. And then Mum asking you to stay for Christmas? I guess it just threw me off.'

'And you felt the best response to that was to make me feel as unwelcome as possible?'

'No, of course not. I just panicked.'

'Oh, that's crap and you know it, Rob! You don't do panic, so why the hell am I really standing out here, freezing my backside off? Just tell me the truth. I think I deserve that, because at the moment, I have no idea what I did wrong that made you treat me like you did last night.'

'You didn't do anything, Izz,' Rob said, his voice soft – well, as soft as it could be in competition with the passing traffic. 'It was all me.'

'Why?'

'Because …'

I tilted my head. 'Really? "Because" – that's your defence? Well, I'm so glad to see that Oxford law degree is working out for you.'

He smiled. 'Smart arse.'

'At least I can put "smart" in front of mine. You're still just an arse right at this moment.'

He laughed. 'Fair enough. I can't argue with that. OK, so, the thing is …' Rob's initial gusto suddenly seemed to halt.

'Is what?'

He cleared his throat. 'Is, that Mum has never been a big fan of my choice in women. Consequently, when she meets one she really likes she has a habit of trying to … engineer things.'

'Fix you up?'

'Yep. And obviously she's nuts about you which means she'd be nuts about us getting together.'

'Oh, Rob. I think you're reading into things. She knows there's no way that would ever happen!'

'How can you be so sure?'

'Because …' I said, allowing the hint of a smile to show for the first time.

'Touché.'

'Because,' I continued, 'your mum even stated last night that she knew I wasn't your type, not having the more "obvious" attributes you tend to go for, i.e. being about seventeen feet tall and looking like they've just popped out of a *Vogue* shoot. She's not trying to set you up. She's just being nice to me. Perhaps if you'd kept quiet about how much you disliked my flat, she might not have even thought of it.'

'Oh, believe me, she would.'

'Whatever. I still don't see why you had to be so unpleasant about it all though! It's nice to know that the thought of being fixed up with me is so repugnant to you, by the way. You really know how to boost a girl's ego!'

'It's not that! Of course it's not!'

I looked at him, wholly unconvinced.

'It's not!' he said, reaching for me. As his hand touched my forearm, I moved it away. I saw a look cross his face.

'What's wrong with your arm?'

'Nothing. I bumped it last night, that's all. Carry on,' I prompted.

'OK,' he said, clearly unhappy with the explanation but realising he wasn't going to get anything else out of me. 'As I said, it's not that I think being with you would be repugnant, to use your words. And honestly, if you think I, or any man, would think that, then you must have bumped your head as well as your arm!'

'Then what? Why act like that? How would you feel if you were invited by my family and all I did was come up with alternatives and excuses for you not to come?'

'I'm sorry. I didn't mean it like that.'

'Then how did you mean it?'

141

'I don't know. I just … I was just embarrassed and feeling awkward that Mum was doing her thing again, even after you'd made it clear you have no interest in any sort of relationship at the moment.'

'Rob, she wasn't doing "a thing". All she was doing was being kind and generous.'

'Yep. You're probably right.'

'I am right.' I paused, 'But what I really need to know now is if this is all going to be a problem for you. It's your home and your family. If having me there is going to just weird you out too much, then it's fine. Really. I'll come up with an excuse and can just pop down for the fitting and the wedding.'

'It's not going to weird me out, Izzy. I promise.'

'Sure?'

'One hundred per cent.' He caught my hands in his, taking care to avoid my arm this time. 'Forgive me?'

'Maybe.'

'What can I do to tip that into a more positive response?'

I thought. 'Promise me something.'

His face turned wary, 'What's that?'

'Just tell me the truth next time?'

Rob dropped his gaze to our hands. 'Promise,' he said softly. 'Does this mean I'm forgiven?'

'I suppose. But only because I like your family more than you.'

'Understandable. So you're still coming?'

'I'm still coming.' I smiled. 'Assuming I don't have pneumonia from standing out on the street talking to you!'

Quickly he bustled me back inside the coffee shop and we re-joined the others.

Chapter 12

'So how come you were in town?' Rob asked.

I pulled a face. 'I managed to drop my laptop last night. Emergency trip to John Lewis this morning.'

'Is that when you hurt your arm?'

'Yeah, I sort of slipped on the stairs.'

'You sort of slipped?'

'Yes. My shoes were soaked and I guess they slipped.'

'Right.'

I hadn't looked at him as I made my explanation but I knew his Spidey senses were tingling. He didn't believe a word of it.

'You should show Mike your arm.'

I flicked my gaze up. Rob held it evenly.

'I take it back. You're still a pain in the arse,' I whispered. 'It's fine,' I said louder. 'Just a bruise.'

'It'd probably be good if I checked it though,' Mike replied. 'Just to be sure. Especially if you're humping about bolts of fabric.'

I shot Rob a look. He shrugged it off. I slipped off my coat and pushed my jumper sleeve up to the elbow. It had taken a turn for the worse last night and was now the most delightful assortment of bruising colours.

143

'Izzy!' Jenny exclaimed.

'Does it hurt?' Mike dropped into medic mode and started feeling my arm and getting me to move it and tell me which bit hurt. Although the latter was pretty evident to all as I attempted to yank my hand away when he got to the worst bit.

'I can't feel any obvious breaks but it's clearly swollen and bruised. I can arrange for an x-ray to double check.'

'I'm sure it's not broken,' I said, cheerily. I couldn't afford for it to be broken!

Mike understood. 'I think we should definitely keep an eye on it though. In the meantime, I'm going to strap it up. It needs to be supported. I've got some magic cream in here too that should help with the pain a little.' He delved into the bag he'd been carrying when the men had entered.

I peered in as he began pulling items out. 'Do you always carry all this stuff?'

'Not usually. The basics normally. But I was refereeing Rob's rugby match this morning. And you never saw such a bunch of big babies in your life,' he said, teasing his mate as Rob pulled a face.

Mike applied the cream and then wrapped my arm and hand in a crepe bandage, leaving my fingers free. It was certainly going to make work more cumbersome but I had to admit, it already felt easier.

'I'll come in and check it when I drop Jenny off in the week and we'll see how it is.'

'Thanks, Mike.'

'So you just slipped?' Apparently Rob wasn't going to let it go after all.

In my pocket, my phone began to ring. I pulled it out, throwing a 'sorry, what can you do?' look at Rob as I stood and stepped past him, answering the call as I did so.

'Perfect timing!' I said quietly to Brett as he yawned down the phone at me.

144

'I aim to please.'

'You got my message then?'

'Yep. Transfer all your stuff onto your new, non-smashed laptop by yesterday? That about the size of it?'

'Pretty much.'

'I can do that.'

'You're a star. I'll owe you one.'

'I might collect one of these days.'

'Fine.'

'I didn't say how I wanted to be paid.'

'I imagine that this morning it involves a large English breakfast somewhere?'

'You see? This is why I should just marry you. You sense my needs.'

'That's not all I sense!' I laughed.

'She cuts me to the quick. And still I return for more.'

'Yeah, yeah. So, where shall I meet you?'

'Where are you now?'

I told him.

'Hang on.'

In the background, I could hear muffled voices and then Brett came back on the line.

'I'm not far from there. Stay there and I'll meet you, then we'll go on for food, and I can get stuck into the computer after that. All right?'

'Sounds good to me.'

'Why are you laughing?'

'Because you had no idea where you were, did you? She must be pretty!'

'She is. And frankly' – he lowered his voice – 'I really wasn't concentrating on where the cab was going last night.'

'You're dreadful, you know that, don't you?'

'I'm exploring my options.'

'Is that what it's called these days?'

'I have to do something to amuse myself until you wake up and realise your Prince Charming has been in front of you all along.'

I was laughing harder now, as was he. 'See you in a few minutes.'

'OK, bye.'

I ended the call and put the phone back in my pocket. Mags' family despaired of Brett ever settling down. He worked hard and rarely saw the same woman more than a couple of times. For all his claims of being my Prince Charming, there was nothing, and never would be anything, between us. Mags' brothers had adopted me as an honorary sister when I was still in nappies, and they were as much my brothers as if they'd been blood. Brett was just being Brett. It was almost a shame though. He was fun and good looking and bright. The ideal guy. Just not for me.

'You look happy.' Rob smiled at me as he shuffled up the couch and made room.

'I am.'

'That's good.'

I smiled back at him. 'Yeah, it is.'

His voice was soft as he held my gaze, his smile remaining in place. 'I really am sorry about last night.'

'I know you are.'

'Izzy, can you join us for lunch?' John asked a few minutes later.

'Oh, that's really sweet, thank you, but I'm actually meeting someone today.'

'Mags can come too,' Rob said.

'It's not Mags I'm meeting, but thanks anyway.'

'There you are! Morning, gorgeous!' Brett appeared beside me, having come in a side door, and promptly placed a big, cold-lipped kiss on my cheek.

I could feel five pairs of eyes watching me. Brett was not what one would call subtle. He began rubbing his hands together to warm them up.

'It's brass monkeys out there! I should be somewhere cosy and warm on this fine Sunday morning.'

'Afternoon.'

'What?'

'It's the afternoon,' I pointed out.

Brett checked his watch. 'Oh, yeah. Time flies when you're having fun, eh?' He winked at me and I shook my head, smiling.

'Either way, it's bloody cold and you've dragged me from a nice warm bed.' He perched on the seat next to me. 'Good job I love you.' He gave me a squeeze and then glanced around.

'Rob, isn't it?' Brett stuck out his hand. 'I remember you from the wedding. I'm Brett, Mags' brother.' Like most brothers, blood related or not, tact wasn't always a strong suit. Having dealt with this for thirty-plus years, it went straight over my head.

Rob shook his hand. 'Nice to see you again, Brett.' He introduced the rest of his family and they all chatted politely. I could tell they were wondering whether this was the 'next man to come along' as Eleanor had put it last night. But unlike Rob, I wasn't about to announce out of the blue that we 'weren't a couple' for no apparent reason. I had no doubt the subject would come up over Christmas and I could explain the situation then. For now, I let it ride.

'Ready then?' I asked.

'Ready for lunch with a beautiful woman? Always!' He winked at Eleanor as he said it, and I caught her blushing coyly.

'You are such a tart,' I whispered to him as I stood.

'You love it!' he said, winking at me this time.

I rolled my eyes and turned to get my coat, only to find Rob standing right behind me, holding it open. 'Oh, thank you!' I said, slipping my arms into the sleeves.

'You're welcome.'

As my hand popped out one of the sleeves, Brett noticed the bandage. 'What happened?' he said, his tone more serious now.

'I slipped last night and bumped it.'

'Bumped it?'

'Yes.'

'On what?'

'The banister.'

'At the flat?'

I looked up at him. 'Wow! Twenty questions! Yes, at the flat. It's all right. Mike a doctor and he's checked it out. It's just bruised.'

'I'm going to keep an eye on it though. Just in case,' Mike offered.

Not helping, Mike. I knew that look on Brett's face from childhood. It said 'I'm going to cover for you here because you're my mate but just know that I know you're lying.' First Rob, now Brett. Apparently I really needed to work on my Woman of Mystery technique. Or at least find a better cover story.

Brett nodded at Mike. 'That's good. Thanks, mate.'

'No problem.'

'Shall we go then?' I said, a little weirded out by people talking about me as if I wasn't there.

'Yep. Ready when you are.'

I quickly made some arrangements to call Jen tomorrow evening and see where we were, and then made a round of goodbye hugs to Mike and the Winchesters. I got to Rob and hesitated for a split second. He saw it, I knew, but he hugged me anyway.

'And we'll see you at the end of the week!' Eleanor smiled widely. 'I'm so excited you're coming to us.'

'Me too,' I replied.

'I'll call you about picking you up,' Rob said, having retaken his seat.

'Great!'

'Nice to meet you all.' Brett waved. He'd picked up my shopping whilst I'd been saying my goodbyes and now held out the other hand for me to take with my non-bandaged one. I did so and we headed out of the café into the bitter chill of the crisp, December day.

'So, how long have you been seeing Mr Beefcake?' Brett asked through a mouthful of Full English Breakfast.

'Sorry?'

'Mags hadn't told me you were seeing the bloke from the wedding. I have to say, good on him. I'm not sure I'd even be talking to a woman who knocked me on my arse, let alone sleeping with her.'

'Excuse me!' I said. 'I am not sleeping with him!'

OK, that came out a little louder than I meant it to. From the corner of my eye, I saw a few people's heads turn. We were in a little corner café that Brett knew did the best breakfasts. He was at least right about that, even if he was way off about me and Rob.

'All right, keep your hair on. I don't think too many women would complain if he showed an interest, so don't get all uppity about it. Even if a five-foot-nothing girl *can* knock him on his backside.'

'Oh ha ha! I'm five-one actually and don't be unkind. You're forgetting I had the element of surprise on my side, not to mention pure rage.'

Brett swallowed. 'Point taken. I'll give him the benefit of the doubt. So, you sure you're not seeing him?'

I gave him a look. 'Uh, yeah. Pretty sure.'

'It's just you looked pretty cosy there earlier.'

I stabbed a hash brown onto my fork and gave Brett an even look. 'I was sitting next to him on a sofa in a coffee shop. It doesn't mean I'm going out with him. For goodness' sake, I'm having lunch with you, and I'm not seeing you either!'

'Completely different thing.'

'Oh really. How is that?'

'It just is. You didn't grow up with him. Besides, it wasn't just the proximity I was going on.'

'I see. So do tell, Oh Wise One Of Relationships.'

149

He waved a fork at me, 'Ah ah ah! You have to be nice to me! I assume you do want this computer done today...'

'Yes, yes. But can we just drop the whole "seeing Rob" thing. Because I'm not. End of story.'

'All right. Perhaps we could talk about how you hurt your arm instead, because you know I don't believe for one minute that you just "bumped" it. And for the record, I'm pretty sure Rob doesn't either.'

I was pretty sure he was right.

Having finally got Brett to believe that I was ok, and had actually started looking for new places to rent anyway, we caught the Tube back to his place and he spent the afternoon getting my new laptop up to speed whilst I kept attempting to be useful only to be told to sit down and rest my arm. Eventually I gave up, chatted to Mags for a bit then scanned the TV schedule and watched repeats of *Friends*. Brett, very reluctantly, sent me home a few hours later, asking me to call him when I got to the door and to stay on the phone until I was inside my own flat. I'd stuck to my story about slipping on the stairs but it was clear he didn't believe a word of it. He hadn't met Pervy Peter but it would seem that Mags had filled him in on all the delights of my neighbour, and my reluctance to alter my account had made Brett even more over-protective than he normally was. I'd already had trouble convincing him that he didn't need to come all the way home with me, only to turn around and go straight back. I really didn't want Brett to meet Peter.

If he thought, which he did, that Peter had had anything to do with my fall, it would be bad. Brett wasn't a violent man. Not in the least. But I was, to all intents and purposes, his little sister. He'd been protecting me and Mags since the day we were born. Just because I was grown up now didn't change a thing in his eyes.

The week flew by in a haze of last-minute appointments, tulle, satin, silk and lace. I'd spent a few nights until well past midnight in the studio. I was exhausted but excitement was doing a good job of fuelling me, along with the odd Red Bull. Emergency rations. We'd got Jenny's dress almost finished, against the clock and the odds, except for some final hand work. That would still take time, but I could do that at the Winchesters'. I owed my seamstress big time. Huge time, in fact. She'd been amazing, and together we had created exactly what Jenny had wanted. The fittings had gone great and Jenny was ecstatic over our creation – not to mention a little emotional. It was hard not to be. I'd seen Jenny despairing of having a dress at all and now she had something she loved. I couldn't wait for Mike to see her in it. Everyone looks at the bride when the bridal party enters, but the groom's face when his fiancée first walks in? That's the best moment. Especially this time.

I laid the garment carrier across the Chesterfield, along with everything else I thought I might need. Glancing around, I tried to think if there was anything I might have forgotten. There wasn't. I knew there wasn't. I'd checked four times already. I sat down at the end of the sofa, next to my rolling suitcase and flicked through one of the magazines on the glass-topped coffee table in front of me.

'Sorry I'm late!' Rob burst through the door, accompanied by a shower of snowflakes, sending the bells tinkling madly. 'Last minute legal emergency.'

'No problem.'

'Is this everything?'

'I think so. I hope so. No. Yes, yes, it is.' He peered at me. 'You all right?'

'Yes. I'm fine. I just … I just want to make sure this is everything Jenny wants it to be. It has to be perfect.'

'Izz. It will be,' Rob said, standing in front of me holding one of the boxes I'd packed up ready to go. 'You're brilliant at this. It's what you do. Don't start doubting yourself now.'

I nodded, focusing intently on a snowflake melting into the wool of his coat. 'Izz?' he prompted when I made no response.

'Yep. Yep, you're right. I know you are. Of course. It's just …' He put the box back down on the floor. 'It's just what? Izzy?'

'No, it's nothing. I'm being silly. Come on, I'll help you load these in.' I bent down to pick up the box myself. Rob moved it away with his foot.

'Oi!'

He raised one eyebrow. 'You're not lifting anything with that arm. Besides, you didn't finish yet.'

I stood up and shoved a hand on one hip. 'Has anyone ever told you how annoying you can be?'

'Yep. Plenty of times. You mostly.'

'Good. Because I'm about to tell you again. You can be really annoying sometimes!'

'Now that's established, you can tell me what you were going to say.'

I let out a melodramatic sigh.

'Ooh! Now that was a good one.'

I whacked him on the arm with my good one and he laughed. 'Oh, that's right, I forgot about your left hook.' He rubbed his nose.

'Hardy ha ha!' I said, doing my best not to let the smile that was dying to bust through show.

'Fine. You win. But you're not to lift any of this stuff. OK?' He glanced down at my feet. 'And don't come outside yet either. The pavements are icy and those shoes were clearly not made for walking on ice.' He gave my five-inch spiked heels another look. 'I'm not sure they were made for walking in at all, to be honest.'

'They're shoes, Rob. What do you think they were made for?'

He raised his head from where he'd bent to get the box and looked at me with a smile. But not just any smile. This was one I'd definitely never seen before from him. And I blushed from head to naughty shoe enclosed foot!

He stood with the box, then bent towards my ear. 'Why, Izzy, I do believe you're blushing.'

'Don't be ridiculous!' I said. 'Come on, slowcoach, or am I going to have to do this myself?'

'I'm going, I'm going,' he said, balancing the two boxes on top of one another as I opened the door for him. His red Range Rover Sport was parked in the loading bay at the front of my studio with its hazards flashing.

'And for God's sake, don't slip over!'

'Aah, it almost sounds like you're worried about me.'

'Not at all. I just don't fancy hunting down diamantes and pearls in the snow, thank you very much.'

'I should have known,' Rob said, and stepped out onto the pavement, laughing as he opened the boot. He loaded in the boxes before returning for the rest, and my suitcase. He glanced at it, as he pulled it along to the door.

'Is that it?'

I panicked. 'What? Should I have something else?'

'No, it's just quite small. For a girl.'

'I pack well. And that's a very chauvinistic thing to say.'

'I was just saying. I've never seen a girl pack this … little.'

'OK, now I'm worried. I wasn't worried before. What if I need something I don't have?'

'It's Dorset. We have shops.'

'True. Fine. Good.'

'And I'm sure you have everything. Whenever I went somewhere with a girl who'd packed a massive great case, which I always ended up carrying, she never used most of the stuff in it anyway! I'm sure you're spot on.'

I nodded. I was pretty good at packing. Even though I hadn't been on holiday in years now, what with college and fees, and then getting the business off the ground. But I obviously hadn't lost the knack, which was good.

'So, who were these over packers then?'

'Too many to count.'

I gave him a look that told him what I thought and he laughed.

'Are these the last things?' he said, holding up the garment carriers. One contained a couple of dresses for me and the other was The Dress.

'That's it.'

'Right. I'll come back and get you in a sec when you've locked up.'

'I can walk to the car, Rob. It's right there!' I pointed at it for emphasis.

'Not in those shoes, you can't!'

'What do you have against my shoes? You're always criticising them!'

'What?' He actually seemed genuinely surprised.

'You are! You're always making comments about them.'

'It's not criticism, though.'

'Saying they aren't made for walking in? How is that not a criticism of something that's specifically made for walking in?'

'Izz. Believe me. It is not criticism. A little fascination at how you manage to stay upright in them, maybe. But really, most definitely, not criticism.'

'Hmm.' I held the door open for him once more as he prepared to leave with his sister's dress.

Just as he was about to step outside, he stopped. I looked up, waiting, wondering what he'd forgotten.

He had that grin on again.

'If you want the honest truth, I think your shoes are sexy as hell.' And with that he strode out to the car as I stood there letting snow blow in the door whilst my brain momentarily freaked out as it tried to decide what to do with that information.

What it decided to do was ignore it and I went back to the rear of the studio to double check I'd locked everything and switched the water off.

'Izzy? You ready?' Rob called.

'Coming!' I threw a last glance around as I walked back through, making sure I couldn't think of anything else I needed to do before I locked up. This was going to be the longest I'd left the studio since I'd first opened four years ago and I wasn't quite sure if I was doing the right thing. Maybe I shouldn't be closed for the whole Christmas holiday? My pulse started picking up and my hands suddenly felt clammy. What if closing up meant that I missed something big? I'd poured everything I had into this business, my time, my money – or rather the bank's – and my love. Did I really want to risk missing out on something?

'You have a funny look on your face. What's wrong?'

'Nothing. I mean, I'm fine. I'm just wondering if this is such a good idea now. What if I miss a call, or someone comes to me with something big and I'm not here because I'm munching on mince pies elsewhere? I've never been closed this long before!' Mild panic was making my voice pitch higher than usual and I was pretty sure it wasn't attractive. Not that that mattered right now. It was only Rob, after all. But still. I took a deep breath in the hope that next time I spoke it wouldn't be quite so helium inspired.

'Are you finished?'

'Umm … yes?' I replied, not entirely sure if I was.

'Good. Then can we go?'

'Argh! Did you not just hear any of what I said?' Uh oh. Still squeaky.

'Yep.'

'And?'

'And. You're worrying about nothing. You have an answerphone, yes?'

'Yes.'

'And that forwards to your mobile?'

'Yes.'

'And you have a contact form on your website?'

'Yes.'

'And the enquiries from that can be accessed with a computer and I know you have your laptop because I just put it in the car.'

'Uh huh.'

'Your studio is appointment only. It says that on the door and it says that on the website so people don't just wander in, do they?'

'Not really.'

'And we've established that you can pick up messages and check enquiries whilst you're away.'

'Yes.'

'So, are you panicking about nothing?'

'Probably,' I said, still feeling a little doubt, even though I knew he was completely, annoyingly, correct.

'Izz,' he said, resting his big hands on my shoulders, and finding little room to spare, 'I know it's hard. I know how much you've worked for everything you've built here. But it'll be OK. I promise. You need a break.'

I sighed. 'I know. I know. You're right. Come on,' I said, picking my coat off the wire coat stand in the corner, 'Let's go before I change my mind again.'

Rob waited on the step as I flicked off the lights and threw all the locks and bolts on the front door of the studio.

'Ready?' he said, raising his voice a little to carry over the wind that was funnelling down my road. 'Yes.'

'Give me your arm, then.'

'What?'

'Your good arm. Hook it around mine.'

I gave him a look. 'Rob, I can walk to the car. It's ten feet in front of me. Even in these "sexy shoes".' I tossed his words back at him with a wink and stepped onto the pavement. His concern was sweet but really not necessary in this instance. I continued to believe this until my third step, at which point I did an impression of a dog taking a corner on lino, and my feet went in very different directions to the ones I had planned for them.

'Whoop! Steady.' Rob's hands were around my waist before I got the chance to fall entirely. But, thank goodness, it wasn't

156

embarrassing. I mean it wasn't like I'd made a big song and dance about being able to get to the car by myself or anything! At least he was behind me and I didn't have to actually look him in the eye.

'If you say anything remotely in the realm of "I told you so", I will break your nose. Again.'

'I wasn't going to say a thing.'

'Good.'

'Would you allow me to assist you to the car safely now?'

'I would appreciate that. Thank you.'

Turning gingerly, I put my hand on Rob's arm, and steadied myself as my feet went sliding on the ice again.

'How in the hell are you managing to march about?' I asked, irritably.

'I had these in the boot,' he said indicating the Hunter wellington boots he was wearing, 'I thought they'd be more effective in this than my work shoes.' He smiled before adding, 'And they're certainly a lot more effective than your work shoes.'

'Here we go again.'

'As I said, not criticising. Just wondering how we're going to get you to the car without you breaking something.'

'I'll be fine. Just let me hold on to you.'

'All right.'

It took one and a half more steps before I was sliding again.

'Oh, for heaven's sake. Sorry about this, Izzy, but we do need to get going.'

'Sorry about wh—' My words were cut off as Rob picked me up and tossed me over his shoulder in a fireman's lift.

'Rob! No! Put me down! Put me down! Now!'

'Your wish is my command,' he said, depositing me in the front passenger seat of the Range Rover, and pushing the door closed. He then crunched around on the snow to the other side and got in. The engine hummed as he turned the key and

157

Rob pumped up the heat controls until warm air was streaming through the vents. My bottom and back were also beginning to warm up thanks to the wonder of heated seats.

'Comfy?' he asked, pulling off his wellies and switching them back for his shiny black work shoes.

'If mortified comes under the heading of comfy, then sure!'

He glanced over as he did up the second shoe lace. 'Why are you mortified?'

'Oh, I'm sorry. I thought that was me you just threw over your shoulder like a sack of spuds. Except potatoes would not be worried about the fact that their underwear was on show to every passing vehicle!'

'Your underwear was not on show. I checked.' He was grinning his head off at this point.

'I'm glad you find it all so hilarious.'

'Oh lighten up, Izz. Relax! It's Christmas! And I think you'd be more mortified if you'd fallen and broken your other wrist or something else. It was a few steps, got the job done and I promise nobody saw anything that they shouldn't have done.'

'Are you sure?' I asked, smoothing out my skirt. I knew it was a bit old-fashioned to be worrying about things like this these days, but I'd always been a bit more reserved when it came to certain things and the thought of flashing my knickers at passing traffic gave me palpitations – and not in a good way.

'Absolutely positive. So can we go now?'

'Yes.' I looked over at him as he hit the indicator and prepared to pull out across the traffic. 'Sorry. I know you think I'm being ridiculous.'

He smiled and shook his head. 'I don't think you're being ridiculous. It's actually kind of endearing.'

'It is?'

A van flashed its lights and let us out across him. Rob remained silent as he concentrated on the other lane of traffic.

'It is,' he answered, now in the stream of traffic heading away from the city. 'It sort of goes with those fifties style dresses you sometimes wear. Kind of demure. Elegant.'

I shifted in my seat and turned towards him. 'What are you up to?'

He glanced over ever so briefly before returning his eyes to the road. 'What do you mean?'

'You. You're up to something. First you say my shoes are sexy, then you're telling me I'm demure and elegant and endearing. And bearing in mind I've just been skating about like a baby deer on its feet for the first time and been chucked over your shoulder like a bit of old carpet, I'm feeling neither elegant nor demure. So, tell me, what exactly are you up to, Mr Winchester?'

I could see his smile even though he didn't turn away from the road. 'The other day I made you a promise at the coffee shop that I would be honest, that I'd tell you the truth about stuff. So I am. That's all. No agenda.'

'All right. Well then, thank you. For the compliments. Not for slinging me around.'

'You're welcome and I'm sorry but you were scaring the hell out of me skating about like that. I was worried you were going to fall and crack your head on the pavement or something.' There was something in his voice that stopped me from sending a pithy rejoinder.

'I'm sorry I scared you,' I said quietly.

'It's all right.' He reached out without looking and took my hand briefly, 'Just promise to wear wellies if we go out for a walk over Christmas..'

'Umm … OK.'

'Izzy?'

'Yes.'

'Do you have wellies?'

'Not exactly.'

'What does "not exactly" mean?'

'It means I don't have wellies.'

'Right. Do you have boots?'

'Yes!'

'Izzy. Please tell me these boots don't have five-inch heels.'

I remained silent.

Rob laughed. 'Fine. We'll find you some wellies.'

I snuggled into the seat and watched the snowflakes hitting the windscreen, their tiny, delicate framework lasting momentarily until they melted or were swept away by the swishing wiper blade. Rob reached behind him and produced another of those superbly soft blankets, like the one he had in his apartment. I really needed to find out where he got them.

'Thank you.' I wasn't cold but the blanket was comforting and I was grateful for his thoughtfulness. I laid it across my legs that I'd now tucked underneath me, having kicked off my shoes shortly after we'd left my studio. The leather seat was warm now and I leant my head back against the headrest, contentedly watching the tail lights twinkling in front of us as Madeleine Peyroux played softly through the speakers. We'd talked a little but I could see Rob was concentrating on the road and the weather so I left him to it. When we'd been chatting, he'd mentioned a video conference with a client in Singapore yesterday. I had suppliers in Singapore so I was well aware of the time difference. I stole another glance and caught him running a hand over his freshly cropped hair.

'Are you OK?'

He smiled over. 'Yeah. I'm fine. You?'

'Yes. But you look tired. I can drive for a while if you like? I'm a good driver. I promise.'

'I'm all right, Izz. Really. I'd stop if I was too tired. I promise.'

Did he think I didn't trust him? After everything he and his family had been through with Jenny, did he really believe I thought he'd ever take a risk on the roads?

'Rob. I'm not worried about your driving. I trust you implicitly. I'm just concerned that you're tired.'

'I'm OK. I had several coffees before we left. At least the traffic's moving pretty well. It shouldn't be too long before we get there now anyway. But thanks for the offer. I appreciate it.'

'You're welcome.' I shifted position again and pulled a snooty face, 'I know it's really that you don't want me driving your car.'

He laughed. 'Uh oh. She found me out.'

I laughed. 'Just remember the offer is there if you want it.'

'I will. Thanks.'

Chapter 13

The ceasing of motion caused me to wake. I swam up from the depths of my snoozing to find the blanket tucked up around me and Rob watching me.

'Nice rest?'

'Oh no! I fell asleep? I was supposed to be keeping you company! I tell you I'm worried about you being tired and then promptly nod off. I am officially the worst travelling companion.'

He laughed. 'No, you're not. The fact that you fell asleep shows you weren't worried about my driving. That's nice. It's reassuring. So that makes you a very good companion in my book.'

'Did you do this?' I asked, nodding at the blanket.

'You looked like you needed the rest. I didn't want you waking up because you were cold.'

'You can be very sweet when you're not being annoying.'

'Gee thanks.'

'You're welcome.' I grinned.

'Come on, Trouble. Dad's put salt on the drive and paths so you shouldn't go slipping and sliding here but I'd still prefer it if you held on to me just in case.'

'I think that's preferable to being over your shoulder, so all right then.'

'Spoilsport.'

I stuck out my tongue. 'What about all the stuff?'

'Mike's here already. I'll grab him and we'll come back and get it in a minute.'

'Are you sure?'

'Yep.'

We got out of the car and, as promised, I held on to him.

'Don't let Mike look in any of the boxes. I don't want him seeing anything he shouldn't!'

'I think he'll be more concerned about getting back in the warm to be honest, but yes, I promise I won't let him look in any of the boxes.'

In the half light from the nearby porch, I could see him focusing on me with those soft brown eyes. 'You're looking at me like I'm being an idiot again.'

He smiled. 'No I'm not. I'm looking at you like—'

'You're here!' Rob's mum came out, half skipping down the path, sensibly also wearing wellingtons.

We both jumped and Rob's sentence remained unfinished as he went to greet his mum. 'Hi, Mum,' he said, wrapping her in a big, warm hug.

'Hello, darling! How was the drive?'

'Yeah, not bad. We were just about to come in.'

'Izzy, Izzy, Izzy!' Eleanor flung her arms out to me. I flicked a look to Rob. I'd had strict instructions not to move without hanging on to him and frankly I didn't fancy the risk anyway. Not that it was an issue as Eleanor was in front of me before Rob could return, giving me a lovely welcoming hug. 'I'm so glad you decided to come.'

'Me too,' I said, honestly.

'Right, let's get you in,' she instructed and Rob quickly stepped beside me and held out an arm for me to hold on to. I'd like to say I was elegant and demure about it, but the truth was, after my escapades earlier, it probably had more a look of hanging on for grim death. He was right. Wellies would have been a good idea. Or at least flats. I did have a pair of the latter but being satin, they weren't really made for trekking through the snow either. I'd not owned a pair of wellies since I was five years old. They didn't really go with my aesthetic, not to mention I'd not had the need for them. I had to admit I felt a bit daft now for not bringing any. But then again, nobody had specifically mentioned I'd need them either. Oh well. I'd got the dress and my supplies. Everything else was a bonus anyway.

'I can hear those cogs whirring again,' Rob whispered as we walked up the path a few steps behind his mum.

'I was just thinking how silly it was of me not to bring any boots. Walking boots,' I corrected.

'Don't be daft. I think you can be forgiven for being rather preoccupied in making a wedding dress appear from thin air in a week! I should have mentioned something before about bringing some. We like to go out for walks, but you don't have to come if you don't want to anyway.'

'No, I'd like to!'

'Good. I'd like you to as well. As will Harold.'

Rob handed me in over the front step into the warmth of the hall and followed, pushing the door closed for a moment.

'Who's Harold?' I frowned.

'Harold! No!' Eleanor said a moment too late as a chocolate lab who weighed about the same as me bounded up to say hello in a wonderfully exuberant manner. So wonderful that I careered backwards into Rob who in turn careered backwards into the front door.

'Harold. Lie,' he instructed, standing us both back up. Harold dropped to the floor immediately, his tail thumping madly on the wood as he watched Rob for his next command.

'Roll over.'

He did. I laughed, already half in love with my latest intro-duction. I crouched down, and reached over to rub his tummy.

'Wait!' Rob cautioned.

I snatched my hand back. 'What?'

'Just know that once you do that, you've got a job for life. He'll expect it every time he sees you.'

I grinned up at Rob. 'That doesn't sound too bad,' I said and promptly gave Harold a good old tummy tickle. His tail thumped faster and faster and he wriggled with excitement.

'Come on, boy. Up you get. Find Mike.' Rob sent him off on a quest. The dog shot off as Rob lent me a hand and pulled me up from where I'd been kneeling on the floor. 'I forgot to warn you about Harold too. I really should have checked you weren't allergic or anything.'

'No, I love dogs! We could never have one because we never knew where we would be sent next and obviously now it's a bit difficult because of working.'

'Yeah, I know what you mean. I love coming down here and walking with him. I'd love to shift to a home office at some point. That way I wouldn't have to go out in the middle of the night when I need to speak to my Asia Pacific clients, all the files would be right there, and I could get a dog then too.'

'Can I come and play with it?' I asked.

'I'd be upset if you didn't.' He winked at me with a naughty glint in his eye.

'Robert Winchester. Did you just proposition me?'

'I don't know. Did I?' His face was all innocence but his eyes told a different story entirely. 'Izzy, I—'

'Hello, you two!' Jenny and Mike came up the corridor. Harold was walking beside Mike, looking thoroughly pleased with himself at having completed his latest task. He left Mike and came and sat by Rob, clearly expecting a treat for his good work. Rob bent and rubbed the dog's chin.

'I haven't got anything, sorry boy.'

Harold tilted his head in an unbelievably cute motion.

'Oh, don't look at me like that.' Rob sounded pained.

'Come here, Harold,' Jenny called. We all looked over to see her holding a miniature bone-shaped biscuit. Harold's feet skidded about on the flooring, much like my own had done earlier on the pavement, as he tried to get a purchase and head off to fetch his reward. Inelegantly, he reached Jenny, and sat hurriedly in front of her chair.

'Wait,' she said, and balanced the treat on his nose. 'OK!'

Harold flipped the biscuit and gobbled it down.

'Good boy!'

Once we'd all finished fussing with the dog, we exchanged our human greetings and Rob and Mike went out to the car to bring everything in.

'Come on in. Mum's saved you two some dinner. You must be starving!'

I'd been so busy this week, I couldn't remember eating a whole lot at all in the past few days but I wasn't about to tell Jenny that. It wasn't just her dress that had kept me busy, but I knew she'd feel guilty anyway.

'Yes, I am a bit hungry, I have to say!'

'Journey all right?'

I followed Jenny through the house to the kitchen where two places were set at the table and her dad was pouring wine into six glasses.

'Hello, Izzy love!' John rushed over and gave me a big sweeping hug. His cheeks were a little flush and I guessed that the glass on the table wasn't his first one of the evening.

'Hello, John! Yes, the journey was fine, thanks. I fell asleep though, which I feel a bit bad about! Sort of left Rob to it.'

'Oh I'm sure he didn't mind! You must have needed it. That's all he would have thought,' John said, handing Jenny and me a glass each.

I smiled and took the wine.

'Where do you want all this stuff?' Rob's voice came from the hallway.

Placing our glasses back on the table, Jen, Eleanor and I headed out to the hallway and met the boys who were now loaded down with cases, boxes and garment carriers.

'It's not "stuff",' Jenny corrected, reaching up for her dress which I lifted off Rob's pile and handed carefully to her, resting it so that it wouldn't obstruct her wheels' movement, 'it's my beautiful dress!'

Rob pulled a face that only a brother could. 'What about the rest of this *stuff*?' He emphasised the last word just to be annoying.

'Do you really want to know that?' she replied, a twinkle in her eye.

Rob laughed.

'Come on.' Eleanor took charge. 'We'll put all the wedding "stuff" in the conservatory, and, Rob, would you take Izzy's case up to the guest room for me?'

'Oh, I can do that!' I offered.

'No problem. I'm putting my things up there anyway.' There was a brief pause. 'Not in the guest room though. Obviously. My room. I'm putting my things in my room.'

Jenny and Mike exchanged a little look.

Eleanor sailed on without missing a beat. 'Of course you are, darling. Now off you go and do that. Wash your hands on the way back and you and Izzy can sit down for your dinner.'

Rob nodded, took the other case from Mike and headed up the stairs with them, his long legs taking the steps two at a time. A few minutes later, I was just coming out of the downstairs loo and bumped into him.

'Hi.'

'Hi.'

'All right?'

'Yep.'

'Rob?'

'Yes?'

'You are OK with all this, aren't you?' My voice was dropped to a whisper. I didn't want to alert anyone else to the fact that Rob was acting a teensy bit odd. Judging by the look his sister had exchanged with her fiancé, I wasn't the only one who'd noticed. And I was pretty sure his mum didn't miss a trick, however smoothly she carried on.

Rob looked at me, smiled and wrapped an arm around my shoulders before kissing me on the temple. 'I'm OK with this. Come on, let's eat.' He dropped his arm and shuffled me ahead of him into the kitchen.

Weak winter sunshine was falling in long thin puddles onto the deep-piled carpet of my bedroom when I woke the next day. The smell of English breakfast cooking drifted up the stairs and woke my stomach. I rolled over in the double bed and looked at the French style clock on the bedside. Half past nine? How did that happen? I never slept past six normally, even when I wasn't going into the studio. Oh my goodness, what would my hosts think of me?

Pushing back the covers in the most reluctant of rushes, I pulled a towel from the pile left on the bedroom chair and headed into the little en-suite. Ten minutes later, I was showered, dressed and had made my face look a little less tired with a slick of Korean BB cream, a swipe of mascara and soft pink lip gloss. I slipped on the hotel-style slippers that had been left by the bed and headed downstairs to be greeted at the kitchen door by Harold who came up to me excitedly. Instead of charging into me, today he sat down, his tail still thumping an excitable rhythm on the tiles.

'Morning, Harold!' I said, bending and giving him a good chin rub. He groaned and pushed his head down further into my hand.

'You've got a friend for life there, you know,' Jenny said, smiling and holding her arms out for a hug. 'How did you sleep?'

'Too well I think,' I said, laughing. 'I'm so sorry I'm late!'

'Nonsense!' Eleanor said, appearing from the larder cupboard, then coming over and giving me a squeeze. 'You clearly needed the rest and anyway, neither Mike nor Rob are up yet either. Although, if they want any breakfast, they'll need to hurry.'

'I'm up.' Mike padded in, barefoot and yawning and came up behind Jenny. Bending forward he gave her a kiss and cuddle.

Eleanor caught me watching them, and patted my arm as she came to stand next to me at the counter. 'We couldn't have wished for a better man for her.'

'He's head over heels. It's wonderful.'

'They both are. Life can be so strange sometimes,' she continued quietly. 'Beautiful things can sometimes come out of the most difficult of circumstances. I mean, without the accident, Jenny might never have met Mike.'

I took the punnet of mushrooms that she was carrying, pulled a knife from the holder on the counter and began chopping them.

'I can do that, dear. You're a guest!'

'No really, please let me. Carry on with telling me about …' I waved the knife towards where Mike and Jenny were now giggling together at the other side of the room.

Eleanor pulled up a bar stool for us each and we sat at the counter as she continued quietly with her story.

'He wasn't really the type of man she tended to go for. They were always these trendy, arty farty types and they always let her down. And then the car accident happened. Poor Jenny. She was in a very dark place at one point. Rob knew Mike had done a lot of work with injured veterans so he thought maybe he'd have some suggestions or something. Well, I'm not sure what he thought to be honest, he was just trying everything he could.

'But the moment Mike walked in, she started smiling. And believe me, it had been a long time since we'd seen her do that. I mean, *really* smile. And he, Mr Professional Medical Doctor, was grinning like a loon. Bless him, Rob's face was a picture! He'd had no idea of fixing either his friend or his sister up, he'd just been trying to help. Which is exactly what he did, just not in the way he imagined. Well, that's not true. Mike got Jenny into some programmes and helped her himself with strength training, as well as introducing her to some other people in a similar situation. It all helped, but falling in love, I think, was the biggest help of all.

'Rob was a bit wary of it to begin with. He's always been so protective of Jenny. I mean, when the accident happened, he was devastated. He felt like he'd let her down. That he should have been able to protect her. We tried to tell him he couldn't be there all the time for everyone but it's just his nature. It always has been. It took him a long time to realise he couldn't fix everything for everyone. But that's never stopped him trying.'

'You raised a good man.'

'Thank you.'

'And you're getting another good one there.' I indicated Mike with a nod of my head.

'We certainly are. Now we just need Rob to find someone lovely too.'

'I'm sure he will, in time.'

Eleanor pulled the boxes of eggs towards her and began putting some on a plate, ready to be cooked. 'I'm not so sure. I don't know what it is. He always goes for the same kind of girl. Beautiful, of course.'

'I'd expect nothing less.'

'Quite,' his mum agreed. 'I mean. They're always these model types, but he's never got really serious about any of them. And between you and me, I'm quite glad. I don't think any of them have been good enough for him.'

'That's understandable.'

'Oh, no, I'm not one of these mothers who thinks nobody will ever be good enough. Just none of the ones he's brought home as girlfriends so far. All a bit shallow if you ask me.'

'I'm not sure Izzy was asking, was she?' Rob's voice made us both jump and made me drop the knife, missing his foot by an inch.

'Bloody hell, Rob!' I said, and then clamped my hand over my mouth. 'I'm so sorry!' I mumbled through it.

'Don't worry, dear. I was about to say something much worse!' Eleanor laughed. 'You shouldn't creep up on people!' she scolded her son, offering her cheek for a greeting kiss.

'He has a habit of doing that!' I said, remembering the first time we'd bumped into each other again. Could it only have been a few weeks ago? I was having trouble remembering a time when Rob wasn't part of my everyday life.

He bent and retrieved the knife off the floor and moved to the sink to rinse it off before handing it back to me.

'Thanks. And good morning.'

'Morning.' He smiled. 'Thanks for missing my toes.'

'You're welcome. Don't listen in on private conversations.'

'It was about me. I'm entitled to.'

'*About* you, being the operative phrase there.'

'Go and sit at the table. I'll bring you a coffee,' his mum said.

'It's all right, I can do it. Anyone else want one?' he called out and got a chorus of replies, including his dad who had just come in the back door, newspaper in hand.

'Morning all!' he called. 'Ah everyone's up! Marvellous. I can finally get my breakfast!'

I must have looked a little horrified that I'd been instrumental in delaying my host's breakfast because he began laughing.

'Don't tease the poor girl, John!' Eleanor chided him before turning to me and taking the mushrooms I'd neatly sliced, 'He was only up a few minutes before you anyway. He just headed straight out to get the paper.'

I gave John a cheeky look and wagged my finger at him. He laughed even more, and took his place at the table next to where his son was now sitting with his hands wrapped around a large mug of coffee.

'I ran into Clive Bennett at the shop.'

'Oh, they're still coming this evening?'

'Yes, in fact it turns out Caroline is down with them for Christmas. He was asking if it was all right for her to come too.'

Jenny groaned.

'Jen,' Rob cautioned.

She looked at me and pulled a face.

'What did you say?' Eleanor asked.

'What could I say? I said of course she was welcome.'

'Welcome is a little bit of an overstatement, but yes, of course she has to be included.'

I was, by now, completely lost as to who the mysterious Caroline was, and nobody seemed inclined to say any more. I guessed that I would find out soon enough at the Winchesters' Christmas Eve party tonight.

Chapter 14

The day passed in a wonderfully relaxed manner. Eleanor had already prepared all the food for the evening so that she could spend the day relaxing rather than cooking. Rob disappeared after breakfast and came back a little while later with a box, which he handed to me.

'What's this?'

'Open it and you'll see.'

'But it's not Christmas until tomorrow.'

'It's not a Christmas present.'

'But it is a present?'

'I suppose. Look, just open the damn box, will you!' He laughed.

It was large so I sank down onto the floor, my feet at my hips in that position that seemed to baffle Rob as to its comfort levels, and pulled the lid off the box he'd handed me. Removing the top layer of tissue, I looked up at him in surprise.

'Do you like them?'

'Yes! I love them!'

The main reason I'd not had a pair of wellies since I was five was because I thought that they were, on the whole, not the most attractive of footwear. I know it seems shallow to worry about what you are wearing whilst tramping through muddy fields and it wasn't that I was vain. I merely liked pretty things. And wellies weren't pretty. Except that on this occasion they were. Grape purple with a front placket of mock lacing, the boots were exactly what I'd have chosen myself. I held them up to show Jenny as she came in.

'Oh my God, they're gorgeous!' She came over, took one from me and looked it over, 'I'm totally getting a pair of these. I don't care that I don't need them!' She grinned down at me on the floor. 'We'll be welly twins!'

'Perfect!'

'Try them on and make sure they fit before the shop closes. I can always swap them if not.'

I slipped off my slippers and stuck my feet out in front of me, pulling the boots on one after the other. Jenny stuck out an arm to help me up and I stood in the living room wearing my favourite fifties style day dress and purple wellington boots, feeling ridiculously happy.

'Do they fit?' Rob asked. 'Walk around.'

I marched around for a few moments, feeling a bit daft but having it not matter because Rob and Jenny were laughing along with me.

'They fit fine,' I said. 'Especially once I put socks on, they'll be perfect.'

'Good.' He smiled and began heading out of the room.

I ran to catch up with him, wellies slapping against my bare legs. 'Rob, wait!'

He stopped and smiled as he looked down at my feet. 'They suit you.'

'I really do love them. Thank you. But I'd rather I paid for them.'

His smile faded a little. 'Why?'

'Because you shouldn't be buying me things.'

'I've bought you one thing. And why shouldn't I? You needed them.'

'Well, we're not … I mean. It's …'

'Not like we're not dating, so that means I can't buy you anything. Is that it?'

'Yes. I suppose so.' I pulled a face.

'Do you ever buy Mags presents? Does she get you stuff?'

'Yes, all the time, but that's different.'

'Why is it different? You're friends. We're friends. I think you get too hung up on the whole boy-girl thing sometimes, Izz. With me at least.'

'With you?'

'Yes. Can I ask you something?'

'Of course.'

'The other day at the coffee shop. That Brett bloke.'

'What about him?'

Rob ran his hand over his hair back and forth quickly, before backing further into the hall and taking a seat on the bench there. 'Are you seeing him?'

'Brett? No! Of course not. Why do you ask?'

'It's just that you seemed very … comfortable with one another.'

I couldn't help but laugh. 'Funny, that's what he said about you.'

A crooked half smile appeared on Rob's face. 'Did he now?'

'He did. And he's like a brother to me. That's why we're comfortable. He's known me literally since the day I was born. We grew up together.'

'Which is why he knew, like I know, that you're lying about how you did that.' He pointed to my arm. Mike had unwrapped it last night and the bruise, although still several shades of the rainbow, was fading and the whole thing felt a lot easier than it had at the beginning of the week.

I gave a big sigh and plopped down next to him on the bench, shuffling my bottom back so that my welly-encased feet could swing. I lifted them up and looked at them, smiling. They made me happy. But there was no avoiding the subject now that he'd brought it up. I took a deep breath and started.

'I went back to the flat that night and met Peter.' I felt Rob go still beside me. I put my hand on his. 'It's all right. Nothing much happened.'

'Nothing much indicates that something did. I'm not feeling reassured here, Izzy.'

I continued on. 'The rain was pouring down. I was soaked from walking from the station and upset because you and I had argued, and he was just going out to the bins. I thought of all the times he'd made my skin creep and, feeling in a bit of a bitchy mood, I closed the door behind me, instead of leaving it open for him. He took exception to it. I let him back in because he was hammering on the glass and I could just see that going everywhere. When I walked away he yanked on my coat and I stumbled back down a stair or two. I whacked my hand when I grabbed for the banister. That was it. I told him I'd kick the crap out of him if he tried anything like that again and I must have bluffed pretty well because I haven't seen him since.'

'You should have told me.'

'No. I don't think I should. You or Brett.'

'I don't want you going back there on your own.'

'I live there. I have to go back. But I promise you, I am looking for somewhere else. Seriously looking.'

'You could stay with me. It's closer to work, and I'd be glad of the company.'

'Rob, that's really kind of you. But I couldn't do that. I wouldn't want to cramp your style for a start.'

He shook his head slowly then leant over and kissed me on the temple. 'We'll talk about this again after Christmas.' He pushed himself up off the bench and headed towards the stairs. I scooted myself off the bench and caught up with him, ducking under his arm and taking a couple of stairs in front of him before turning around, my eye line now more on a level with his, for once.

'What are you doing?' He asked, laughing.

'Thank you for the boots. They're gorgeous!'

'You're welcome.'

I leant forward to bestow a thank-you kiss. Apparently my impression of a baby deer had stuck with him because his hands automatically went to my waist, steadying me, as he smiled at me in a way that was soft and familiar. And I swear that, even though that smile was ricocheting around in my brain, I really did have every intention of going for his cheek. But somehow, with me going for one cheek and him thinking I was going for the other, my lips ended up square on his.

For a split second my eyes flew wide open but immediately closed again as my hands slid from his shoulders to the back of his neck, pulling him closer. Rob's hands tightened on my waist the moment our lips touched, and as the kiss deepened, one arm wrapped itself around me and pulled me close. The other was now resting on my lower back and I could feel the warmth of his splayed hand through my dress. I pulled away slowly, my eyes locked on his. I wasn't entirely sure what had just happened and I wanted to see if Rob's expression gave me any clue. Nope. Just that lazy smile. Which right now was really making me want a repeat performance. Did he have any idea just how sexy that smile was? I was pretty sure the answer was no. And more to the point, how had I managed to come this far without noticing exactly how sexy that smile was?

There I had a pretty good idea. I'd been so busy burying myself in work and trying to forget the humiliation of the past that I'd cut myself off from any sense that there might just be a chance of real happiness in my future. But maybe, just maybe, I wasn't too late.

'Like I said, thank you for the boots.'

'Like I said, you're very welcome.' He leant in, gave me another very quick, very soft, kiss straight smack on the lips and then moved past me and headed up the stairs, throwing me a grin as he did so.

'Come on, those boots are getting their first outing.'

We all traipsed out, bundled up against at the cold with hats, mittens, coats, and scarfs and spent a lovely couple of hours in the forest, wandering along one of the accessible trails, watching the deer and the ponies and running around with the dog – who was having such fun with all his visitors, that he didn't know who to run to first. Back at the house, we spent the next few hours gathered in the living room, drinking real hot chocolate and enjoying the fire that John had lit.

I finished my drink and lifted the project bag that contained Jenny's veil onto my lap. With most of it hidden from Mike, I began stitching on a few more of the tiny beads that would form part of her headdress.

'We really can't thank you enough for what you've done, you know, Izzy,' Eleanor said. I looked up and saw tears shining in her eyes. Her husband noticed too and put his arm around her.

'It's all right, love,' he whispered, and then kissed her temple, just as Rob had kissed mine earlier. Just before he'd really kissed me.

I dropped my glance back down to my work as I thought about that. About how it had felt. About how I felt.

'Having me here is more than enough thanks,' I said, truthfully, and flicked a quick smile at them as emotions bubbled through me.

'I know you work hard, but it's a lovely job to have I think,' Eleanor said.

'It is.' I agreed.

'Do you think you'll make your own wedding gown?'

I saw from the look on her face that she realised what she'd said immediately. Caught up in the warm glow of the fire, the season and the upcoming celebration of Jenny and Mike, Eleanor was just carried away with thinking romantically.

'Oh my dear!' Her hand flew to her mouth. 'I didn't mean … I–'

'Oh, Eleanor! Don't be silly! It's absolutely fine. Honestly! Please don't upset yourself.' I could see she was completely mortified by having accidentally brought up the subject of me and marriages. But what I'd said was true. It was fine. I was OK with it now. 'Right now I'm more than happy to be making dresses for other people and just concentrating on my business.' I gave her a reassuring smile and went back to working on Jen's headdress.

'I'd better take the dog for a walk.' Rob got up from where he was sitting beside me. Until this point, Harold had been contentedly sleeping with one paw on my foot but as Rob moved and he simultaneously heard the word "walk", he was up and ready to go, scooting around Rob's legs and almost tripping over his own feet in his excitement. 'Come on, boy,' Rob called.

'Do you want some company, mate?' Mike asked. I saw a look pass between them. I didn't know if it was a military thing but Mike seemed to have that unreadable expression on his face, just like the one Rob occasionally wore. It was, though, apparently only unreadable to me. Rob seemed to understand it completely.

'No, you're all right. I've actually got a couple of calls to make anyway, but thanks for the offer.'

'No problem.'

'Don't be too late. The guests are arriving from six.'

'Understood.' Rob gave his mum a little smile and salute and headed out towards the kitchen, Harold still dancing around his legs. A few minutes later, we heard the back door open and close.

'Harold's going to be pooped tonight, that's for sure,' John commented.

'Oh. I shouldn't think Rob will go far.'

'No, probably not. Well, the dog won't complain.'

He certainly didn't complain but he was spark out in his bed, which had been put in the utility room for the evening, and snoring contentedly when guests started arriving for the party a few hours later.

* * *

'Wow!' Jenny said when I came into the kitchen.

'Is it all right?' I said. 'When I asked Rob what sort of dress code it was, he was a bit vague. I kind of worked out that it was a sort of cocktail dress affair. But I have something I can change into if you think this is too much?' I'd picked out a strapless number in blue silk that was shot through with purple, and had tied a silk chiffon bolero over the top.

'Don't you dare change a thing!' Eleanor walked in behind me. 'You look gorgeous! It's perfect.'

I smiled and breathed a sigh of relief. 'Oh good! Now, is there anything I can do?'

Rob must have gone further than his parents thought he might because when we'd all started heading off to go and get ready, he still hadn't returned. He'd texted Jenny to say that he'd met a friend from school and was going to go for a quick drink and to let their mum know he'd be a bit late, but still back in time for the party. I must have been in the shower when he came back because I hadn't heard him go past the door to his own room. I'd wanted to stick my head out and just check that he was OK. I couldn't shake the feeling that him walking the dog this afternoon had been a sudden inclination rather than a planned excursion. Something about it had just seemed a little off. He'd seemed a little off. As it was, I hadn't had the chance. Until now.

Rob was leaning against the wall, chatting to a man I'd not met. Dressed in a gunmetal grey suit that was beautifully cut and definitely not off the peg, he looked pretty damn gorgeous. The blue shirt he'd chosen to go under it provided just the right amount of contrast. He'd opted to forgo a tie and had left the collar open, managing to look relaxed but formal all at the same time. I felt a spark zip through me as I remembered the feel of him against me, kissing me. He caught me watching him and smiled. But it wasn't the smile of earlier. He pushed himself off the wall and excused himself from the company, heading towards me.

'You look nice,' he said.

I did my best not to let the smile on my face drop. I'd got a 'wow' from Jenny, and a 'gorgeous' from Eleanor but apparently only ranked as 'nice' with Rob.

'Thanks.'

He didn't appear inclined to say any more so I took the initiative. 'Great suit, by the way.'

'Thanks'

'Italian?'

He tilted his head. 'Yes. I had a business trip to Milan a few months ago. Thought I'd go crazy. How did you know?'

'I'm interested in men's tailoring. I keep up with things,' I teased. 'I wouldn't want to do it day in, day out, but I keep an interest.'

'Because you're happy right now creating wedding dresses for other people.' He paraphrased the reply I'd given to his mum earlier. And I wasn't sure why.

'Yes.' I looked at him a little unsure. His expression gave nothing away.

'Rob,' I said, lowering my voice a little so that no one could overhear. 'About earlier.'

'Earlier?'

I waited.

'Oh, you mean when you kissed me?'

I kissed him?

'Yes, but I seem to remember you being on the other end of that kiss.'

'Absolutely.'

When he seemed disinclined to say any more, I prompted him. 'And?'

He pulled a face, half smiling, half confused. 'And what, Izz? I really hope you're not dissecting that? I've said before you read too much into things. Like with the boots. You needed boots, I got you boots. But then you're worried about some rule you've

181

made up in your head that gifts can only be received from friends if they're female.'

'That's not entirely fair.' I tried to defend myself.

'Yeah it is, Izzy. You read too much into that, and you're reading too much into this. Yes, we kissed. It was nice. Don't ruin it by breaking it open to see how it works.'

'It was nice?' I repeated. Nice was apparently his word of the evening. And it had sure as hell felt a lot more than *nice* to me and from his response, nice didn't cover it for him either, at the time. I mean, I know there was more attraction there than just 'nice'. I felt it. And I'm not just talking metaphorically. I mean I *felt* it.

'Didn't you think so?'

'Of course I thought so but I also thought—'

'Robert! There you are. Mummy said she'd seen you. I hope you're not hiding from me.'

The brunette that had just walked in on our conversation with her impossibly long legs and shampoo-advert-worthy hair then endowed us with a tinkly little laugh. I'd never heard anyone actually laugh like that outside of a 1950s film.

'Caroline. What man would ever want to hide from you? You look stunning, as always.' Rob's attention was firmly shifted. And apparently he'd found a new word. I'd got 'nice', she got 'stunning'. Even if it was true. She did the laugh again. 'Isn't he the charmer?'

I smiled widely. 'Quite.'

She raked her eyes over him and I chewed the inside of my lip, feeling superfluous and trying to think of a way to leave without it seeming like I was flouncing off.

'Has it really been five years? You know you haven't changed a bit. Still as gorgeous as ever. So, doesn't an old friend get a hello kiss?' she asked him, the question so loaded I was amazed it didn't clang on the floor.

He didn't reply with words. He didn't have to. The kiss was

enough. For me too. A bubble of petulance threatened to pop out and I was milliseconds away from asking him if that was 'nice' too when I squashed it back down and flushed it away with a large gulp of champagne.

'Now, Rob, you haven't introduced us?' the woman chided him, her arm snaking possessively around his waist.

'Caroline, this is Isabel Bryant. She's a friend from London. Izzy, this is Caroline Bennett. Her parents live the other end of the village. We went to school together.'

She held out her perfectly manicured hand with its Christmas red nails. 'We did a lot of things together!' She laughed, shaking my hand.

'Nice to meet you.' I smiled, lying through my teeth. I might have been stupid when it came to thinking Rob felt more than he did. More than I did. But I hadn't missed her meaning in the apparently conspiratorial comment she'd just shared with me. I'd seen it in her eyes. *We have history. Back off!* Well, that was fine. I'd seen something in his eyes too as he looked at her. And I couldn't blame him. She was flat-out gorgeous. And just his type.

I was such an idiot. Rob was right. I did read into things too much. He'd kissed me back but it hadn't really meant anything. And I'd started it, for heaven's sake. It was my own fault. He was kind and being friendly and accepting a kiss between two single people. That's all it meant to him.

But that moment, that kiss, this whole experience of being here with him, had woken me up to the fact that I was, to my utter surprise, in love with Rob Winchester. And he wasn't in love with me. Perfect.

'It was nice of Rob to invite you down for the holidays,' Caroline said, baiting her hook and casting the line out again.

'Actually it was Mum and Dad,' Rob put in, faster than I could open my mouth.

'Oh! How sweet.' Caroline's smile spread even further and her hand splayed and rested on Rob's belt, just above his hip.

'Yes. It was.'

'Jenny had a bit of a disaster with her wedding dress. Izzy is making her a new one. It saved a lot of hassle for everyone if Izzy came here to do it, fittings and so on, apparently.' He shrugged his shoulders at Caroline, as if to say 'what do I know about weddings?'.

Seriously, Rob? She's got the idea that I'm not a threat. There's no need to make me sound like I'm bloody staff! I threw him a dagger-laden glance. I couldn't tell if he understood it or not.

'No, that would make sense. And how sweet of you to do that for her.'

Hello? Can we all say 'patronising'?

'Not really. It's my job. I'm a bridal designer. She's paying me to do it.' OK, not the full story but I didn't like the air of superiority Caroline Bennett was surrounding herself with. And Rob really wasn't helping.

'I see. I've been hearing all about this wedding,' she said, pouting at Rob.

Ha! She didn't have an invite. Good. Childish, I know. But still. Good!

'It's a shame I won't get to see it.'

'Jenny said the local newspaper is coming, so you'll at least get to see some pictures.' I gave her a smile that I knew from hours and hours of dealing with difficult and stressed women came across as genuine. Even if it wasn't. I knew exactly what she was angling for – an invite to be Rob's plus one.

I'd seen Jenny's face and heard her groan when her dad had mentioned he'd had to extend the invite for tonight to include Caroline. I was pretty sure she wouldn't want this woman at her wedding. Either way, it was her decision to have her there. Not something that should be imposed on her by her brother not thinking with his brain.

'Is that so? How lovely. Then I'll have to look out for that.'

She smiled at me. Clearly she'd had far less practice at it because there was no way anyone could have missed its coldness.

She turned to Rob and whispered something to him which resulted in a smile. I felt sick. I needed to get away. Their attention diverted with each other, I took the opportunity to knock my drink back in one.

'Oh! Empty glass. Better rectify that,' I said. 'Would you excuse me?' I didn't wait for an answer but headed off to the kitchen where I found a bottle of bubbles chilling in an ice bucket. Filling my glass, I knocked it back again. I half-filled it once more and put the bottle back in the bucket. I munched on some peanuts and peered back towards the party. Caroline and Rob were still looking cosy and perfect, whilst in the background, Michael Bublé was crooning away. I caught the lyrics – 'Please fall in love with me this Christmas'. Great. You know your love life is toilet bound when even the ever-chirpy Mickey Bubbles starts mocking you. Picking up my glass, I headed out to the hall and delved into the handbag I'd left hanging on one of the coat hooks. Pulling my phone out, I texted Mags.

Hi sweetie. How's things?

True to form, she responded within seconds.

Absolutely bloody crazy. B/f coping well. Good sign. A laughing emoticon followed this snippet. I smiled, glad that my friend, my very man fussy friend, seemed to really have found someone. And someone that could cope with the chaos that ensued when her whole family got together. That really was a find.

How's it going with you?

My fingers hovered over the keys. I switched to the contact screen and focused on the "call" button. What should I say? I knew she'd want to know. I actually had a feeling that she already did know, or at least had an inkling about how I felt for Rob. She was good with sussing out people. Probably because she didn't trust them straightaway. The fact that she'd always liked Rob more than Steven should have told me something. Especially when Brett said the same thing last week. As if thinking of him hit a chord in the universe, my phone buzzed again.

Brett says have you snogged him yet? What does he know that I don't????

Oh great. Thanks Brett. How to explain this? Well, yes I have. Except all it's done is make me look a complete idiot. But the problem is I've now realised I'm head over heels for him but he's not interested. He thinks I'm 'nice'. However, he thinks his neighbour is a whole lot more than nice. And I'm desperately wishing I'd come and stayed with you because then I might never have come to the realisation that I'm in love with him and then it wouldn't hurt as much as it does right now.

I went back to the text screen on my phone.

I think the only thing Brett knows is how to drink a lot more than you. Let me ask you – has he been drinking?

It's Christmas Eve! Of course he's been drinking!

Well, there's your answer. Seriously. Nothing to tell.

I wasn't about to ruin Mags' Christmas. If she knew I was miserable, she would be too, and I wasn't having that.

Let me know if that changes.

She ended with a wink. Oh crap. She did know how I felt about him. I could see several bottles of wine in our joint future.

Although I have fallen for Harold …

Who's Harold??? Tell me tell me.

I pulled up a cute picture I'd taken of him out on the walk earlier and sent it to her.

Awww, adorable! Not exactly what I had in mind but at least an improvement on your previous choice.

This time a pokey tongue face ended the reply.

Ha ha! Although, true.

Better go. Will speak to you tomorrow. Happy Christmas Eve, Magsy. Love you lots! And give my love to everyone else. Xxxx

And to you! Have a great time there! Love you too … Brett

says he wants you to deliver your love personally … for which I apologise. LOL xxx

As I said, definitely drunk! LOL! Xxx

Honestly, it would be so much simpler if Brett actually meant that – which we all knew he didn't and I felt the same – which I didn't. I read the text again. *'Have a great time there'.* I should. Mags was right. That's exactly what I should do! I put the phone back in my bag and picking up my glass, set my sights on having a good time.

Chapter 15

'There you are!' Jenny called, waving to me from across the room. I squeezed through with an assortment of 'excuse me's and came up to her, taking the hand she was holding out to me. Mike gave me a little look from his position next to her, perched on the arm of a chair, and laughed. Jenny was plastered.

'I thought you'd gone!'

'Gone? Where would I go?' I laughed. 'Especially in these shoes!' I waggled my heeled foot in the air. 'There's a foot and a half of snow out there already.'

'Well I'm glad you haven't gone. Especially now Caroline Bennett's shown up.' Mike pulled a face at me while Jenny made a 'Bleugh' noise.

'Jen!' I said, shooshing her, but laughing at the same time.

'Weeellll,' she said, as if that explained it all. 'Have you met her?' she asked.

'Oh yes,' I said, taking a swig of my drink.

'Then you know exactly what I mean. God knows what Rob sees in her.'

'I think that's pretty obvious.'

'Apart from the obvious.'

'Hate to tell you, Jen. For a lot of men, the "obvious" is more

188

than enough. No offence, Mike.'

'None taken,' he replied, shrugging his shoulders as if at least in part agreeing with me.

'I thought we'd seen the last of her when she dumped him before.'

'She dumped him?'

'Yeah. Effectively. But I guess she's back as she's now draped all over my brother yet again.' Jenny took a swig of her drink. 'Oh joy.'

We all looked towards where Caroline and Rob were standing, laughing and chatting with another couple. Jenny was right. Draped was the right word. And the worst part, aside from the fact that he seemed to be thoroughly enjoying it, was that they actually looked good together. Both tall, gorgeous, sexy. They looked like they belonged together.

'Oh shit. They're coming over.' Jenny yanked me down onto the pouffe that was beside her. 'Do not leave me with her.'

'Mike's here. It's—' I caught a glance at her face. 'Nope. Right, got it. Not leaving.'

'Thank you.' She squeezed my hand.

I had a horrible feeling I knew what Rob and Caroline's intention was in coming over to see his sister. It was true I didn't know Caroline. But I'd met people like her, and all I'd heard so far only backed up my theory. Even Mr and Mrs Winchester didn't like her, and they seemed to like everyone. Hell, they'd invited me to stay with them on the basis of one evening! I wrangled with myself as to whether to say anything. I had no intention of stirring the pot but I didn't want Jenny put in a difficult position either.

'Jen. I've a feeling that Caroline might be after an invitation to the wedding. Especially now.' I finished, as we all watched her lift her thumb to Rob's mouth, ostensibly to brush off a crumb but there was no mistaking the sexuality in the move. And there was definitely no question that Rob understood it. His lips curved and he lifted a hand to cover her own. He leant over and whispered

189

something. She laughed that laugh again and they continued their path towards us.

'Over my dead body,' Jenny said, a steel in her voice that I'd not heard until now. I glanced across at Mike. He gave me a tiny shake of his head.

'Jennifer!' Caroline enthused but made no move to either hold out her hand or hug Jenny. That, along with it being the first time I'd heard anyone use Jen's full name, told me everything I needed to know.

'Hello, Caroline.'

'Congratulations on your wedding.'

'Thanks.'

I reminded myself never to get on the wrong side of Jenny. I was pretty sure that if I went outside right now and played snow angels in my cocktail dress, it would still be warmer than this conversation.

'And is this the lucky man?' Caroline swung her hair and batted her lashes at Mike, all the while keeping a possessive arm around Rob. Quite the achievement.

Jenny glared at her.

'How do you do?' Mike shook her hand but there was no warmth there. It was all very formal.

I was obviously missing something. Rob shot him a look. Mike gave him a blank one in return. What the hell was going on here?

'Robert tells me Isabel is making your dress?'

'Yes. Rob's right. Izzy is. It's beautiful.'

'I'd love to see it.'

Uh oh.

'Sorry. Big reveal on the wedding day!' Jenny smiled and took a sip of her champagne.

I followed suit. Over the top of our glasses both of us watched as Caroline gave Rob puppy dog eyes.

'Oh good grief,' Jenny whispered.

'Jen?' Rob began.

'Yep?'

I made a casual glance around. This was going to be awkward. More than that, it was going to cause an atmosphere between Rob and Jenny, not only for Christmas, but also for the wedding. After everything they'd been through, how could Rob let this woman manipulate him like that? If it was clear to me earlier that Jenny didn't like her, then he certainly knew. I couldn't believe that he'd put his chance of getting a shag before the happiness of his sister on her wedding day. Apparently neither could Mike.

'Rob, mate. Can I borrow you for a sec?'

Rob turned from where he'd begun addressing Jenny. Mike had stood and was now waiting for Rob to accompany him. It was clear to all of us that although a request, Mike wasn't expecting no for an answer.

Rob waited a beat, his gaze fixed on his friend's, before he gave a quick smile and said, 'Sure.'

He turned to go. 'I'll be right back,' he said to Caroline before following Mike through to the other room.

When they returned a few minutes later, they were both wearing their impassive masks. Mike retook his position and slipped his hand down to take hold of Jenny's.

'Right. Back. Sorry about that,' Rob apologised to Caroline. 'I've just seen the Mitchells arrive. Let's go and say hello.'

Whatever conversation had taken place between the two men, Rob now clearly had no intention of finishing the request he'd begun. Mike, normally so warm and friendly, calmly sipped his drink. Caroline really must be something. And she was not happy.

'Actually, I've got a headache coming on. I think I'm just going to go home.' Wow. Sulking. Mature.

From the corner of my eye, I saw Jenny hide a smile behind her champagne glass.

'I'll take you.'

'No. It's fine.' She smiled at Rob with all the warmth of an ice

191

pop. 'I'll see if Mummy and Daddy want to stay. If they do, I'll just call a taxi.' She put a hand to her head dramatically.

'Oh for …' The rest of Jen's comment was lost in her glass.

'Come on. I'll take you.' Rob put a hand on her back and steered her towards the front door, grabbing the keys to his Range Rover and his jacket as he did so.

'Guess it was lucky that he didn't drink tonight,' I said.

'He always takes the Andersons home after Mum and Dad's party. They're elderly and don't drive anymore. Caroline knew that. She knew he'd take her home too and probably keep working on him to get her an invitation.'

Jen and I swapped a look then both hurriedly made our way to the front door and peered out of the adjacent windows, hiding ourselves as much as possible behind the curtains, one each side, before peeking out.

'Oh she's turned the waterworks on.' Jenny sounded disgusted. 'If he falls for that, I'll bloody kill him. I do not want that woman at my wedding.'

'She won't be at the wedding, sweetheart,' Mike said from his position on the stairs, an amused look on his face as he sat watching us both acting like bad spies.

'How do you know? I can't believe he's even going out with her again!'

'No, I know. But I promise you. She's not invited.'

Jenny opened her mouth to speak.

'And she won't be,' he finished.

Watching Rob hand Caroline in to the same car he'd so carefully helped me out of yesterday, I could only wish that I felt Mike's confidence. Rob closed the car door and walked around to the other side. A few moments later, the sound of gravel crunching on the drive signalled their departure.

'What about the Andersons?'

'He won't forget.'

I waggled my head. 'I have a feeling Ms Bennett's headache is going to clear pretty fast and that she's probably got the ability to make him forget a lot of things.'

'Possibly,' Mike replied.

So not the answer I wanted to hear.

'But not things that matter.'

'OK,' I said, flopping down opposite them onto the bench. 'Clearly there's a story behind all this. Come on, spill.'

Mike and Jenny exchanged a look.

'See! Aha! There is!' I pointed, vaguely aware that after acting like a bad spy, I was now sounding like a bad detective.

Mike indicated for Jenny to make the decision. A sobering thought broke through.

'Wait!' I held up a hand. 'I mean, if this is something family, personal, then don't. Just don't tell me. I was assuming it was just gossip but from that look on your faces, there's something deeper here, and it's really not my place to know. So!' I stood up. 'I am going to head back to the party!'

'Izzy. It is family but I want you to know.' Jenny held out her hands to me again. I glanced at Mike and he nodded, a gentle smile on his face.

I crossed to where Jenny was and, taking her hands, I sat on the floor in front of her, my heels kicked off to the side.

'None of us were thrilled when Rob started seeing Caroline. She's vain, boring and self-obsessed. As much as it pains me to say, we all know my brother is good looking. He was still serving when they started dating and she loved all the formal balls and the pomp and circumstance of it all. Not to mention the fact she got to meet a lot of men in uniform. When he came out, she was a bit put out but, of course, once she knew he'd be a solicitor in London she was happy again. It was up to her standard. We just couldn't understand what he saw in her. He's intelligent and funny and we know she couldn't possibly stimulate that side of him – all you have to do is spend five minutes in her company to know that.

'Anyway. Then I had my accident. Rob was incredible. I know what it must have done to him. What it would have done to me if things had been different. But added to the fact that he's always thought he should be able to protect me from everything, then well, I can only imagine what ran through his mind. Mike knows that side of it more. They were both out of the army by then and living close, doing voluntary work with veterans, so their friendship continued. Which, I am very glad about!' Jenny touched Mike's hand to her face. It made my eyes fill and I made a mental note to pack plenty of tissues for the wedding.

'Anyway. Rob was obviously spending a lot of time at the hospital. Mum and Dad were having a hard time with it all initially, so he was trying to keep them together, keep his business going and make sure I was getting the best care possible. Mike said he looked pretty terrible some of the time.'

'He wasn't sleeping much, I know that,' Mike added. 'And he was worried, obviously. They weren't sure for a while how much damage Jenny was going to suffer permanently and what would recover.'

'Initially they thought I might not have the use of my arms either. Mum and Dad, well, they just fell apart a bit.' Jenny wiped a tear away.

'Jen, please don't. Don't tell me if it's going to upset you. It's Christmas Eve. It's supposed to be a happy time!'

'I'm fine. I want to tell you. I want to explain about Caroline, and show you I'm not just being a bitch.'

I had to laugh. 'I don't think you're just being a bitch! Even if you were, it's OK. It's your wedding so you should have final say as to who is and isn't invited. Besides, I knew it wasn't just that when Doctor Genial here wasn't pleased to see her.'

'Doctor Genial?' Mike laughed. 'I quite like that. I might use that. Get some nametags made up.'

'You should.' I winked at him.

'Anyway. Basically everyone was in a bit of a state. Rob had been seeing Caroline for about two years, on and off, at this point'.

'Wow. I didn't realise they'd seen each other for that long.' No wonder she was warning me to back off. They really did have history. I'd been hoping they'd had a one-night stand at the most.

'Yeah, a while. We'd just assumed that although she didn't seem all that deep to us, perhaps there was more to her than we'd seen. Turned out there wasn't. Mum and Dad were a bit surprised that he always came to the hospital alone but figured at the start at least, perhaps Caroline was actually being sensitive and leaving us to ourselves for a while, giving us time to get over the shock, and let me get a bit stronger. But then she still didn't come. Rob asked her to, apparently, but she always made excuses. And then she wanted to go on holiday!

'I was in a coma for a few days when it first happened and then obviously there was a lot going on. Rob was there all the time he could be. Mum and Dad said he should rest and so did I when I was lucid enough. Even in my drugged-up state I could see he was knackered and hurting. But instead of supporting him, after the first week, once I woke up, it turned out that Caroline had started questioning how much time he spent at the hospital and giving him grief. Making him feel guilty for wanting to be with his family at the most horrible time we've ever had! He was so busy supporting everyone else, he was making himself ill and he had no one supporting him! The one person who should have was more concerned about herself and going out, or on holiday, than she was about the man she was supposed to care for.

'It all sort of came to a head one night when Rob didn't turn up at the hospital. Of course, Mum and Dad went into an absolute panic that something might have happened to him. They rang Caroline but she said she hadn't seen him. She was in a huff because he'd been supposed to call her but he hadn't. Mum said it had sounded like she was in a bar. Anyway, they tried everyone they could think of, including Mike without luck. Mike had been worried enough to go over to Rob's place and get Security to let him in. It was clear that Rob hadn't been home and it was late by this point so Mike headed over to Rob's office. Just as he and a security guard were getting to Rob's office, one of the cleaners came running out, shouting something.

'They were all Polish and I only know a few words. But I recognised one of them as "Dead",' Mike filled in.

'Oh my God!' My hand flew to my mouth.

'Mike and the guard rushed in. Rob was on the floor. Luckily the cleaner had overreacted. Rob had actually collapsed from exhaustion. It was likely he'd been there for hours.'

'And yet Caroline hadn't bothered to check on him even though it was obviously apparent to everyone he wasn't doing so well.'

'Exactly. She'd just got the hump that he'd refused to take her to the Bahamas the week after my accident and hadn't called her that day. He hadn't called her because he was unconscious on the floor!'

'So, what happened?'

'I got him admitted to the hospital I worked at,' Mike said, taking up the story. 'We set him up with fluids and rest, ran some tests just to check nothing else was going on. He was all right. He just hadn't been eating or sleeping much. Existing on coffee alone was only ever going to keep him running for so long. I rang his parents and told them he'd just fallen asleep but that he really needed to rest – which they knew. I felt bad lying to them but telling them their son was in hospital with exhaustion when they're sat around the bedside of their seriously injured daughter didn't seem the best plan at the time. When Rob was a bit more with it, I told him what I'd done and said he should call them and explain. He didn't want to. As it was, they didn't find out until much later. I have to say, I had some explaining to do when I met them again properly!' He smiled, then looked over at Jen. 'I knew I had to get it right though because I'd just met this one and I wasn't going to screw that up.'

'It turned out Caroline *had* been at a bar. With one of her exes, in fact, whom she'd called whilst in a strop with Rob. As Mike was rushing her current boyfriend to hospital, she was checking in to The Cavendish with a previous one. And after all that, he thought I would let him invite her to the wedding! I don't even know what he's thinking going anywhere near her again! He's bloody nuts!'

I tended to agree. I couldn't even begin to imagine what Rob, all of them, had gone through with the accident. Surely if you see someone you care about in pain, don't you automatically want to alleviate that pain, even if you can't fix it, at least make it easier, somehow? Although I couldn't understand it, I could believe it. The thing about my job was that you saw the good, but also the bad, of human nature. I'd seen some really ugly green-eyed monsters in my studio over the years. Caroline's behaviour had the distinct whiff of the same.

'She was jealous of the attention he was giving his family.'

'Exactly. Unbelievable, isn't it? Honestly, Mum and Dad will go mad if they know he's taken up with her again.'

'Well, not much we can do about it!' I said, standing up very inelegantly as I found out one of my feet had gone to sleep. Mike put an arm out to help me as I stood and rubbed my foot back to life. When I felt the blood start moving around again I slipped my feet into my shoes and declared that we all needed another glass of champagne. Seconded by Mike and Jenny, we all went back through to the party.

I was exhausted after putting on a fake smile for so many hours. Rob's dismissal of our kiss, Caroline's well, everything – and then Jenny's story had worn me out. I was with her in not understanding how Rob could want to be with Caroline after she'd shown him so little care at such a difficult time. Maybe he thought she'd changed. Or maybe he didn't care whether she had changed or not because it was just about sex so it didn't matter.

I could see that. Actually it made sense. Rob never seemed to have had any long-term relationships, in all the time I'd known him. That's why I'd been surprised to hear that he and Caroline had lasted nearly two years. Not that that seemed to have had a lot of depth to it either, by the sounds of it. At least not on her side. His mum might be right. He just might not be the settling down type. Some people weren't. And it stood to reason that I'd fall in love with just such a man.

The room was quiet now. All the guests had gone and we'd all mucked in helping Eleanor clean up. Initially we'd planned to go to Midnight Mass but the snow was getting heavier all the time and Jenny and Mike were both pretty tired. He'd had a long week with a few double shifts and it was starting to catch up with him so we decided to leave it. Rob had, as Mike said he would, remembered his promise to take the Andersons home and had returned on the dot of ten to collect them but promptly disappeared again. Glancing out at the snow and pretending not to be worried, John sent his son a text.

'Says he's fine and not to wait up.' His parents didn't seem thrilled but they did at least seem relieved. 'I'm going to video call my parents in a bit, if that's all right?' I said as everyone said their goodnights.

'Of course it is, darling! I hope they're having a wonderful time.'

'Me too. I'll just wait a bit longer and make sure they're up.' My dad wasn't really one for lie-ins, but I wanted some time alone before I spoke to them. Just to get my head in order.

John had banked the fire down but it was still warm in the room. I wandered through to the kitchen, running my hand over the cool granite counters, killing time, trying not to think of where Rob was right now. Who he was with. And most of all, trying not to think of the fact that he wasn't with me – in any sense of the word, and never would be.

'Hi!' I called quietly, waving at the screen, and seeing my hand in the little screen become a blur.

'Hello, love!' my parents chorused. They looked happy and relaxed. It had definitely been the right thing to do to bully them into going.

'How's the holiday?'

'Oh, it's been wonderful!' They caught me up with all the things they'd been doing so far and some of the things they had lined up. 'It will be so funny having a barbecue for Christmas dinner!'

'I bet!' I laughed, before immediately starting to cry.

'Izzy, love! What's wrong?!' Mum sounded so upset I felt terrible, even worse than I already had which was saying something.

'Nothing!' I took a deep breath. 'Nothing. I just really miss you right now. It's only because it's Christmas and stuff. I'm fine. Honestly! Just being silly. Probably overtired, that's all.'

'Have you been overdoing it?'

'No. Just the usual.'

'Definitely overdoing it then.' Mum chided softly.

Probably not the best time to tell them of the several nights past midnight this week then. 'Anyway. Tell me more about what you've been doing.'

I chatted to Mum and Dad for another half an hour before we said goodbye and arranged another chat in a few days' time. I said goodbye, tried not to get tearful again, and waved until Dad finally pressed the end button after neither Mum nor I wanted to. I looked at the blank screen for a few moments and then turned the tablet off entirely. Up on the mantelpiece, the antique clock shuffled its hands into place and began softly chiming half past midnight.

I wandered back into the kitchen and looked out of the double doors that led onto the lawn. The snow was coming down heavily and the tracks Harold had made earlier were nearly all covered. Little flickers of crystal caught the moonlight and reflected back as they settled on the mini drifts now being created in the Winchesters' garden. I thought of Mum and Dad having Christmas dinner on the beach and of the upcoming wedding. I thought about Jenny's accident, of Rob collapsing, of Mike telling a white lie to protect the people who would eventually become his in-laws. And then I thought of Rob again. How it felt when he held me, when he teased me, when we laughed. I was so stupid to have believed that it had ever been anything but friends to him. Even the kiss. I knew his preference for leggy, slightly vacuous types and how different that was from me. Why on earth had I kissed him like that? Why did I give myself the opportunity to feel what I was missing? I slid down the glass door and laid my head on the cold pane. The click of toenails announced Harold's presence. He plodded in slowly and stopped, looking at me for a moment before making his way over. He nudged my face with his nose and sat so close beside me he was practically on my lap. Gently he laid his big square head on my shoulder. I wrapped my arms around his warm, solid body and sobbed.

Chapter 16

'Izzy?' Rob's voice drifted down into my dreams. Oh, great. I couldn't avoid that deep rumble even in my sleep now.

'Izzy?' It came again. I opened my eyes to find myself looking into Rob's, and the room bathed in an eerie light from the snow that was now banked up against the patio door I was leaning on. Harold was lying with his head on my thigh and watching us both, his eyebrows rising alternately as he looked from one of us to the other.

'What are you doing down here?' Rob asked, his voice soft in deference to the rest of the household.

'I … err …' I pushed my hair back off my face and surreptitiously checked that there wasn't dribble running down my chin. Clear. Good, that was something. 'I was talking to my parents on video. I must have nodded off.'

'Right,' he said and glanced over to the table some yards away where my tablet was sat.

'I was watching the snow for a while.'

'You've been crying.'

Rob's tone suggested that denial wasn't a viable option.

'Yes, I have. I miss my parents.' Which was true. He didn't have to know the rest.

'Is that all?'

Bloody hell that was an annoying habit.

'No. But it's not important.'

'It is to me.'

No, Rob. Don't do this. This is how I fell for you in the first place.

'No, it's not.' I gave him a little smile and pushed myself up off the floor. My bum was entirely numb.

'Why won't you tell me?' he asked.

'As I said, because it's not important. How was your evening?'

He stiffened. 'All right,' he said, without looking at me.

'Good,' I whispered, cheerily. 'Well, I think I'd better go to bed.'

Rob nodded, letting me past.

'Night, Rob.'

I bent down and gave Harold a big cuddle. 'Thanks, boy,' I whispered, planting a kiss on the top of his head. Swiping my tablet from the table, I began walking away.

'So, I'm guessing I don't get one of those?'

When I turned back to face him, Rob indicated the dog's head. He was standing in shadow and I couldn't make out his expression. But I didn't need to be able to see his expression to guess that he thought this was all just a bit of fun. Two could play at that game.

'I don't think so,' I replied, keeping my voice light. 'After tonight, I'm pretty sure I'd fail very miserably by comparison.'

I turned and took a few more steps, 'By the way,' I said, looking back and tapping the side of my neck, 'you might want to put something on that.'

Rob looked confused.

'There's lipstick on your shirt collar. It can be a pain to get out.'

He didn't say anything.

'I'll leave a can of hairspray outside my door. Soak the stain with that as soon as you can, then wash it. It usually does the trick.'

'Right. Thanks.'

Walking away, I tried not to think about how that lipstick had got there. 'Merry Christmas, Rob.'

'Merry Christmas, Izzy.'

Lying in bed, I stared out of the open curtains, watching as snowflakes drifted past the window, and the trees cast flitting moonlit shadows across the room as their branches danced with the breeze. Thoughts tumbled around in my head until eventually I drifted off to sleep.

I was up, showered, dressed and sitting talking to Harold before anyone else stirred.

'He's not known for his conversation,' Rob's deep, sleep rough- ened voice said from behind me.

I didn't turn, just carried on playing with the dog's ears which he seemed to be enjoying immensely. 'Possibly not. But he is a very good listener.'

'Is there something you want to talk about?'

'Nope. I think Harold and I are all sorted, thanks.' I stood and turned around, taking a step back when I realised Rob was closer than I'd thought.

'I meant with me.'

My innocent expression probably didn't fool him but I went with it anyway. 'No, I don't think so.' I smiled. 'Coffee?'

He nodded and padded over to grab a mug from the cupboard, his bare feet making little sound. For such a big guy, he was really good at being quiet. I thought back to the offer he'd made yesterday, before the whole kissing thing happened, about me staying with him until I found somewhere else. Had I not gone and spoiled the possibility by realising that I was in love with him, I thought he'd probably make a pretty good roommate. Well, I guess I should just chalk that up on the 'never to be' list too.

'Here,' I said, handing him a freshly poured coffee from the pot I'd put on when I got up.

'Thanks.' He sipped it and I smiled as I saw the relief on his face from his first hit of coffee.

'You should probably switch to decaf occasionally, you know.'

'I should? What on earth for?' Rob looked at me as if I'd just suggested he go outside and play naked snow angels.

'To give your system a rest.'

'You seem to be missing the whole point of the coffee.' He laughed. 'This' –he pointed to his mug – 'is to kick my system into life.'

'It was just a thought. I notice you drink a lot of coffee and I'm not sure exactly how good for you it is.'

Damn Jenny and Mike and their enlightening me that Rob, despite being built like one, wasn't an indestructible powerhouse. And I had noted that he drank a heck of a lot of coffee. With long hours, and a handful of weird ones thrown in, I knew how it could be. I'd been exactly the same but a few months ago I'd made an effort to cut back and actually felt a whole lot better in myself.

'You look tired.'

I'd thought I had anyway. 'Thanks!'

'No, I didn't mean that the way it sounded.'

I pulled a face that indicated I wasn't entirely sure what other meaning 'you look tired' could possibly have.

'I just thought you'd be sleeping in a little later today. I mean, it was late when I got back and I'm pretty sure sleeping upright against a cold pane of glass with your bum on a hard tiled floor isn't conducive to the most restful of nights.'

'I'm fine.'

'Are you? You seemed pretty upset last night.'

'Absolutely!' I gave a big, happy grin to prove it. 'I was just a little overtired and missing my parents at Christmas. That's all. Just being silly.'

'It's not silly to miss people you love.'

'No. I suppose not.' But it is silly to miss people when they're standing right in front of you because it feels like they've already gone.

'Do you think there is anything I could be getting on with for your mum, you know, towards the dinner or anything?' Changing the subject seemed like a good distraction right about now.

'Umm …' Rob looked around. 'I highly doubt it, to be honest.'

'Oh.' Great. I looked both tired and incompetent apparently.

'No, no, no!' he started. As usual, it appeared my enigmatic, impenetrable expression had masked my feelings perfectly. 'It's not that I don't think you can do anything. It's just that I'm pretty sure there won't be anything that isn't already done. The military thing runs on Mum's side of the family and whilst she didn't join up, she's definitely got the genes! Events like this will have been planned with precision and various counter measures in place.' His mouth was serious but his eyes were lit with humour.

'I see. So, what can I do to make myself useful?'

'Useful?' he asked, incredulity clear in his voice.

This morning was just getting better and better.

'Yes,' I replied, a little defensively. 'Is me being useful really that hard to believe?'

'What?' Realisation dawned. 'Oh shit! No, not what I meant. Christ, I'm saying everything wrong this morning.'

I refrained from making a barb about over exertion clouding his brain. Remaining silent, I sat on the floor and went back to playing with Harold's ears.

'Izz, you've made a wedding dress when there very nearly wasn't one. I think you have "useful" covered for several years to come.'

'Hardly the same thing. I can still peel potatoes.'

'I know. And you can peel as many as you want when you move in after Christmas.'

'Rob. I'm not moving in.'

'I thought we talked about this yesterday.'

'No. You brought it up yesterday. I said no. You said we'd talk about it again but now you're acting like it's already been agreed.'

Rob rubbed the dog's head gently but I could see his jaw tensing.

'Please don't think I don't appreciate the offer. I really do.'

'Izzy, you can't go back to that place. Not on your own. I don't want you there. It's not safe.'

'Rob, with all due respect, what you want doesn't come into it. No, don't take offence, please,' I placed my hand on his arm as he made to move away from where he'd taken a seat next to me. 'I know you mean well and I know that you worry about me, which is sweet—'

'It's got nothing to do with being sweet.'

I let that go.

'I told you. I bluffed my way with Peter for now and I'll find something really soon. I'll even have you come and check it out for approval first if you like.' I bumped against him, trying to tease him out of the dark expression his face had taken on.

'I'm not going to get you to change your mind on this, am I?'

'No. Sorry. And it's not that I don't think it wouldn't be great at your place. I just need a place of my own.'

Oh, and to not be in the same place that you're testing the bedsprings next door with Caroline Bennett or whatever other long-legged beauty walks into your life next because that, right now, is not something I can deal with.

He looked round at me for the first time, a half smile on his face. 'Wow. One weekend with me was enough to keep you away for ever. I must be a worse housemate than I thought.'

'Don't be silly. It's got nothing to do with that. Actually,' I said, 'that was honestly one of the nicest weekends I've had in a long while.'

His half smile spread further over his unshaven face.

'You even put the toilet seat down!'

'Yeah, my mum has a thing about that, as does Jenny – so when she moved in for a while, it was the best option for a quiet life.'

'Is my son taking my name in vain again?' Eleanor breezed into the kitchen, ruffled the dog's face and then came and kissed us each good morning.

'Merry Christmas, my darlings!'

I couldn't help grinning at her effusive manner. 'Rob, dear. Are you going to have a shave?'

'Umm, I wasn't planning to.'

His mother looked up from where she was getting out crockery, pans and other cooking paraphernalia.

The only word she said was 'Oh', but there was a whole wealth of meaning behind it.

I dropped my gaze and stifled a laugh.

'I guess I'm going to have a shave then.' He gave me a wink as he stood, his easy-going manner winning out again. I watched him leave – he really did have the nicest bum. I blushed as I caught his mum glancing in my direction. I fussed with the dog for a moment, then went to wash my hands and asked what I could do.

Dinner was in the oven and smelling divine as we all sat around in the living room, exchanging gifts. I had brought my own, partly as a thank you for the invite but I certainly hadn't expected to be so thoroughly included by the Winchesters. I was completely spoiled and loving every minute of it. Sitting next to Jenny on the sofa with the lads sprawled out on the floor in front, and the dog having the best time playing and shredding the used gift wrap, I was relaxed and, for the most part, happy. I'd decided to put aside my feelings for Rob, as much as I could, for today at least. I didn't want to spoil this time for me, or anyone else. The next few days would take care of themselves. I was going to give Jenny another fitting tomorrow and then do the final alterations and finishing touches. It was going to keep me pretty busy and I knew, from bitter experience, that keeping busy with my work was a good tactic for when the rest of my life was sliding away from the plans I had for it.

Jenny and I were oohing over the beautiful necklace Mike had bought her when Rob emerged from scrambling under the enormous Christmas tree with a large, flat box. He walked across the floor on his knees and laid the box on mine.

'What's this?' I asked. 'You already gave me plenty.' Thanks to Rob I now had a pile of books I'd been wanting to read, a subscription to the Hallmark channel so that I could watch romantic comedy films whenever I chose and a gorgeous basket of Neal's Yard goodies that all smelled absolutely wonderful. I knew this because Jenny and I had started opening and smelling everything immediately.

'It's just a little something extra.'

'Rob, really. You shouldn't have.'

'All right then,' he said, and put one large hand on it with a move to taking it away.

'But as you have,' I said, grabbing the box back with both of mine, 'it'd be rude of me not to accept it.'

He looked up from the floor at me under those luscious eyelashes and smiled. A bolt of heat shot through me and ended up in places that really didn't seem appropriate for the setting. I looked away and, laughing, pushed his hand off the box. A bright red ribbon was tied around the white box. I gave one end a tug and it fell away. Lifting off the lid, I met with nothing but tissue paper. I swung a glance at Jenny who was looking as eager as I was to see what was inside.

'This isn't your other dress, is it?'

'Come on, come on!' she said, grabbing my wrist.

'All right, all right!' Laughing, I risked another glance at Rob who was still sitting at my feet, but now looked almost apprehensive.

Three layers of tissue paper later and I gasped. There in the box, laying beautifully folded, was a replica of my favourite cardigan that Rob had shrunk that first night I'd stayed over. I gently lifted it out and held it up, the softness of the cashmere caressing my hands. The only difference to the original was that this one had the most delicate of crochet trims around the bottom hem and the sleeves. I had loved my previous one, but this? This was perfect. In the back of my mind, I heard Jenny and her mum commenting on it but I wasn't focusing on that. My head was spinning on how Rob had found such a similar one – I knew they didn't sell mine anymore, because believe me, after the laundry disaster, I'd searched high and low. But it wasn't just that. It was that he'd even thought about it. I didn't think I'd ever had such a perfect, thoughtful gift. And of course, it had to be from Rob. Argh! I wanted to kill him! But mostly I really, really wanted to kiss him.

'Do you like it?' he asked, quietly.

I suddenly realised that I hadn't said anything. 'Oh yes! Yes! It's beautiful!' *No tears, please don't do this to me now.* I swallowed them down but I knew Rob hadn't missed it. I was pretty sure he didn't miss anything. 'I just don't understand how you got one? I searched high and low for a replacement.'

'Yeah. Me too.'

'A replacement?' His mum asked.

Rob explained what he'd done. She pulled a sympathetic face at me. 'Thanks, Mum. Like I didn't feel bad enough already.'

'No! No you shouldn't!' I told him. 'This? This is even better! I love it! But where did you find it?'

'I didn't. Actually my secretary came to the rescue. She got into knitting a couple of years ago. I took the mickey out of her a bit, but in fun, you know. Apparently it's cool now?' He looked bemused and shrugged. 'Anyway, the joke was on me because she completely saved the day. I took your toddler sized jumper in and told her what happened. And after she gave me the same look as Mum just did, she said she could make a new one, if I gave her your size.'

'But you don't know my size.'

Rob suddenly developed an intense interest in the ribbon I'd dropped on the floor. 'I kind of saw it on your underwear when I got everything out of the washing machine.'

'Oh God,' I mumbled, and flushed the same colour as the ribbon.

'I wasn't intending to see it. I didn't realise your underwear was in there until I went to empty it and then—'

'Rob, I'd stop if I were you, mate.' Mike, and everyone else, had huge grins on their faces that they were doing their best to hide.

'Right. Yes, well. I told her that, said "think Kylie" and … this is the result.'

I had to admit the embarrassment of Rob seeing not only my underwear, but also the sizing, was worth it if this was the end product. And being compared to Kylie didn't hurt my ego too much either.

'Your secretary is a genius!'

'Funnily enough, that's what she said. And then said that being such a genius she should be entitled to an extra week of holiday next year.'

'Which you gave to her, I hope!'

'Of course.'

'Such a soft touch.' His mum chuckled.

'Not at all,' he said. 'If Izzy likes this, then it was worth it.'

'I do!' I said, flinging my arms around him without thinking, taking in the clean, citrusy smell of his shower gel and savouring the strength I felt as his arms wrapped around me. 'I love it. Thank you,' I whispered, before reluctantly letting go.

'You're welcome,' Rob replied, his eyes dark as he looked at me. My mind, and body, rushed back to what had happened the last time he'd said those words to me and it was all I could do not to lean those few inches and taste that pleasure once more.

The loud, shrill ringing noise of a cooking timer shattered the moment and Eleanor jumped up. 'Dinner will be ready shortly. Boys, could you set the table, please?'

* * *

By Boxing Day the snow had stopped and the sun was out. After clearing away another delicious lunch, Rob and Jenny's parents sat quietly with the papers whilst the rest of us piled out into the garden to build a snowman. Harold jumped about eating snow and digging little tunnels in the drifts, popping back out every now and then to check we were all still there, his face adorably covered with twinkly white crystals. Sitting next to Jenny who was bundled up in her new coat with its glamorous fur-lined hood, I was wearing a white Puffa jacket I'd bought in the sales last year. I still hadn't quite decided if it was really me, but at least I was warm. Jenny tapped my shoulder. I turned to see her holding out a snowball the size of a small cannonball.

'I have a supply here ready to go.' She grinned. 'Whenever you're ready.'

'Sure?'

'Of course! If Mike wants a chance of seeing what was in that Rigby & Peller bag, then he'll know better than to aim at me.'

I waited a beat. 'Umm, doesn't that mean he'll be aiming at me instead?'

She laughed. 'No, of course not! We're just the catalyst. Rob's going to be the target!'

'Oh no!' I joined in her laughter. 'That doesn't seem very fair!'

'Just pretend Caroline Bennett is standing in front of him.'

I launched a snowball with absolute precision, smacking Rob square in the chest.

'What the—?' He looked up to find Jenny and I sitting as innocent as angels.

'Yeah right. Because I believe that act!' he said, marching over, his boots crunching the snow down heftily. I returned his look evenly. He narrowed his eyes. We'd moved our little stash of snow weaponry behind me and I was leaning back casually to hide it, my purple wellies stuck straight out in front of me, face to the watery sun, for all intents and purposes enjoying the weather and company. He stood in front of me, blocking the light.

'Would you mind moving just a little?' I said, waving my hand and indicating to him to let the sun back in to my little patch.

From the corner of my eye, I saw Jenny make a small movement with her hand and a snowball landed with a thump on the back of Rob's jacket, heavy enough to make him bump forward.

'Score!' Mike cheered from across the garden. Rob spun around. 'Oi! You're supposed to be my mate!'

'True. But she's prettier than you.' He pointed at his fiancée.

'Right. All alliances off then,' Rob said. 'I can work with that.' And he took off at a run, scooping up snow into a ball as he did so – which he stuffed down the back of Mike's jacket as he rugby tackled him to the ground.

'See? Told you!' Jenny giggled. 'Now, fire!' And we let loose our stock of snowballs at them both until we were out of ammunition.

We were just heading back in as Rob and Mike jogged across the lawn, Harold bounding excitedly beside them. Wet from head to foot, they both looked relaxed and happy.

'Don't think I don't know who started that, Miss.' Rob raised an eyebrow at his sister.

'I'm sure I don't know what you mean.'

'Yeah right. I'd go and dump you in the fishpond if I didn't think Mike would try and kick my arse.'

'Try, he says,' Mike replied, laughing.

Rob pulled a face, the humour still evident in his eyes.

'In light of that, I'm afraid you'll have to sacrifice your teammate.'

Jenny and I shared an unsure look just before I was scooped up in Rob's arms and found myself heading for the fishpond.

'Rob! Put me down! Now! Don't you dare!' He got to the pond and started bending so that the ends of my hair were just hovering above the water. I'd linked my hands around his neck and was now clinging on, and making requests to be put down. Some of which were a lot politer than others. A koi carp broke the surface of one of the breathing holes in the pond. We considered

212

each other for a moment before it disappeared again and I made another attempt to get upright.

'Bloody hell, Izzy! Stop wriggling, or I really will drop you!' Rob said as I squirmed about. I took the combined advantage of him steadying himself upright, and years of ballet lessons to whip my legs out in a kick, unhooking them from his arm. I gave him a shove, causing him to let go so that he didn't end up in the pond himself and then took off as fast as my welly-encased feet would take me. The Winchesters had a beautiful garden but I suddenly wished it were smaller as I pelted towards the kitchen.

About ten seconds later I was flat on my back on top of Rob, also flat on his back on the snow, his arms wrapped tightly around me.

'You're quite feisty when you want to be, aren't you?' he said behind me. I could hear the smile in his voice.

'You're quite an arse when you want to be, aren't you?'

He laughed and the reverberation in his chest caused a funny sensation in my own. At least, that's what I told myself caused it.

'I need longer legs.'

'No you don't.'

'I'd move a lot faster.'

'You wouldn't be you.'

'Yes, I would. I'd just be a taller, faster me.'

I made a startled noise as he rolled in the snow, shifting our position, flipping me over in the process.

'Which means you would take longer to catch.'

'Well, duh. That's rather the point!'

He laughed again. 'Did you just "duh" me? I'm thinking we might just take a trip back to that fishpond …'

I started wriggling as he tried to grab me.

'You look like a marshmallow in that jacket.'

Well, I guess that answered my question as to whether the coat had been a fashion fail or not. I paused in my wriggling to give him a look.

'No, it's good. I like marshmallows,' he said, trying to dig his way out of the hole he'd just put himself in. 'They have soft, squishy centres.'

'No!' I squealed as a cold hand snaked under my jacket and started tickling. The reaction caused me to fling about even more, which Rob thought was hilarious until I accidentally kneed him in the groin. His breath caught and his whole body went still before he rolled to the side with a groan.

'Oh God! I'm so sorry! Your hands were cold and I'm really ticklish. Are you all right? Rob?' Another groan.

I shuffled across and bent over him. 'Are you OK?' I asked again, softer this time.

He rolled in the snow, so that he was on his back, his legs still drawn up. 'If you don't like me, you could just say so, you know. It might be less painful on the whole.'

'Don't say that. And this time was an accident!' He really did look in pain. 'Are you all right?'

'It's fine.' The strain in his voice told me it was far from fine. 'I hadn't decided on the whole kids thing anyway. Thanks for sorting that out for me.'

'Is it really that bad? Is there anything I can do?' The pain on his face was clearly genuine, as was that gorgeous crooked smile that broke through it. I put a hand on his chest. 'But if you say anything remotely in the realms of rubbing it better, I will leave you here to freeze.'

'Never crossed my mind.'

I raised an eyebrow at him.

'I really wish I'd dropped you in the fishpond now.'

'I seem to remember you were closer to ending up in it than me,' I said, casting a glance down at him.

Rob's hand caught around my waist, pulling me down onto the snow as he moved so that he was now looking down at me. I could feel the snow soaking into my jeans even more, but I didn't want to move. I knew it was pathetic but if this was all

214

I ever got, the only chance I ever had to look up and see Rob looking down at me, then I was going to take it.

'Are you all right?' he asked, his voice softening. 'You look funny.'

'Of course I'm all right!' I laughed. 'You know you need to work on your compliments. In the past couple of days I've looked tired, like a marshmallow and now funny.'

He didn't reply but I saw his gaze drop to my mouth, momentarily. 'Izzy ...'

A flame of hope blazed, as the smile I gave him was returned. 'Look, I—'

'Rob!' his mum called out into the garden. Rob turned his head, then quickly shot up and away from me before I could take a breath. 'Caroline's here,' his mum finished. Her tone was pleasant but had an underlying quality, as though she'd just discovered that Harold had temporarily forgotten he was toilet trained. I pushed myself up into a sitting position and saw Caroline watching us, a look of forced amusement on her face. Rob put his hand down to help me up but I waved it away and shoved myself up. My whole lower body was now soaked through and I'd started shivering.

'Oh God, you're freezing.' Rob made to put his arms around me but I stepped away, towards the house.

'No, I'm fine. I'm going to go and take a shower and warm up.' I crunched off and heard his boots falling heavily behind mine.

'Izzy.'

I purposely waited until we were within earshot of the open door of the kitchen.

'Umhmm?' I answered, leaning on the doorframe to pull my boots off.

Rob gave me a look. I returned it. The silence said it all. Whatever it was that he wanted to say, he couldn't say in front of Caroline, or anyone else. And I was done with it all.

'Just a friendly game of snowballs,' I said to Caroline as she scanned the state of me. 'Rob lost.'

'Is that so?' she replied, apparently unconvinced that snowballs was the only game being played. And as unlikely as it seemed, for once, I agreed with her. I had no idea if there was another game going on here or not. But what I did know was that I wasn't playing anymore. This might all be a joke for Rob – 'nice' as he put it – but it wasn't for me. For a moment there I thought … well it didn't matter what I thought. The fact that he'd sprung away from me the moment he saw Caroline spoke far more than anything he could have said. And he might be happy with the odd snog, a 'friends with benefits' thing, if that was what he was thinking, but that most definitely wasn't my scene. Not even with Rob. Especially not with Rob.

'You didn't arrive. So I thought I'd come to you. I guessed you'd become distracted.' She looked at me as she said this. It was obvious she thought that I was the distraction and also obvious that she couldn't understand why.

'Oh hell. Yep. Sorry. Give me five minutes,' Rob said, and headed out to the stairs.

'Are you all right, dear?' his mum asked, 'Would you like a hot drink or something?'

'I'll have a shower first but then I might take you up on that.' I smiled at her and turned to head off to my room, not missing the glare Caroline was sending my way.

'Bye, Caroline. Have a lovely evening,' I said, sounding as genuine as I could.

'Thanks. I'm sure we will.'

Touché, Caroline.

216

Chapter 17

I'd spent the last several hours on Jenny's dress and my back was killing me. My thoughts had been darting about since the snowy encounter with Rob earlier and I needed to get it out of my mind. I thought a walk with Harold might help loosen up a few tense muscles and clear my head. I made my proposal to the Winchesters and received several offers of company which I thanked them for but declined. The only company I wanted tonight was Harold. I just hoped we didn't meet a long-legged lady dog because I really couldn't take two hits of rejection quite so close together today.

Taking the dog out had been a good move. I was getting exercise which was good and it was actually clearing my head. I knew I had to get a grip on this thing with Rob, seeing as how it was perfectly clear that, whatever he'd been thinking in the snow, it was unimportant enough to get knocked into oblivion the moment he saw Caroline. It was stupid of me to ever think that he'd look at me in that way anyway. Every woman I'd ever seen him with was a variation on a theme of Carolines. A fact his mum had backed up when she had commented on his predilection for the "obvious" after he'd hastily made it plain that he and I were not a couple.

I was nothing like her – or them. And I didn't want to be. OK, yes, I wanted longer legs but show me a woman that doesn't! The rest of it I was actually quite happy with. But I wasn't someone that would make Rob look twice – removal of stockings aside. That wasn't something I could change, and I had to deal with that. And I would. First off, I decided, crunching along with Harold, I would go back to seeing Rob just occasionally. That might happen on its own, of course. I mean, Rob had been trying to contact me because he wanted to check I was doing all right. Now he knew I was. And then the rest of it mostly came about by accident and because of the wedding and that would be over soon.

I knew I'd be keeping in contact with Jenny as we'd grown close, which I was really happy about, and I absolutely loved Mike. Their happiness inspired me. I couldn't wait to have a picture of them up on my studio wall. But keeping in touch with Jenny didn't mean I had to keep in touch – too much – with Rob. At least not until I got over him. Right, so basically I was planning to call him in about five to ten years.

I let out an audible groan. Harold stopped and looked round at me, snow frozen on his whiskers. 'Just ignore me, Harold,' I said, which he took as a command and went back to investigating the snow as we marched along.

The walk I'd planned and the one I ended up on were very different in distance, as I somehow managed to take a wrong turn and found myself wandering into the village. It was lit with white Christmas lights and a beautiful, huge Norwegian Pine stood in the square, looking like an enormous cake decoration with snow on its branches and a star twinkling from its summit. I slowed my pace and peered in shop windows, Harold patiently matching his walk to mine as I cast my eyes over books, antiques and jewellery. A couple of restaurants had their signs lit and appeared to be open, as was the local pub, signalled by the few souls desperately trying to gather warmth from a patio heater in the outside designated smoking area.

I wandered around in a loop and started to head back, passing an Italian restaurant on my way. I stopped to have a look at the menu. Pricey but the choice looked delicious. I walked on, glancing in as I passed the window. It looked busy, considering the period and the snow so I took that to mean it must have a pretty good reputation. Which was probably why Rob had chosen to take Caroline there. Her chartreuse coloured dress caught my eye, and I couldn't help but stare. She was leaning towards him, her hand resting on his, his face serious. The candlelight highlighted their matching cheekbones. They looked perfect together. Eleanor might not be keen on Caroline, but I was pretty sure she'd get some beautiful grandchildren from the deal. Caroline lifted her hand and laid it on Rob's cheek. I backed up quickly, feeling sick, and promptly fell over the dog who had been sitting patiently the whole time I'd been torturing myself.

I lay in the snow for a few moments, feeling a little dazed, and a lot idiotic. Harold nuzzled my face. 'I'm OK, boy.' I shoved myself up and picked up the lead, brushing snow off myself as the two of us turned back towards the Winchesters' home.

It certainly seemed longer going back than it had coming and I hoped I was actually heading in the right direction. I'd texted Jenny to say we'd walked further than I planned so that they didn't worry. I kept Harold in his reflective dog coat to the inside of the lane. My marshmallow jacket, whilst not reflective was at least white so I hoped that we'd be visible enough to any cars that did pass, not that we'd seen a whole lot of traffic at all throughout the evening. Most people, sensibly, seemed to be staying indoors.

The sound of a car approaching from behind made me shift a little more to the side of the lane. It slowed, so I stopped and shuffled the dog and myself further in again even though there was plenty of room by now. Whispers of anxiety started to build within me. I wasn't really worried but I couldn't shake off the knowledge that I was in the middle of nowhere, on my own, except for a dog. I had a good idea that Harold, soppy as he was, would challenge anyone who threatened me but there was no way I was putting that gorgeous dog in harm's way. The vehicle still didn't gain speed and I reluctantly turned my head to see what was going on.

The car pulled level.

'You scared the crap out of me!' I blasted Rob when he buzzed the window down. 'I thought you were a kerb crawler or something.'

'What are you doing out?'

'I'm not on day release from the local prison. I am allowed out.'

'You know what I mean.'

'I fancied a walk so Harold came too. But I got a bit lost and ended up going a bit further than planned.'

'You look frozen.'

'I'm all right.'

'Come on, get in. We can go the rest of the way back together.'

'No really, it's fine. It's not far now.' I paused and looked up at Rob, who was now out of the car and opening the boot for the dog to jump into anyway which he did with enthusiasm. 'Is it?'

'Not in the car, no. And Harold's in there now so I don't think walking down here on your own is a good idea.'

A nice warm car, which I had noticed immediately was Caroline-less, did seem appealing right now. But I didn't really want to mess up Rob's seats with my wet clothes. To be honest, I didn't want to him to know I was wet at all as that would mean having to explain my clumsiness – which, after an evening spent with Caroline, would merely serve to highlight my lack of grace.

'Why are you wet?' He frowned at me.

Bugger.

'Yes, that. I sort of fell over the dog. And don't think I can't see that smile just because it's dark.'

'I'm sorry. Are you hurt?'

'I'm fine. Luckily the snow cushioned my fall. But, as you pointed out, I am now wet which is why I'm not getting in your expensive car and ruining the seats.'

'You won't ruin them. They're leather. It'll wipe off. Come on, get in please, Izz. I don't want you getting ill because you got cold and wet. Jenny would kill me for a start.'

'I'll be fine. You fuss too much.' He opened his mouth to say something. but I got there first. 'So where's Caroline?'

'Home,' he said, indicating with his hand for me to get in, which I did.

He shut the door, walked round to the driver's side and stepped up into the car, pulling the door closed behind him. We drove along in silence which Rob seemed disinclined to break. I, on the other hand, didn't last two minutes.

'Did you have a nice evening?'

'Nice enough.'

The silence returned.

'So, you went for dinner?'

'Yes.'

The words blood and stone came to mind.

'So, what did you talk about? Anything interesting?'

'No, not really.'

'Right.' That made sense. From what I'd seen and heard of Caroline, conversation wasn't especially her strong suit, and I guessed that wasn't Rob's main interest in her anyway. I gave up, laid my head against the glass and rode the rest of the way home in the silence that had now once more descended.

We arrived back at the Winchesters', the car tyres crunching over snow and gravel as Rob pulled up. I slid out of my seat and followed him to the back of the car to get Harold out. Rob popped the boot. The dog was sprawled out, snoring. Rob chuckled.

'You really did wear him out.'

'Is he all right? I mean, he'll be OK?' I'd never had a dog. Could you over-walk them? I didn't know.

Oh my God, they'd invited me for Christmas and I'd broken their dog!

'He's fine!' Rob rubbed my shoulder, reassuringly. 'He's just had a lot of excitement over the last few days and he's catching up on his sleep. He always falls asleep in my car for some reason. Bearing in mind you did the same thing, I'm beginning to wonder if it's got something to do with my scintillating company.'

'Always a possibility.'

'Thanks.'

'You're welcome.'

'Come on, boy.' Rob cajoled the dog a little, and as he shuffled towards the opening, Rob scooped him up and lifted him down out of the vehicle. Harold toddled off in the direction of the house as Rob reached in, grabbed the lead and closed the boot. He pressed a button and a soft sound signalled the car was now locked.

'You need to get out of those clothes. Wet clothes, I mean,' he amended hastily.

'On my way.' I hesitated. 'I haven't broken Harold, have I?'

Rob laughed and gave me a squish. 'No. You haven't broken him.'

I nodded, pushing away from the hug as politely as I could. All I could smell was Caroline's perfume.

'It's perfect!' Jenny said, looking at herself in the mirrors her dad had produced after a rummage in the loft, garage and next door, and which now gave Jen a full view of herself in her wedding dress.

'I just need to take in that tiny bit I've just pinned and then we'll be done.' I had to admit I was glad. It had been a lot of work and I'd been up until two the last couple of nights making sure it was finished with the decorative work we'd designed. Jenny had said to leave it off but that wasn't my style. We'd decided on a design and that was exactly what she was going to get. The look on everyone's face as she stood there, supported by her dad and brother, told me the long hours had been worth it.

'Right, let's get you out then.'

Rob and his dad left the room for a few minutes as Eleanor and I helped Jen out of the dress, and her braces, and she pulled her T-shirt and leggings back on. The men wandered back in, just as I was hanging the dress back up from a window catch. Or trying to. I really did need longer legs.

'Need a hand with that?' Rob asked, taking it from me and hooking it easily.

'Jen, have you seen—' Mike took a step back as a cacophony of noises and shouts greeted him. He'd had his head down, looking at something on his phone, when he'd stepped in – but at the noise he looked up, startled. The moment he'd walked in, I'd yanked Rob's bulk in front of the dress and then stood in front of him, my arms spread. Logically I knew I wasn't adding much effectiveness but panic won out over logic. After hiding the dress from Mike for the past couple of weeks, I wasn't about to have him see it two days before the wedding.

'Sorry, sorry!' Mike slapped a hand over his eyes and made to go out backwards.

'Don't do that! You'll trip and that's all we need!' Eleanor bustled up to him. 'Keep your hand up. The conservatory is out of bounds, Michael!' she chided him gently.

'Sorry. Forgot.'

John rolled his eyes, smiled and wandered out after them.

When they'd gone, Jenny looked worried. 'Do you think he saw it?'

'No, I don't.' She didn't look convinced. 'Really, Jen, I don't. He had his head down when he came in and by the time he looked up, this lump' – I thumbed at Rob – 'was blocking his view of the dress completely.'

'Er, excuse me? Lump?'

I ignored him. 'Honestly, Jen. He didn't.'

'Jen, don't worry. Not only was I in front of it, but Izzy was in front of me, with her arms spread out, so that made all the difference.'

Jenny's face lost its concern, replaced with a giggle. I gave her brother a look. 'You're hilarious.'

He pulled a face back and then did an impression of me jumping in front of him with my arms out.

His sister giggled again. I covered my smile, and looked at his bare feet.

'Mind your feet. I wouldn't want you to step on a pin.' My tone suggested otherwise. Only because I knew it wasn't going to happen. My mega magnetic pin cushion had been scooted over the floor several times as I already had anxiety about the dog coming across one. Rob wiggled his eyebrows at me.

'I'll get onto this now,' I said, pointing at the dress. 'It won't take long.'

'I'm going to go and find my fiancé and have a talk.'

She wheeled out and I looked at Rob. 'Do you think he's in trouble?'

'Only for about a minute. He didn't see anything. No harm done.'

'Sorry about manhandling you. You were the biggest thing close to hand.'

He laughed. 'First I'm a lump, now I'm a thing. Talk about being objectified.'

'Oh pfft! You love it.'

'Maybe.'

I tossed a look over my shoulder before reaching up for the dress. He leant over me and got it back down.

'Thanks,' I said, taking it and turning it inside out to look at where I needed to make this final alteration.

'It looks amazing, Izz. You're amazing. I can't believe you've done all this in so short a time.'

'Needs must,' I said, concentrating on the dress.

'You've made her so happy.'

'Rubbish. She's marrying someone she's crazy about. That's what's making her happy. I'm just helping with the decoration of something that's already beautiful.'

'Izzy, she wanted a beautiful dress. You've given her one. It's …' he paused, 'added to her happiness immensely.' He was looking out of the window, and I knew he was waiting for me to argue.

I smiled. 'OK, I'll give you that one. And it's been a pleasure. She deserves it.'

He laid his hands on my shoulders. 'You're a good person.'

I wobbled my head. 'I try.'

He laughed and squeezed my shoulders, suddenly stopping. 'Blimey, Izz. Your muscles are one solid knot.'

That, I did not need telling. My neck had been aching badly for the last couple of days, and my back wasn't great either.

'Yeah I know. It'll go off.'

'Put that down a minute.'

'No, I just need to get this done. I'll be done in a bit.'

'Do you ever do anything you're told.'

'Very occasionally.' I smiled, concentrating on my work.

Rob made an exasperated sound and flopped into a chair across from me. I glanced up a few minutes later as I heard his breathing even and slow. His head rested on his hand and his long lashes cast shadows on his cheek. His mum was right. He did work long hours. I stood and switched off the light that was over him, and left the task light on, enabling me to get on with my work.

A couple of hours later, and I was done. I put the dress back in its garment carrier to protect it and pulled out the hanger to hook it back up on the window, stretching to reach. I glanced around for something to stand on. The chairs were all far too heavy to move without making a noise and waking Rob. I opted to lay it across one of them for the moment and then go and ask John to come and hang it up out of the way for me.

'Do you want that hung back up?' Rob asked, his voice sounding sleepy and sexy as he came over to take the dress from me.

'Yes. Please. Did I wake you?'

'No. Are you finished?'

'Yep. All done.' I stood back, my hands automatically going to my neck where the pain was shooting from. My head had started thumping about half an hour previously and I really just wanted to lie down.

'Come here.' Rob tugged me gently towards him, and placed his hands on my shoulders. His fingers and thumbs began carefully kneading at the knots. I started to pull away. This really didn't seem a good idea.

'I'm all right, Rob. Really.'

'Izz, sit down a sec.'

I obeyed, for the simple reason that I felt like I was about to fall down anyway. His hands moved over my skin, the touch gentle but firm. I still felt like crap with my head pounding but my neck was definitely feeling better. In fact, the more he did it, the better I felt. Everywhere. Which wasn't good.

Not good at all. Except …

'Oh God, that's good.' The words slipped out before I could stop them.

Rob chuckled and I realised how it sounded.

'Oh no!' I jumped away, my face flushing and the movement exacerbating my head. 'That, um, sounded …'

'Fine to me.' He gave that deep chuckle again.

'Rob, don't.' I flopped back down into an armchair, tucked my feet up and closed my eyes.

'Izzy?' His voice was serious now.

'I've just got a bit of a headache.'

The back of his hand felt soothing and cool on my forehead and I wanted him to leave it there forever.

'Stay there,' he said and disappeared off.

I had no intention of staying there to be administered to. Flicking off the light next to me, I pushed myself out of the chair, groaning as the pain in my head sliced with every move I made. The moonlight flooding in through the glass guided me out of the conservatory and I padded quietly through the kitchen and out into the hall and up the stairs. A little lie down and I'd feel much better. It had been the truth when I'd said it had been a pleasure making the dress for Jenny, but there was no denying it had taken a lot out of me to get it done in time. And, it turned out, discovering you're in love with a man who isn't in love with you and is in fact cosying up to someone else can be quite tiring too. And thinking about all those things then kept you awake at night so, all in all, it wasn't an ideal situation. As much as I'd loved being here, I was looking forward to getting back to London and putting some sort of normality back in my life and some sort of distance between me and Rob.

'I see you took my advice, once again.' Rob's voice came up the stairs with more than a hint of exasperation to it.

'I'm just going to lie down for a while.'

He stepped on to the landing. 'Mike's going to take a look at you. I told him you didn't look good.'

'Thanks! I bet you told him that Caroline looked great though!' I threw my hands up in the air and carried on walking away from him into the bedroom. Then I sprinted for the bathroom and threw up. When I came back into the bedroom, Mike and Rob were both standing there waiting. This day just kept getting better and better.

'I'm fine. I'm just going to have an early night. Mike, would you mind making my apologies to everyone?'

'Of course. Once I check you over.'

I glared at Rob. 'Mike, I said I'm fine.'

'You don't look fine and you just threw up. Sit, please.'

'All boys together,' I replied grumpily and made a show of sitting down heavily on the bed.

Mike took my temperature, pulse, checked my breathing and blood pressure and asked various doctor-y questions while I sat on the bed, just wanting to go to sleep. I'd told Rob he didn't need to stay but, taking a tip from me it would seem, he chose to do his own thing and stayed anyway, leaning on the wall and watching the proceedings. I was too tired to ask him twice and was pretty sure he'd ignore me for a second time anyway. I had a feeling he was going to want to talk about my Caroline quip, which was even more reason for me to avoid that conversation by going to sleep.

'I can't find anything obvious. All your vitals are good although your temperature is a bit up which I'd like to keep an eye on. I think you've probably just been overdoing it.' He paused. 'Don't think we don't all know you've been up until the small hours working on that dress.'

My eyes widened. 'But I was quiet!'

He smiled. 'Yep, you were. But everyone could see how much more tired you were looking every day. It doesn't take a brain surgeon to figure it out. Which is lucky, because that's not my area of speciality.'

I dropped my head down to my chest. 'Great. I thought it was just him who thought I looked like hell. I didn't realise there was a consensus of opinion.' I let myself fall to the side and snuggled my head into the pillow. Oh that felt good. Almost as good as Rob's neck rub. Almost. There wasn't much that could feel better than that. Not anything that was available to me, anyway.

'I think that's a pretty good idea,' Mike said, 'although actually getting into bed would be more beneficial. I recommend staying there until as late as possible tomorrow too. You need to be fit for this wedding. I can see Jenny postponing it if you're not!'

I pulled myself upright and looked up to where he was now standing over me. 'Understood. Thank you. Sorry if I was a grump. I'm just tired.'

'You are. Tired, I mean. Not a grump. Although, technically

228

you are that too but as I'm part of the reason behind your tiredness and therefore grumpiness, I'm happy to let it go.'

'Thank you.' I gave him a hug.

'You're welcome. Now, get some rest.'

'Yes, Doctor.'

Mike chuckled, and left the room, briefly nodding at Rob as he did so.

'You heard the doc,' I said. 'I need to get to bed, which means jammie time so if you wouldn't mind …' I made a little waving motion with my hand.

'I'm going to be just outside. Shout when you're changed.'

'What? Why?'

He'd already closed the door behind him. I wondered how long he'd wait out there. The way I felt, I was pretty sure I was going to be asleep soon so all I had to do was delay him coming in until …

'If I don't hear from you within three minutes, I'm coming back in anyway.' I heard a chuckle in answer to my scream of frustration.

I changed into my pyjamas then cleaned my teeth. This seemed like the best plan just in case Rob made good on coming back into the room before I called him. At least this way I'd be fully clothed. It actually turned out to be unnecessary because he did wait and I did call him. Five minutes later. Petty? Yep. Just chalk it up alongside grumpy.

I was burrowed into the duvet with only half my face peeping out when I called him back in. He poked his head around the door.

'Hi.'

'Hi.'

'You OK?'

'Yes. But you didn't need to call Mike.' I pulled the duvet down under my chin to unmuffle my words.

'I was worried about you.' He stepped into the room and soft light from the bedside lamp caught his features, all of which showed concern. My stomach knotted and I knew it wasn't anything to do with being overtired.

'You don't need to be. You heard Mike. I'm fine.'

'That's not exactly what he said.'

'I just need some sleep. Something you're preventing from happening.'

'So this is all my fault.'

'Yes, it is,' I said, with more feeling than intended.

Rob walked into the bathroom and came back a minute later with a glass of water which he put on my bedside. Crouching down beside me, he tucked the duvet around me a little more and then gently laid a hand on my forehead, pushing aside a curl that had come loose out of my hastily tied plait. He didn't say a word about what I'd said about Caroline.

'Rob, about what I said.'

'Ssh, it doesn't matter. Just close your eyes.'

Chapter 18

When I woke up at three o'clock the next afternoon, I was alone and feeling much better. Twenty hours, give or take, of straight sleep was a cure for many things it would seem. I had even come up with a plan for making this evening more bearable; all I had to do was avoid Rob and Caroline for most of the evening and then head out around half eleven so that there was no chance of having to watch them locking lips as they welcomed in the New Year. From what I'd heard, it was a fairly large gathering so avoidance shouldn't be too much of an issue. I could do this. I had a plan!

'Izzy! How are you?' Jenny said, coming up to me as I popped my head in to the living room. Her hair was drying in rollers on her head. I giggled and poked one of the foam sausages.

'Much better. Thanks. Sorry about being such a drama queen.'

'Don't be silly, darling.' Eleanor came up, putting her arms around my shoulders. 'Of course you weren't! I should have kept a better eye on you.'

'No! Please don't feel bad! It was nothing to do with you. In fact, I got much better treatment here than I would have at home, so I ought to be thanking you.'

She squeezed my shoulders. 'Are you sure you're all right now?'

'Yes. Positive.'

'Then I'll make us all a nice cup of tea. We've got some peace and quiet for a bit. The boys have all gone out mountain biking.'

'Perfect!' I glanced out of the window and saw the snow still thick on the ground. 'Rather them than me though. Test run for tomorrow?' I said to Jen, pointing at my own head.

'Yep,' she said, her hand going to the rollers.

'Nervous?' I asked, folding myself into an armchair.

'Not really. Is that weird?'

'Not at all.'

'I thought maybe I'm supposed to be.'

'Of course not. Everyone's different. I think it's great that you're relaxed about it all.'

'I may of course turn into Bridezilla overnight.'

'You wouldn't be my first, and I'm certain you won't be my last. Don't let this petite frame fool you, I'm tougher than I look!'

Jenny giggled. 'Noted.'

We set about getting ourselves comfy with our tea, books and blankets. An hour later, the peace was shattered as three noisy blokes and one excited and very tired dog came clattering into the kitchen.

'Don't let Harold in here until you've washed him off!' Eleanor called.

'Already done,' came the call back.

We heard the kettle boiling and a few minutes later, the men all traipsed in, each one looking thoroughly mud splattered.

'The ground's frozen. How did you three manage to find mud?'

'It's an art.' John bowed.

'Nice look, sis.' Rob chuckled and made a face at Mike.

'Thanks,' Jenny replied, before slapping Mike's hand away from where he'd now started fiddling with the rollers.

'You look a lot better, I'm relieved to see.' Rob crouched down beside my chair.

I turned, seeing his handsome mud-splodged face close to mine. 'Thanks. I'm feeling a lot better.'

'So you're coming tonight?'

'I am. Your mum's been telling me that there are several eligible bachelors around so I thought I might look out for some mistletoe.'

'Did she mention they're all in their eighties?'

'How very ageist of you.'

'You're definitely feeling better,' he said, standing back up. 'I'm going to take a shower.'

And off he went, the others taking a cue and heading off to various en-suites to do the same. Harold watched them go before wandering over to his bed and stepping in. He turned around three times then flopped down heavily, and within five minutes was on his back, feet in the air, snoring softly.

The hotel ballroom had been turned into a real winter wonderland with surprisingly real looking icicles, glittering lights and several large ice sculptures. It was hard to believe that tomorrow it would be transformed once again into the reception venue for Mike and Jenny's wedding. The men were staying here this evening and us girls were all piling back to the house so that we could get ready in peace tomorrow. Mike's two sisters, Jenny's bridesmaids, were arriving tomorrow. Luckily their dresses had been drama free.

Mike and Rob had taken all their gear down to the hotel earlier in Rob's car and Mike now came to meet us.

'Don't you all look lovely!' He spread his arms and gave Eleanor and me a hug, and shook John's hand, before bestowing even more compliments on his bride-to-be. I watched as he did so, the love so evident in both their faces.

'Where's Rob?' Eleanor asked.

Mike glanced up, an awkward expression on his face. 'Oh. He … err … went to pick up Caroline.'

233

'What?' Jenny thumped her fiancé on the shoulder. 'I thought that was all over.'

It was?

'Oi! It's not my fault,' Mike replied, rubbing his shoulder.

'No, I know. Sorry.' She pulled him to her again and kissed him, whispering something to him that, whatever it was, apparently ensured forgiveness, judging by the now dopey look on his face.

'Well!' Eleanor said, gathering me on one arm, and John on the other. 'Let's go and introduce you to some people, shall we?'

Several hours later, I was having a much better time than I'd expected to. The Winchesters had effected introductions with what seemed like the entire village and I even had a few likely commissions from it, including an entire bridal party and two Ascot dresses. I also seemed to have acquired an admirer. Callum Andrews wasn't as drop dead on the spot gorgeous as Rob, but he was nice, making me laugh and happily flirting with me even though I wasn't returning the flirts. The last thing I wanted to be doing right now was leading someone on. It was clear Callum had got the message but, as we were both enjoying the banter, he'd apparently decided to continue anyway. Rob had finally come up to me a little while ago, followed closely by Caroline of course. She gave me one of her icy smiles before looking my dress up and down.

'Your dress is beautiful.' The fact that she practically choked on the words gave me a clue to the fact that her compliment, amazingly, was genuine.

'Thank you,' I replied.

Clearly bored with me, she turned her attention to my company. 'Callum, darling! I haven't seen you in so long. Are you still running that funny hedge fund of yours?' She slid her hand along his arm and batted superbly thick false eyelashes at him.

'That's right,' he replied, expertly extricating his arm and picking up his champagne glass, 'although we tend to avoid calling them funny. It makes our clients nervous.'

'Do you mind if I borrow Izzy a minute?' Rob asked Callum, placing his hand on my back and steering me away without waiting for an answer.

'Oh, Callum! You're so funny!' Caroline's voice followed by the tinkly laugh trailed behind us. I glanced back. Callum gave me a look that said 'Help' and threw Rob one that said something else entirely.

I pulled an apologetic face at him, and signalled that I'd just be two minutes. I caught Rob observing the exchange, that impassive expression back on his face. It seemed that Caroline was a little bit friendlier when she'd had several glasses of alcohol, a fact that Callum didn't seem to be especially enjoying.

I looked up at Rob, waiting for him to say something. When he didn't, I turned to go. 'I really ought to get back to Callum.'

'Worried Caroline's going to snag him?'

I levelled a look at Rob. 'Yes. That's exactly what I'm worried about,' I replied, my voice dripping with sarcasm. 'Unlike you, he doesn't seem to be quite so swayed by her beauty and giraffe length legs. Lucky for me.' I turned to go. Rob caught my arm.

'I'm sorry. That wasn't what I came to say at all.'

I turned back to face him but said nothing. For once, I managed to keep silent until he was forced to say something.

'I just wanted to say that you look beautiful. I mean, you always do, but tonight' – he smiled – 'in that dress? It's no wonder Callum's falling over himself for you.'

'He seems nice.'

Rob shrugged. 'He's all right.'

I laughed. 'Robert Winchester, are you jealous?'

'What?'

'You are!' I glanced back over at where Caroline was still cooing at Callum. 'Look, she's just probably had one too many cocktails and getting a little friendlier than normal. She even complimented me so she's obviously not feeling quite herself.' I wiggled his arm, trying to get a smile.

'Callum's loaded. I mean, ridiculously so. Caroline's been after him for years.'

'Oh come on, Rob. You're not doing too bad yourself. I'm pretty sure you could keep her in the style to which she's become accustomed.'

'I … what?'

'What?'

'You think Caroline and I are an item?'

'Rob. Please. I'm not stupid, and neither is your family. They're not happy, which I'm sure you've already gathered, but it's your life. You have to do what's going to make you happy. Now if you don't mind, I'm going to rescue Callum.' I walked away from Rob, and relief flooded Callum's face as I made a point of returning to his company. I didn't miss the look Caroline threw me but I didn't much care. Rob could deal with her.

'I thought you'd abandoned me!' Callum offered his arm and manoeuvred us away from them both.

'I wouldn't do that! Now come on, I believe you promised me a dance earlier.' Callum smiled and held out his hand, leading me to the dance floor.

A few dances later, I begged off and found a seat whilst Callum went to find us both a drink. Jenny and Mike appeared at my side.

'You seem to have made a friend.' Jenny raised her eyebrows.

'Friend being the key word.'

'Does he know that?'

'He does.' And he did. I'd reiterated it on the dance floor. I had no wish to lead Callum on. He'd made what might have been a difficult evening pleasant and even fun. There was no way I was going to repay that by hurting him.

'What's wrong with him?' Jenny asked.

'Callum? Nothing! I like him. I'm just not sure he's for me.'

'He seems to think otherwise.'

I made a dismissive sound. There wasn't anything wrong with

Callum at all. He really was very nice. But he wasn't Rob and I knew that getting together with Callum now would be unfair on both of us.

'Rebounds are a bad idea,' I said.

'Rebound?' Jenny repeated.

Oh shit! Did I say that out loud? I'd only had a couple of champagnes the whole night, preferring to stick with water this evening what with the wedding tomorrow, but apparently I was still a little too chatty.

'Yes. I mean. You know, the whole wedding non-wedding thing.'

'Right,' she said, glancing at Mike. I could tell they didn't believe a word.

'What time is it?' I said, changing the subject.

Mike tilted his wrist. 'Ten to twelve.'

'I need to go,' I said, jumping up from my chair.

Mike pulled a face and laughed. 'Why? I don't think you have to worry about turning into a pumpkin at midnight. Or do you? I mean, everyone's been going gaga over your dress ... maybe there is a fairy godmother involved somewhere.'

Jenny blinked at him, then gave him a playful whack. 'How many have you had? You do know you're getting married tomorrow, don't you? Hangover Chic is not a good look.' She turned to me. 'I apologise for my inebriated, apparently delusional fiancé. But he did have a valid question.'

'Oh, Jen.' I flopped back down on the chair. 'I just need to go.'

She looked at me for a long moment. 'OK,' she said softly, 'give me a hug before you do though.' I hugged her close and told her I'd see her in the morning.

'Here you are!' Callum appeared in front of me as I straightened.

'Callum! I was just coming to find you.'

He threw a grin at Mike and Jen. 'Lucky me!'

'I'm heading home, but I wanted to say thank you for your company this evening. I really enjoyed it.'

237

'You're leaving before midnight on New Year's Eve? Is that even legal?'

'I know it's frowned upon but I'm pretty sure it's still legal.'

'I think we ought to check for sure. Where's that brother of yours?' he said to Jenny, casting his gaze around the room. 'He's a legal bod, isn't he?'

'No!' I said, a little bit too enthusiastically. The last thing I needed was Rob turning up and giving me a grilling as to why I was leaving early. I'd already blabbed once this evening. There was no guarantee of it not happening again. Jenny and Mike might know I was fibbing but I was fairly sure they didn't know the reason. Rob, on the other hand, with his knack of knowing exactly what I was thinking, might be harder to deal with.

'I mean, I'm pretty sure he's more entertainingly engaged at the moment.'

'Caroline certainly is.' Jenny said, indicating a spot in front of her with her glass where Caroline was flirting madly with a very good looking bar tender.

'A barman?' Mike asked, voicing the thought we were all having.

'Oh, that'll be just for tonight. He doesn't earn anything near what she needs.'

'Jen,' I cautioned.

'No. Jenny's absolutely right.' Callum said, 'We all grew up in this village. Caroline's been like this for as long as I can remember.'

'But what about Rob?' I asked.

'Oh, they probably had an argument because he didn't get her invited to the wedding. She's making him pay.'

'I see. Actually he said something earlier about him and her not being an item.'

'They're not an item. They're sex.'

'Meet my fiancée.' Mike laughed. 'She tells it like it is.' They clinked glasses and he kissed her. I loved Jenny but I really could have done without having that image put in my head.

'Anyway! Like I said, I'm off.'

'But it's nearly midnight. You may as well stay now!' Callum tried, encouraged by Jenny and Mike.

As if on cue, a loudspeaker turned on and a countdown began which everyone enthusiastically began joining in with.

Ten!

'I really need to go.'

Nine!

'Oh, come on, Izzy. Have a heart!' Callum turned puppy dog eyes on me.

'Now, that's not fair!' I chided.

Six!

'Just a peck on the cheek, I promise!'

Five!

'Callum.' Four!

'I'm really sorry, mate!' Rob interrupted, rushing up to us all and sliding a little on the polished floor. 'But I've been waiting years for this.'

As party poppers banged, streamers hooted, and balloons rained from the roof, Rob took my face in his big, warm hands and kissed me, gently at first but with an intensity that increased quickly as he slid his hands down and wrapped his arms around me, holding so tight I was literally pinned against him. And all I wanted was more. He moved slightly and I freed my hands, sliding one around his waist, and the other reaching up to the back of his neck. I wanted to pull him closer, feel him everywhere, and prolong the headiness that I knew was nothing to do with either glass of champagne. Finally he pulled away gently, and just looked at me, a searching, concentrated look that I knew was for me, and only me. He let go, then quickly caught my hand and pulled me gently to the side, away from the main crowd. His arms immediately went around me again, but I held back. We'd been here before.

Chapter 19

'If you say that was nice, I take no responsibility for what happens next. You know that, don't you?'

'It *was* nice. Wait!' Seeing my expression, his face went serious. 'Izzy. I'm sorry. I probably shouldn't have done that.'

Yep, we'd definitely been here before. I made to move away. 'I think I should go.'

'No! Izz. Let me explain.'

'Rob, I'm not here for you to make Caroline jealous. I'm not—'

'What?'

'Isn't that what this is all about?'

'No!' he said, rubbing his hair. 'This is about the fact that I've been in love with you since the moment Steven introduced me to you four years ago. It's about the fact that I had to sit and watch whilst he got to go home with you. And that I had to sit and watch when he left you standing in that church, and that I had to tell you he wasn't coming and watch what that did to you – and me, come to think of it.' He rubbed his nose and gave a little smile.

I, meanwhile, was just staring at him.

'Izzy. If it had been up to me that day, I'd have gone back out there and married you myself because that's all I've ever wanted.

240

I knew it about a week after meeting you and nothing's changed.'

Eventually I found some words. 'But, Caroline? You and her. You're … I mean.'

'We're nothing. I hooked back up with her because when you explained your five-year plan to my family, it was pretty clear that there was no room for a relationship in there. I was pissed at myself because I thought I'd got over you and that brought it home that I wasn't over you. I'll never be over you.

'After the wedding thing, I left you alone which was, well, you have to believe me, was really, really hard. All I wanted to do was hold you and tell you that everything would be OK. That I loved you and I'd *make* it OK. Better than OK. But I knew you didn't want to hear that. Not then and probably not ever. So I kept away. But I couldn't stop thinking about you and I really did want to know how you were, but you wouldn't talk to me.

'That night I saw you again I wasn't worried because I thought, "it's been months, I'm over it all, it was just a crush". But it wasn't. The moment I saw you again standing there, extremely ill-prepared for snow, I was as deeply in love with you as ever. I really did do everything I could to get you home that night but I'm not going to lie and say that I'm sorry I couldn't. Because I'm not. Having you there that whole weekend was wonderful. Coming back from a run and seeing you sitting on the floor, looking sexy as hell in my sweatshirt, it was just … everything I've ever wanted. Well, not everything. I mean, we were in separate bedrooms for a start. That's definitely not something I wanted. But I knew you weren't interested in anything then—'

'You weren't either!' I interjected, trying to process everything. 'You told me so. You said you weren't looking for anything other than friendship.'

He pulled me towards him, tipping my face up to his. 'Izz, I'd made you cry within minutes of meeting you again! I thought, I don't know, I thought if I put you at ease about me not wanting anything more from you, then in time you might actually open up to the possibility.' He ran a hand over his hair again and gave a half-hearted laugh. 'I don't know. It made sense to me at the time.'

'But this week, on the stairs when I kissed you? You might go around kissing people willy nilly but I don't. Didn't that give you a clue I liked you? It gave me a pretty big one.'

'You didn't know?' he asked.

'Not really, no.' I pulled a face. 'I realise how silly that sounds. I suppose I've just been concentrating so much on putting bad things behind me, I couldn't see when something good was standing right in front of me.'

He smiled and bent for another kiss which I sank into before a thought crossed my mind, which, considering the way Rob was kissing me right now, was pretty surprising in itself because for the most part I wasn't thinking at all.

'Wait!' I pulled away. His face showed confusion and I began to smile at what else it showed. Pure unadulterated lust. I was fairly sure my own expression was similar but I needed to get this straight. I'd cocked up mightily in my previous choice and although, as I had promised him I wouldn't, I wasn't making any comparison between Rob and Steven, I needed to make sure this time.

'After I kissed you on the stairs, which, for your information, I know you thought was a whole lot more than nice, however much you tried to cover it.' I dropped my gaze lower momentarily and he grinned. 'That same evening, you had Caroline Bennett all over you, and you weren't exactly fighting her off. Quite the opposite in fact. And you went to dinner with her. Don't deny it because I accidentally saw you in the restaurant when I was out for a walk. I was backing up from the window when I fell over the dog. So that's your fault.'

'Of course it is.' He gave a little shake of his head. 'Izzy, you kissed me. I had been wanting that for so long, it's untrue. And all it took was a pair of funky wellies. If only I'd known.'

I pulled a face.

He continued, 'You gave me hope with that kiss and then two hours later you smashed that hope by telling everyone you were happy just making dresses for other people and focusing on your five-year plan, which clearly had no room for me in it. What was I supposed to think?'

'Rob. You never said anything when I kissed you. How was I supposed to know you wanted more? Every woman I've ever seen you with is a version of Caroline. Why on earth would you be interested in me? And as for what I said? I'd just been publicly reminded that I'd been left at the altar. I know your mum didn't mean it, and I know it wasn't my fault and I'm glad it happened as it turns out because I don't think it would have been a very happy marriage for very long. But it's still hurtful to be stood up like that and made a fool of. I didn't know what to say and your mum was so mortified I just said the first thing that came into my head. I had no idea how you felt! I wish I had because then I would have been able to say that everything was actually perfect because I was about to have mad monkey sex with the best man.' I paused. 'Although bearing in mind it was your parents, maybe I would have phrased it a bit differently.'

'Agreed.'

'You're right, I should have said something after that kiss.' He wrapped his arms around me, pulling me in close. 'But I was so worried about scaring you off. I know you've been through the mill already and I thought taking it slow would be the best policy. But it wasn't. I should have just told you. Which is what I'm doing now. As for the rest? I've never even noticed a pattern with my girlfriends before until everyone kept bringing it up this Christmas. It wasn't a conscious decision, it's just something that sort of happened. But believe me, every single thought I've had about you has been entirely conscious. And I'm interested in you because you're beautiful and funny and talented and sweet.'

'Oh. OK.' I knew that wasn't the most gracious or romantic

of replies, but it was all my brain could form right about now.

He smiled, but it faded a little as he spoke again. 'Do you think you might ever feel the same?'

'The same? About you?'

'No, about Harold.' He pulled a face at me.

'That's easy. I'm totally in love with Harold.'

'Ha ha.'

'It's true. But the thing is, I'm also totally in love with you too.'

'You are?'

'Of course I am! Why do you think I was so bothered about you and Caroline?'

'I just thought you didn't like her. I knew Mike and Jenny would fill you in on the back story.'

'There is that. It does bother me that she treated you like that. And then that you were stupid enough to go back to her.'

'I didn't go back to her, Izz. I promise. We didn't sleep together.'

'That was definitely her lipstick on your shirt the other night.'

'Yes. We kissed. I was lonely and upset and pissed off.'

I rolled my eyes.

'But I took her home and left her there and I went on and sat in the pub drinking orange juice until they threw us all out. I swear. I took her out to dinner because I needed to tell her there was no getting back together which is what she wanted, and I didn't want to do it here tonight. If she made a scene I wanted it to be as far away from Jenny's wedding reception venue as possible.'

'But you brought her here tonight.'

'I'd offered her and her parents a lift the other night. Of course, she held me to it.'

'And you're too much of a gentleman not to honour it.'

'Her parents had already cancelled their taxi. Izzy. Please, you have to believe me. I've been trying to find the right moment and the right words to tell you all night.'

I did believe him.

244

'So basically, we both just should have said something sooner.'

'I guess,' he said, bending his head and kissing my neck in a way that sent tingles right to the tips of my toes.

'This "you being a gentleman" thing?'

'Yes?' he replied, moving back up my neck.

'Does that only apply to Caroline?'

'What?' His head shot up as he looked at me. 'Of course not! Why would you say that?'

'Because I seem to remember you being very ungentlemanly when I was trying to extricate myself from wet stockings the other week. A gentleman would have looked away. You gawped.' I raised an eyebrow.

He groaned and lifted me so that I was pressed against him, but our eyes were level. 'You know you nearly killed me with that move, don't you?'

'It wasn't a move!'

'No, I know. That's what made it all the more deadly! You need to know there was a whole mountain of restraint on my part going on there.'

He put me down and I looked up at him through my lashes and grinned. He returned it and buried his face in my neck again.

'Rob, we probably ought to get back to the party.'

He made a non-committal sound.

'Rob.'

He brought his head back up and met my gaze. 'I have a room here.'

I tilted my head at him. 'Wow. You must think I'm easier than I am.'

'You're the one that brought up wild monkey sex!'

I laughed. 'I didn't say tonight.'

'Oh my God.' He dropped his head down gently on my shoulder which was helped by my sky high heels. 'You're killing me, you know that, don't you?'

'I have to be at the house early in the morning for everything.'

He brought his head up and looked at me, a mix of emotions on his face. 'Yeah, I know. I know.'

'Please don't think I don't want to,' I whispered.

'So you are easy?' he teased.

'Only for you,' I teased back.

He groaned.

I smiled at him and then placed my hands either side of his face. 'Look. This face, not to mention that body, has been driving me just as crazy for the past week. Don't go thinking you have the monopoly on lust, Mister.'

'Is that so?' he said, casting a glance around and steering us back farther into the corner.

'That's so.' I just about got out before things went a little fuzzy as Rob's hot, lusting mouth covered mine and the solid, strong bulk of his body pressed into me with wanting and heat.

'Your room. Now.' I shoved at him.

He pulled back, his eyes darker than I'd ever seen them. Not saying a word, he took my hand and set out back towards the throng of people. Weaving through the crowd, Rob's hand tightened on mine as I took about four steps to every one of his. He glanced back, checking I was OK and smiled. I stumbled a step as the promise of that smile sent waves shooting through me.

'You all right?' He stopped, seeing my stumble.

'Yes. Fine. Go.'

He kissed me, and set off again. I needed this man and I needed him now.

'There you are! We've been searching all over for you.' Rob's family were all suddenly in front of us. 'Us girls were all just heading home. Early start tomorrow! Are you ready to go, Izzy?'

I froze my smile in place. 'Yes!'

Rob's hand tightened around mine. 'I'll come and help you find your coat. We'll meet you out by the car, Mum.'

'All right, darling.' Eleanor looked at us both. 'We weren't interrupting anything, were we?'

I felt the blush start to make a rush for it.

'No, not at all.'

'Oh, good. Although I am glad to see that you two finally saw sense.'

'Pardon?' Rob and I said together.

'Oh, for goodness' sake, Robert. I'm your mother. I knew you were head over heels for this one the moment I saw you together at the flat. I don't think you realised until you were down here though, did you, Izzy?' I shook my head, mesmerised by the power of Mother Knowledge.

'And obviously Mike and Jenny already knew.'

Rob nodded.

'Wait, what? You did?' I asked them.

'Of course! It was obvious the first weekend we met you. For Rob at least.'

'It would have been nice if someone had told me!'

'That could only be Rob' – Mike clapped his friend on the shoulder – 'which he seems to have finally got around to. At last.'

'Yeah, yeah.' He motioned at his friend, laughter in his eyes. 'Come on, Izz, let's get your coat.'

'Did you know they all knew?' I asked Rob as we queued for my coat.

'Not Mum and Dad, no. But yes to Mike and Jenny. They called me when I was driving back from your place.'

'And said what?'

'Had I asked you out, if not, why not? You know. The usual.'

'I see.'

'Can I ask something else?'

'Of course,' he replied, taking my coat ticket and handing it to the staff member.

'What exactly did Mike say to you about inviting Caroline to the wedding? He seemed pretty sure you weren't going to bring her when you both got back.'

'Thanks.' Rob took my coat from the busty blonde who handed

247

it over, completely missing the come-on look she gave him. He held it out and waited for me to put my arms in, before wrapping his arms around me from behind and trailing butterfly kisses just behind my ear. When he spoke it was soft and low.

'He asked me what the hell I was doing and said that if I carried on with Caroline, I'd lose any chance I might ever have with you.'

'I love Mike.'

'Yep. He's a very good mate.'

'Now come on before I whisk you up to my bed anyway.'

I turned in his arms. 'I am sorry about that.'

'It's OK,' he said, gently stroking my face with the back of his fingertips. 'Well, it's not OK, obviously, but it is probably better this way. I'm not going to want to let you go when I finally get you there.'

'That sounds exhausting.' I grinned.

'Not necessarily.' He flashed me a look full of promise. 'Besides, when I take you to bed, I really, really want to wake up with you. I don't want you having to hurry out on me. So, as hard as this is—'

I raised my brows just a fraction.

'As difficult,' he changed the word, running his hand over my backside as I snuggled against his warm, broad chest, 'as this is, I think it probably is for the best.'

I kissed him on the tip of the nose and we went back to meet up with the others at the car.

Chapter 20

I'd been involved in bridal design my whole working life and had attended more weddings than I could count. Add that to my own experience, which could easily have tainted my entire outlook on weddings as a whole, and you'd have thought I'd be a bit jaded by the whole thing. But nope. I still loved a wedding. And I still cried. Almost every time. And this time there was a whole extra layer of emotion to deal with.

Jenny's nerves had held out but her emotions were close to the edge. And when she saw her big, tough brother's eyes fill with tears the moment he saw her, she was done.

'Oh, Rob!' I teased, 'now look what you've done.' I grabbed a tissue and gently patted around Jenny's eyes, being careful not to damage the gorgeous makeup she'd done for the day.

'I'm sorry, I …'

'Rob' – Jenny flung her arms wide – 'Izzy's teasing you.'

'You look amazing,' he said, wrapping his little sister in one of those fabulous hugs of his.

'You look great too!' Jenny said, pulling back and holding on to his hands, taking a good look at him.

She was right. He looked pretty damn delicious. The light navy suit was expensively cut and fit him perfectly. I wasn't sure I'd ever seen a guy look quite as good in a suit as he did. Of course, I might be a little biased. But boy, he looked hot! And judging by way Mike's sisters were staring at him, I wasn't the only one who thought so.

'Hi, Marie, Carly. It's nice to see you again,' Rob said, smiling their way.

'Hi, Rob.' they chimed, throwing under-their-lashes glances his way. Several years younger than Mike, the sisters made no attempt to hide their attraction for Rob. And to their credit, I didn't get the viper looks I was almost expecting when he stepped over to me and slid his arms around my waist.

'Good morning,' he said softly, the heat contained within the melting chocolate of his eyes making me feel almost liquid. 'I missed you last night,' he whispered into my hair. His fingers tightened on my waist and I got an idea as to just how much. My eyes widened and he grinned, which did nothing to help stem my immediate desire to yank him into the nearest bedroom.

'Hello, Rob!' John wandered into the room. 'Mike all squared away?'

'Hi, Dad. Yes, he's all set and ready to go. I've left him in his brother's capable hands now.'

Carly and Marie snorted at the fact their youngest brother was being called capable. Rob smiled at them and sent them swapping looks and giggles with each other again.

'So, everyone ready to go?'

We got Jenny in the car with her dad and the bridesmaids, and Rob then handed his mum and me up into his Range Rover, put his sister's wheelchair and braces in the boot, then followed the limousine the short distance to the church. When we got there, he parked and we all piled out. John got the braces out and Rob leant in the limo door, scooped up his sister, and carried her to the side door where the vicar let us in and Jenny set about fitting the braces.

'Eleanor, why doesn't Rob take you to your seat now?' I hoped that he would get the hint. His mum was getting quite weepy and doing her very best to hold it all in. I knew that if Jenny saw, there might be no coming back with the reparations to any of our makeup!

Rob swept the room with an assessing glance. 'Good idea. Come on, Mum.'

'You don't think I need to stay?'

'No, Mum. She's got Dad and me and Izzy and the girls. Let's get you in place so you have a good view of Jen walking down the aisle.'

'Oh!' Eleanor clutched a handkerchief daintily to her nose.

Rob looked at me, a faint show of panic on his face. I shook my head at him and took over. Bless him. He was used to being in control but this was way out of his comfort zone and, in trying to make his mum feel better, he'd succeeded in saying just the wrong thing. I crossed the small room to where they stood.

'Why don't I take you, Eleanor? Jenny can sort the boys out to where she wants them, and Carly and Marie can get themselves in place too.' I gave them a conspiratorial look and they nodded happily.

'All right. If you think that's best.'

'I do. And I've been to one or two of these things now.' I winked, succeeding in getting a little giggle from her. She took the arm I offered, and Rob gave me a 'thank you' look.

I safely delivered Eleanor to her seat before returning to where Jenny was now just standing. Rob and John each held an arm out which she held as she steadied herself. They watched her, concern and utter love showing on their faces. Jenny saw me standing at the doorway.

'Well?' she asked, tears shining.

'Jen, you look *so* beautiful. You really do.' I'd lost count of the amount of brides I'd said similar things to, and they all had, indeed, looked beautiful. But this time, with Jenny, there was something more. The training and determination she'd put in to get to where she now was made her shine. She'd fought for this and she'd won. I bustled over and began arranging the dress perfectly.

'Thanks to you!' she said, looking down at the dress, and to where I was crouching, adjusting it. 'You'd look gorgeous in a bin bag!' I teased. 'But I'm pleased you like it.'

'I love it!'

'I'm glad,' I said, straightening and adjusting her veil. 'I'm really glad.' I gave a wide smile to hide the fact that tears were now threatening my own composure.

The vicar popped his head around the corner and nodded to me. 'Right! Now that everyone's looking totally fabulous, shall we go?'

Everyone got into position, and I tweaked Jenny's dress one final time before stealing a quick kiss off Rob and hurrying to my place on the pew next to Eleanor. Mike caught my eye as I sat. Giving him the international sign for perfect with my finger and thumb, I blew him a kiss. He grinned and gave me a thumbs up.

The first chords of Wagner's 'Bridal Chorus' filled the small village church followed by a flurry of creaks and swishing of fabric as the congregation stood to view Jenny's arrival. People bobbed their heads and craned their necks, trying to catch the first glimpse. And then she stepped into view. A gasp rippled through the crowd and tears began to stream. Jenny's secret plan to walk down the aisle to meet her groom made just the impact she was hoping for. I kept my eyes on Mike as Jenny came into view. And then he saw her. His eyes filled, and I saw his hands grip as he did his best to keep the tears under control. Jenny had already given him orders not to cry because it would definitely set her off! It was hard to see how his smile could be any wider, as steadily his bride, accompanied by his best friend and his father-in-law to be, walked down the aisle to meet him.

I'd finally found a quiet corner in which to sip my champagne and reflect on a most perfect day. Rob had been a wonderful, and very busy, joint best man, sharing a witty speech with Mike's brother, not to mention making Carly and Marie's day by being the one to say how lovely they looked and deliver their bridesmaids' gifts, complete with a kiss. The bride and groom had just left for their suite and the dance floor was pounding to the strains of YMCA.

'Blimey!' Rob flopped down heavily into the seat next to me, resting his head back against it and closing his eyes. 'Being a best man is exhausting – even when it's joint!'

'But on the bright side, at least nobody punched you this time.'

Eyes still closed, he raised his eyebrows in consideration. 'Always a bonus.'

I took the opportunity to study him as he lay back, his arm running along the back of the sofa, so that it was behind my head. He looked worn out, but also more relaxed than he had in days.

'Why don't you go upstairs and lie down for a little while. You've been on the go all day.' I placed my hand on his cheek and ran my thumb between his temple and cheekbone.

Catching my hand without opening his eyes, Rob turned his head and kissed the palm of my hand. My breath hitched for a second as he did so. He caught the change and smiled. When he opened his eyes, they were filled with heat.

'Did I tell you how beautiful you look today?'

'You did,' I replied, smiling.

'I want to tell you every day.'

'All right.' I laughed. 'If you must.'

His expression turned more serious. 'I mean, I want to be able to wake up and tell you. I want you to be the first thing I see each morning and the last thing I see at night. That's all I've ever wanted since I first saw you.' He shifted in his seat a little.

'I know this is sudden to you and, like I said, I don't want to scare you away.'

'Is this because you don't like where I live?' I teased, smoothing my hand over his recently clipped hair, enjoying the fuzzy feel of it on my palm.

'No. Although you're right, I don't like where you live. But this, all of this' – he took my hand and kissed my fingers – 'is because I love you, Isabel Bryant. I want you to move in with me because I love you. I want …' He faltered, his eyes focused on my hand still enclosed within his much larger one.

'You want what?' I prompted.

Rob looked up at me through those ridiculously long lashes. 'Oh, you don't want to ask me that.' His voice was thick and full of meaning.

'I'm sure I don't know what you mean.' I blinked at him, innocently.

He made a guttural, primal noise and scooped me up off the sofa, onto his lap. 'Then how about we go up to my room and I'll explain it to you.' His lips pressed onto mine, and I opened, letting his tongue in to play. As his arms wrapped me tighter against him, I could feel the hardness of his chest pressing against mine through my dress and his shirt, and all of a sudden, there seemed to be way too much fabric involved. Especially considering that wasn't the only thing I could feel.

'I think I might need a very detailed explanation,' I whispered, teasing his ear with my teeth.

'I'm nothing if not thorough.'

I shoved myself back off him and stood. He paused a moment to make some adjustments, then quickly pushed himself up and took my hand, heading for the stairs.

'The lifts are this way,' I said pointing, as we half ran straight past them.

'The stairs are quicker.'

'Ha! For you maybe.'

'For both of us,' he said, sweeping me up and taking them three at a time.

'Happy second of January,' Rob's sleepy voice whispered in my ear.

'Happy second of January? Is that a thing?' I laughed, running my hand over the expanse of chest that lay uncovered in the twisted bed sheets.

'We could make it a thing.'

'We could.'

'What are you doing next year, same time?'

'I don't know. Do you?'

'Waking up next to my wife, I hope.'

I sat bolt upright, grabbing the sheets against me as I did so. 'What?'

He rolled his head on the pillow to face me. 'Too soon?'

I frowned. 'You really want to marry me?'

'Of course! The sooner the better, preferably,' He pulled me back down gently so that we lay side by side, facing each other. 'It's always been you, Izzy. I want it to always be you forever.' He pushed the curls that had fallen over my cheek back over my shoulder. 'I know that I should probably wait, and do this properly, somewhere romantic, with wine and a ring – but I can't wait. I've waited so long for you, and we promised we'd tell each other everything. So I'm telling you now. Or at least I'm asking you … Will you marry me?'

He was looking at me with that gaze that seemed to go right through me, one hand holding mine, his other tracing up and down my arm. For once, I could tell that he didn't know what I was thinking. I leant closer and kissed him, enjoying the thrill I got from the look it brought to his eyes. 'I will. And I even promise not to punch the best man.'

'So long as you promise to marry this best man, that's good enough for me.'

I smiled at him lying next to me, and knew that he was more than good enough for me. He was everything.

'I think that could probably be arranged. And guess what?'

'What's that?' he asked, sliding his hands around me and pulling me over on top of him. I propped myself up on his broad chest as he let one hand rest on the curve of my back and the other teased a strand of hair that was tickling his skin.

'I know the perfect place to get a dress!'

Loved *Winter's Fairytale*? You'll love ...

The Best Little Christmas Shop

Icing gingerbread men, arranging handmade toys and making up countless Christmas wreaths in her family's cosy little Christmas shop isn't usually globe-trotter Lexi's idea of fun. But it's all that's keeping her mind off romance. And, with a broken engagement under her belt, she's planning to stay well clear of that for the foreseeable future ... until gorgeous single dad Cal Martin walks through the door!

Christmas takes on a whole new meaning as Lexi begins to see it through Cal's adorable five-year-old son's eyes. But, finding herself getting dangerously close to the mistletoe with Cal, Lexi knows she needs to back off. She's sworn off love, and little George needs a stability she can't provide. One day she'll decide whether to settle down again – just not yet.

But the Christmas shop in this sleepy, snow-covered village has another surprise in store ...

Out now!

Dear Reader,

We hope you enjoyed reading this book. If you did, we'd be so appreciative if you left a review. It really helps us and the author to bring more books like this to you.

Here at HQ Digital we are dedicated to publishing fiction that will keep you turning the pages into the early hours. Don't want to miss a thing? To find out more about our books, promotions, discover exclusive content and enter competitions you can keep in touch in the following ways:

JOIN OUR COMMUNITY:
Sign up to our new email newsletter: http://smarturl.it/SignUpHQ
Read our new blog www.hqstories.co.uk

𝕏 https://twitter.com/HQStories
f www.facebook.com/HQStories

BUDDING WRITER?
We're also looking for authors to join the HQ Digital family!
Find out more here:

https://www.hqstories.co.uk/want-to-write-for-us/

Thanks for reading, from the HQ Digital team

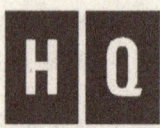